THE Keeper OF Fire

BY THE SAME AUTHOR

The King of Nigh

The Mermaid's Plight

THE Keeper OF Fire

BOOK ONE OF THE DOLPHIN CODE TRILOGY

DAVINA MARIE LIBERTY

ARCHWAY
PUBLISHING

Archway Publishing books may be ordered
through booksellers or by contacting:

Archway Publishing
1663 Liberty Drive
Bloomington, IN 47403
www.archwaypublishing.com
1 (888) 242-5904

Because of the dynamic nature of the Internet, any web addresses or
links contained in this book may have changed since publication and
may no longer be valid. The views expressed in this work are solely those
of the author and do not necessarily reflect the views of the publisher,
and the publisher hereby disclaims any responsibility for them.

Any people depicted in stock imagery provided by Getty Images are
models, and such images are being used for illustrative purposes only.
Certain stock imagery © Getty Images.

ISBN: 978-1-4808-5983-8 (sc)
ISBN: 978-1-4808-5984-5 (e)

Library of Congress Control Number: 2018902565

Print information available on the last page.

Archway Publishing rev. date: 2/28/2018

For Cindy Rusert
My Teacher of Life

The World of Nigh

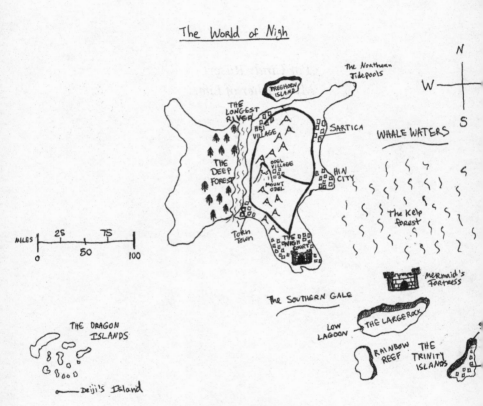

Map drawn by Davina Marie Liberty

PROLOGUE

Long ago, before the Mermaids crawled onto the shore, nudged and supported by the great Whales of their time; before the rise of cities and villages - even before the falcon majestically spread his wings to claim the sky, the balances of all that is good or can be evil were set into the stars.

The Scales were erected by Mowat himself, in an effort to forever maintain what was good, what was gray. He still did not know what to make of this decision, this action he once thought inevitable but now seemed destructive. He found himself looking out over the earth, his thoughts stressed, and shoulders tense. The stars seemed to dull when Mowat frowned.

A Dolphin peered out from the emptiness of space next to him.

"This world is not entirely evil yet, Mowat," the Dolphin who called himself Arill advised. "It has actually been cause for our relief since the Mermaids took their chances to escape this peril."

"No, not evil yet," the Necromancer agreed. "But things can escalate beyond even my control. And what if things do turn for the worse? What if the Keepers fail? We need to keep a watchful eye. We are attempting to set a careful balance here, a precarious weight between extremes."

"I see." Arill remained quiet, but Mowat knew his friend well enough to know he harbored more thoughts than he would bring to conversation.

He stared at the Dolphin for a moment as he hovered about the stars. Frowning once more, he turned back to his scales and checked the weight. He added a single stone.

"There we are. In years to come this balance will shift. We

must devote ourselves for the inevitable day when the Mermaids will recount to themselves what they have done and the entire world must face it. One can hope they will stray from evil and all will live in harmony together, but that is not the nature of these new creatures. We must be realistic."

Mowat called forth the moon and gazed into what lay beyond. Arill looked on solemnly.

The man was aware of what was to come in these long years ahead, and he shuddered when he knew fear.

Many years passed and Mowat watched the tides and the changes.

Man had risen from the sea, lost their fins and scales, established families, villages, cities and a government of people. On the surface it seemed they had gained more than they abandoned, and he was nearly pleased at this. But they had also lost their memories.

It became clear as the years went on that Man was different than their mystical brethren. They rose from the oceans and became something new, something devoid of magic and mystery.

Painfully unaware of the existence and presence of all magical creatures, Mankind reduced these people to topics of wonder; slivers of memory from long ago brought to myths and legends.

Nothing more than campfire lore.

Mowat stared across the divide from his separate mountain. He glowered at Relant, the Keeper of Fire. Lightning flashed in the distance against the eerie blue-gray sky. He brushed aside the wet, white hair that clung to his face as he stared at the black form. He gripped his staff firmly.

Mowat could only just make out Relant's dark silhouette looming over the valley below. The dark Keeper's talons dug into the parallel mountain, dripping streams of blood, the darkest Mowat had ever seen.

He could see the Hourglass of Time above them, the sand slipping away into the Odel valley. He saw a woman grow ill, her husband die, and she herself bed-ridden and slowly fading away as her daughter cared for her over the years.

The plans were in motion.

He dared to speak against the howling wind. "Relant," he began.

Relant raised his two wicked talons and joined his claws together. He thrust his palms outward and growled, "*Debeo!*" and a haze of black, silvery fire blazed toward Mowat's form.

"*Lateo!*" Mowat cried, deflecting it with his staff. It flew harmlessly over Relant's shoulder.

Mowat sighed and a gust of wind ruffled his hair. He growled, "I have recently sensed a deep magic cast upon the four elements of the earth."

"And what is it to you if such a spell has been cast?"

"Be reasonable, dark Keeper. You know what we are bound by."

"And must we play by the rules, dear Teacher?" Relant sneered. "I have every right to meddle in the affairs of humans as you do. And forget the Code. You never practiced the loyalty the Code proclaims anyhow, hypocrite! You will never find the one to rejoin them. Why waste your time?"

"Relant," Mowat warned through gritted teeth, "I know such a creature as you has very little use for such a thing as *honor*, but I am here only to ask for a simple reconsideration."

Relant opened his mouth and let out a high-pitched, eerie cry.

"You know your song does not affect me," Mowat growled. "Why do you even try?"

"Someday you may drop your defenses. And on that day I will catch you unawares and sing as I do to the Merpeople." Relant flashed him a nasty grin.

Mowat's tone changed drastically, and his features hardened. He became angry, frightening, the clouds behind him darkening. Thunder rumbled. He knew he looked as one to fear, but Relant hardly flinched when he began to shout.

"You dare to threaten them after all this? I have heard far too many reports of the slaughter in the Unknown World. Many mystical creatures have fallen victim to this spell you have cast, this fever. Why forget the Code? What is your purpose?"

The Code they were referring to was the new order that arrived when half the Merpeople became Man. When the people of the sea washed ashore, they became so beyond what the rest of the world knew as to their origins and ways of life that they all but created a new world for themselves. As Mowat saw these things unfold, the Dolphins wrote a Code of ethics; a Code derived from their life in the sea, promoting peace and unity. A Code he hoped they would not forget, of all the memories lost to them.

It stated that, differences aside, the humans and mystical creatures still belonged to the same earth. And though they could not co-exist, they were both susceptible to higher influences.

However, the Code also only allowed so much intervention between those few who hovered above the realm of humans and mystics alike; the Keepers. Mowat swore to this and took it on faith that Relant would too. All were under the same powers. It was one world, however divided.

"Relant," Mowat continued, "it is a parallel! You must leave the people alone! By taking their lives and their strengths, you weaken the wills of the entire world!"

It began to snow.

Relant laughed a deep, slow laugh. "You now have the idea, Mowat. Brilliant."

It began to hail.

Mowat glanced to the third mountain, the quiet volcano of the Eastern Ranges, Mount Odel. He looked and saw the one he chose, the one who was to bridge the gap between everything.

"It will not work," Relant warned, catching his gaze. "There is not a single one who can withstand the trials to unite the people of this earth. You try so hard with your visions of honor, and yet Man reveres me like a *god*. And now, they will die in this spell I have cast. You, Mowat, are *nothing*." He laughed, blood dripping sloppily from his mandibles down to his chin.

Mowat's eyes flashed with the lightning; the sound he made was as thunder. "RELANT!" he boomed.

Relant laughed again. "Indeed, Mowat, Teacher of *Life*," he sneered. "You have at long last discovered my plan of *death*."

PART ONE

CHAPTER ONE

The World

I t was dawn when Deiji J Cu of Mount Odel awoke from her pleasant dreams of the sea. She smiled and shoved aside the threadbare coverlet and threw her feet to the dirt floor of the hut.

She hurried toward the door, stopping briefly to peek at her ailing mother who was still asleep.

The girl ran outside, not wanting to miss the sunrise, and sprinted across the cool green grass. The fresh dew was heavy that morn, and the hem of her sodden nightdress slapped sharply against her ankles.

Deiji laughed loudly as she stopped at the edge of the cliff. *"Wandelen si um mi ha!"* she sang out to no one, and she lifted her arms to rejoice in the sunrise, the burning white sun with its luminous edges that lit up the valley below, bringing the distant trees of the Deep Forest into daylight.

Rarely was she free from her stiff, old-fashioned, fat, and ultimately proper aunt Micid, who constantly pushed her toward becoming a well-mannered and virtuous young maiden. Micid, who kept her on a short leash and governed the girl carefully. Micid, the short-tempered spinster.

In fact, her aunt had left the farm the evening before to

search the royal courts of Nigh for a profitable marriage arrangement for Deiji.

In these troubled days, the worth of a bride, a young and healthy bride, had nearly tripled, making any young woman un-afflicted by the fever eligible as a tool to gain some wealth for her family.

The small farm that they lived on wasn't producing enough to support them, and Deiji's mother, J, needed a frequent doctor in her illness. As much as they strained in labor to draw the fruits from the earth, the money simply didn't exist.

The courts of Nigh were over one hundred miles away, on the southern tip of the Known World. Every royal person in the world resided there, and many of them, fearing the end of their royal bloodlines, were willing to pay quite a sum for such a one who would produce an heir. Especially a beautiful one.

And Deiji was beautiful. She had been accounted as beautiful for as long as she could remember, in all of the region and neighboring villages.

What a silly thing to see in a person! She only ever saw her reflection in the gaps between the clusters of scum on the pond, so perhaps she did not quite see what they meant. But still…

Due to her long dark hair, mysterious eyes and bright smile, many suitors came to present marriage proposals to her aunt Micid. Enough men in fact, that Micid quickly came to recognize the opportunity living under the straw roof of her very own hut.

Deiji had no qualms against propriety, no complaint toward virtue, but it wasn't a life she would have picked for herself. Her spirit yearned for freedom.

She was predisposed to loathe the notion of prearranged marriages, or even marriage at all, having seen her childhood friend Maia take vows in the village church the year before to a complete stranger. Maia's parents had arranged the affair, a marriage to a man of a better position in the town, easily fed and well-to-do.

Maia had seized the life eagerly, and with good cheer; for she had waited with an intense patience for such an arrangement, and had played out many silly daydreams that Deiji found tiresome. She was able to live in the neighboring town of Sartica, and her husband was master of that whole region. With her new allowance she was able to care for her family, who remained behind in the Odel Village.

Deiji waited in fear and displeasure for her turn. Her aunt had taken Deiji and her mother in after Deiji's father died of the mysterious illness. J was already in the first stages of the sickness when they moved from the base of the mountain to the middle. Deiji had been seven.

On this new dawn she drank in the fresh, early morning air, a renewal to her very soul. She stretched onto her tiptoes, letting the wind tease her rough, un-brushed brown hair.

She turned and walked back toward the hut, and skipped a few small stones across the top of the green pond they used to water the livestock. After the ripples faded she went into the barn to prepare feed for the animals.

The day passed uneventfully as usual. Deiji worked around the property, smiling sometimes in her daydreaming and humming an idle tune.

Around noon she looked up from where she knelt pulling weeds from the lettuce bed. She quickly examined a few of the wilted heads and sighed. Brushing the dirt off her hands, she headed into the hut to check on J.

"Ma? How are you doing?" she asked as she entered quietly. She helped her sit up in bed to drink from the basin.

J swallowed once, twice, then sat back against the head-board, her eyes closed. Her nose and mouth were lined by flaky red scabs, the telltale sign of the fever victims. "I am only tired, Ju Ju," she said softly and coughed a little.

Deiji stood to go.

"Wait!" J's eyes opened suddenly. She frantically flailed her arms about, trying to get a hold of her wrist.

Deiji quickly set down the basin and water sloshed onto the dirt floor.

"Mother, what is it?" She sat down next to the writhing woman and took her hand.

"My child, your name... never forget your name..."

"Okay, mother," Deiji replied, nodding. This was not unusual.

J often launched into a flurry of senseless words and instructions in her delirium. At times it could be quite scary. Deiji, however, was ultimately sympathetic. She was aware of the effects on the victims of this great plague, and had heard rumors of it having spread as far as Rint City.

"Whatever happens to me, just don't forget," her mother gasped. "You have an important name. It is your middle name, J, it is my name. It..." Her voice faded away and she moaned, her head falling to one side. Her eyes fluttered and closed. She was asleep.

"Okay, mother," Deiji whispered, and she kissed her forehead gently, picked up the basin and left.

The Night Court

Micid Nun Cu stood before King Jebhadsen as a group of doctors and herbalists shuffled out from the grand entrance hall of the Nigh Court.

"She is the daughter of my deceased brother, Your Highness," she explained to the elderly king. The wide door closed with a bang that echoed throughout the hall.

"That is well. I have heard rumors of her astounding beauty."

"A vision from heaven, my lord," she said slyly.

"And is it well that she be so far from her family? The consequences of no dowry state that after our agreed purchase fee, there will be a cut in ties. You will be unable to depend on her for support, or food during famine."

"It is well, my lord." Her smile grew slightly.

As she bowed to show her graciousness, her eyes caught sight of an older, thin man lurking in the shadows off to the right hand side of the throne. He was watching her and listening intently.

"Then we are agreed," King Jebhadsen said sharply, catching her attention. "One hundred Emeralds, square."

Micid flushed with pleasure, and could barely speak forth the word, "Agreed!"

Telius stepped out of the shadows. "Please, sire, may I?"

The king nodded and waved him forward. Micid's eyes shot from the king to this new man with uncertainty.

"I need to know," Telius said gruffly, "about this girl."

"Yes, good sir," Micid sank into a curtsy. "She is sixteen, talented in her work, extraordinary in her embroidery -"

"Please," Telius sneered, cutting her off. "I don't need the seller's pitch. Just tell me she is better-looking than you, milady."

Micid stood as if she'd been slapped and her expression froze, then darkened.

"Why, yes. Indeed she is." She stared at the weathered man's face for a moment. "Quite," she added coldly.

Telius smirked for a moment; then his expression turned serious. "Then we have much to talk about. Tell me of her family. Her history. Tell me all you know of her."

12

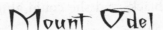

Mount Odel

Over the days while her aunt was gone, Deiji tended to the two pigs, three chickens and the donkey. She drew water for the washing, cared for her mother, and went into the nearby village to buy a bit of bread for aunt Micid's return, as was the custom. With her basket on her arm and her shawl around her shoulders she set out one morning on foot.

She enjoyed her weekly walks to the village, because it was a peaceful, inspiring walk and she savored the time alone. From the ridge that wound down Mount Odel, she could see for miles around; even a tiny sliver of the sea, which always made her smile, for she had never been to the shore.

Glancing into her purse, she saw the monies Micid had allotted her for food and medicine during her absence. She had but three white Pearls and two black ones. Most of it would go toward the medicine for her mother, and there would hardly be any left for the bread. She sighed.

Odel Village was nestled into a little crook in the green valley below, and the snow-capped mountains of the Eastern Ranges that loomed above them seemed to reach the heavens themselves. Mount Odel was a quiet volcano, and though smoke often loomed out of its top, it remained silent.

Looking out above the lush-green tree line, she saw a falcon rise up and up, and farther still, until he was nothing but a speck in the sky above.

"I wish I could be up there with you," she said wistfully, envious of his freedom.

As she lowered her gaze, her eyes caught sight of something black and ominous clinging to one of the mountains across the valley. She shielded her eyes against the sun and peered at the thing.

It was a deep black, and she could almost make out two wings folded at its sides.

Her heart began to pound as she thought of what this creature might be, what it could mean. She blinked and it was gone. She scanned the skyline and the mountaintops, but there was nothing.

"Maybe it was a Dragon," she thought excitedly.

An odd girl in her time, she spent much of her childhood years eagerly listening to the village elders and other townspeople tell folk stories of Centaurs, Elves and Merpeople. She loved these tales and ideas of this mystical world they spoke of. And well she knew there were undiscovered parts of this world. It only seemed logical that there could be undiscovered peoples as well.

The Unknown World was a thing they were aware of in its existence, but not of its content. No one seemed much interested in fording the Longest River and venturing into the Deep Forest. Rumors of terrifying social separatists, barbaric heathens who ran amok were the common explanations given to those who questioned.

But Deiji imagined she knew. She believed that all the mystical creatures in the stories that were so amazing were there, on the other side of the river. Where a better place for them to be, than on the other, quieter half of the divided continent? And where would the stories come from anyhow, if they had no basis in fact?

Deiji was constantly pouring over the world maps, sloppy as they were, in the blacksmith's shed. She spent much of her childhood memorizing its simple geography. She had many questions about its uncompleted half, more questions than answers given.

The blacksmith humored her, for the most part, and even let her have a go with his carefully crafted swords sometimes.

But most of her questions were left unanswered, silenced angrily by those around her, and after emerging from the frustrated frenzy of childhood she stopped asking. But secretly she still wondered. There was a kind of hope in it, a hope that maybe she was right, and the world of Nigh held more than anyone knew.

Deiji smiled at this thought as she made her way down the mountain, watching the falcon return to earth.

She paused at a nice flat spot on the trail and opened her basket. Digging to the bottom, she pulled out a scrap of her father's old leather coat.

Wrapping the piece around her arm three times, she held it out and let out a wild screech that echoed across the valley. The falcon answered, playing their little game.

Looking up, she saw him spiral downward until he was near her. He circled her a few times suspiciously, as if assuring himself that it was, in fact, Deiji. The falcon slowed, and swooped onto her outstretched arm.

"Hello, Polk!" she laughed, and stroked his feathered breast with two fingers.

Polk leaned forward and caught a few strands of her hair, clipping at them with his beak.

Deiji laughed. "Okay, okay!" she cried in mock exasperation.

She had rescued this young falcon from beneath a tree in the middle of a rainstorm the previous season, where he had fallen from his nest. Deiji had taken him up in her apron and hid him in the corner of the barn, feeding him dead mice and moles. He had come to trust her.

Polk fluffed his feathers and gently snipped her ear. She reached into her apron pocket and unwrapped her handkerchief to reveal a dead field mouse. He snatched it up in his beak.

Just then, something to the left of the trail moved and she saw a flash of red. A tall feminine figure in robes of green slipped from a brushy goat trail onto the path.

Startled, Polk spread his wings soared up and over the tree line out of sight.

"Hello, Maia," Deiji said heavily. It was her friend, with her long and unusually red hair. She stood tall and proper, wearing jewels in her ears, as her status allowed. A maiden wearing a white smock stood beside her. They watched Polk fly away.

"Hello, milady," Maia said curtly, and she sank into a slight and graceful bow, her stunningly silky hair falling over her ears. "I see that Polk has come to you once again. He will never come to me." She sighed dramatically.

"We're old friends," Deiji said tolerantly, tucking the leather strip back into the basket. She honestly wasn't sure if she was referring to Maia or the falcon.

"Are you on your way to the village?" Maia asked pointedly. The girl in the apron cleared her throat.

Deiji glanced at Maia's escort, who was staring politely at the ground, and she sighed inwardly.

Since the day her parents signed the betrothal papers Maia had become quite proper, embracing and observing all social niceties eagerly, as was fit for her new station.

When they were children they had ran about the hills and the villages in all manner of disregard and messiness. They had both loved to laugh. Even when Deiji moved up the mountain they still maintained their friendship, enjoying little adventures and make-believe stories about Dragons and the Pegasus. And now, ten years later, things had changed. Deiji wasn't sure if it were for the better.

"Yes," Deiji said finally, breaking out of her reverie, "I am." In seeing Maia's somewhat indignant glance she continued in haste, and much in her own defense, "my aunt Micid is due back from her journey sometime this week. I am buying fresh bread for a meal upon her arrival. Are you going to the village as well?"

"No, I am not. I am off to see my brother at my former residence before the noon sun shines. He has the fever."

"Ah. My best wishes for his health," Deiji replied courteously, but inside her heart nearly broke for her friend, and for the realization that she could not outwardly show her compassion.

"I thank you, milady," Maia curtsied briefly. "My best to your mother," she added.

"My thanks," Deiji bowed, and turned to go.

"One would think," Maia called back haughtily, stopping Deiji in her tracks, "that one would dress a bit more... *carefully*... the month when they are about to make their debut into society." She looked Deiji up and down, her lip curled in distaste.

Deiji glanced down at her torn and dirty dress, her shoeless feet. She saw her friend's perfectly pressed emerald robes and her sleek leather shoes and she blushed. Maia smirked.

"Well one would think," Deiji snapped, her embarrassment turning quickly to anger, "that one could do as they wished and not be subject to nonsensical social ridicule!" She glared at her old friend.

"Very well," Maia said decently. She turned to her servant with a curt nod. "Come." The girl and her matron disappeared beyond the path.

Furious, Deiji made her way to the village muttering obscenities under her breath. By the time she arrived at the gates, however, she was somewhat calmed. There were more pressing matters at hand.

She peeked around the corner of the wall and saw exactly what she expected: village boys. Ruffians. Idle, rude younger boys of no apprenticeship who harassed those in and around the village, mostly in fun and games, but these ignorant little boys knew no limits.

She looked about and saw a cart loaded down with produce – a farmer on his way to market his cabbage and carrots. As he passed through the gate, Deiji crouched and walked hurriedly next to his cart, shielding herself from the mischievous boys who often threw handfuls of mud at passersby. She grinned as she passed through the gate undetected.

The Village of Odel was a cluster of less than a dozen rickety shacks at the mouth of the valley. The wide paths that worked their way between the buildings were worn down from years of feet and wagon wheels.

Everyone in the region visited the village annually for food, trade, family and church. Deiji wanted to take her time on this day, but she knew her mother might need her soon. Besides, the crops must be watered before sunset, and she wouldn't be making it back until evening as it was.

She stopped at Pav the baker's hut. "Hello, Pav," she said to the dirty robust woman who had flour on her nose and apron.

What Pav lacked in intelligence, she made up for in size and gossip. She assuredly knew all the details of all the mishaps of every family in the valley.

"Hello, Deiji! Any news from the mountain? My, you are filthy! Are you here to buy bread? How is your mother's health?" she asked these things eagerly, quickly, wiping her floury hands on her soiled apron.

"Maia's brother Emor has the fever," Deiji murmured idly.

"Ahh!" Pav cried out, delighted in the new news. "What sad times are these! And has your aunt returned yet? I bet she has found you a husband!" She shook her finger knowingly at her.

Deiji sighed a bit and leaned over the counter and surveyed the baskets full of bread.

She did not cling so easily to the life the villagers spread out in front of her. She refused to admit it to herself, but with the apprehension she felt within toward her aunt's return, and the news she would surely bring, Deiji knew she would not sleep tonight.

Though young, she knew herself well enough to know that this was not the life she wanted. She was such a kind who would live on to be an old maid, tending her vegetable garden and taking long walks each day. One day she might have a horse, and travel alone to Toten Town or the Trinity Islands. Such a quiet, albeit adventurous life she saw for herself, however unusual.

Deiji wanted the world.

Pav's noisy babbling cut into her daydreaming.

"... and your mother does need a doctor! I say, it is time you caught up with your little friend Maia! It will be quite the thing if Micid gives you to a man of the court! Ah, so much money!" She clasped her hands together delightedly, looking to the ceiling as if toying with a fantasy in her head.

"A round wheat loaf, please," Deiji said, suddenly impatient to be gone.

Pav busied herself in plucking a nice, round loaf from the shelves, expertly wrapping it into its brown paper, and presenting it with a toss onto the counter.

"You know," Pav began again, turning toward her ovens, "the miller's wife was in here the other day, and *she* said ..."

Deiji quickly set one black Pearl upon the counter and hurried toward the door, shoving the bread into the basket as she walked.

Out upon the dusty village street, Deiji saw several village elders playing a sort of game on the roadside, smoking their wooden pipes and positioning their colorful clay pieces.

They sat here every day, talking of fanciful tales, of mystical creatures of times long past, or of the One who was to come, prophesied and chosen by the gods to save the world from this new sickness.

Today she could overhear snatches of conversation about the yearly earthquake that plagued the regions of Nigh.

"It must come from the Unknown World! They say it hits strongest in Toten Town, right next to the river! They suffer the most damage every year..."

Deiji longed to pause and converse with these wizened elders, with all their speculations, but she had business to be done with.

She sprinted into the apothecary for a bottle of meaded syrup and a vial of bronze herbs. She handed over her last Pearls to the busy shopkeeper and set on toward the gate.

Near the wall she caught sight of the village church and hesitated. She walked inside and left her basket in the vestibule. Inside it was eerily quiet, cutting out the noise and the light from the village. A single patron lit a candle near the altar and did not notice her arrival.

She smoothed her wrinkled dress and knelt for a few moments in one of the last few pews.

As fanciful and wide-minded as she was, Deiji was not an avid churchgoer. Her family's visits here were few and far between, but Deiji did enjoy the idea of a deity, however unknown.

She knelt reverently, not praying, not thinking, only meditating in silence. She sat for an extra moment, then made a quick, silent imploration for her mother.

"*Bigerriones Omino,*" she cried inside her heart. "*And save me, too.*"

She left the church with a cloud of heaviness around her. She walked with laden feet, her mind a hundred miles away.

As she neared the front gate, she looked up sharply at an elderly man she did not recognize. He was leaning against his curved wooden staff, swaying as he was maliciously pelted with handfuls of mud and livestock refuse by the village brats.

"Please! Stop!" the old man croaked, pleading as he held up a hand to shield himself. Laughing, one of the boys threw a rock that hit him square in the cheek. He cried out, lost his footing and fell in the mud.

"How dare you!" Deiji cried out, dropping her things and raging toward them in large, angry strides. "An elder! You leave him alone!"

She plowed headlong into the boy who threw the rock and they fell into the mud in a flurry of fists and feet. Deiji socked him in the nose and he fell back. She straddled his chest, hitting him, and her fingers reached into the mud beside him. They closed around a handful of steaming cow dung and she crammed it into his open mouth.

The boy choked as Deiji got to her feet and threw herself toward the young spectators. "Who's next!" she cried, infuriated. "WHO'S NEXT!?" She snatched up a rock, ready to hurl it at them.

The boys scattered. The one on the ground gagged and spat out the unholy meal Deiji had prepared for him and ran after them all, clutching his bloodied nose.

Deiji picked up the staff and rushed to the old man's side.

"Sir?" she asked, reaching to help him up. "Are you alright, sir?" His clothes were soaked with refuse and mud. He looked her in the eye as she lifted him up.

For one brief second they locked gazes. In a single, splendid moment that felt a whole eternity, she caught a glimpse of his world.

Vast reflections of the revolving universe and all its planets.

So many stars shining in the galaxy. She was caught up in a moment that felt centuries long.

"Sir, your eyes…" Deiji choked in awe. She tried to get a closer look, but he tore away from her, rushing toward the village, suddenly sure-footed and able to walk.

"Sir?" she called out to him, still holding his cane, but a wagon rolled between them, and after it passed he was gone.

The Necromancer

Mowat called forth the moon. He gazed into it deeply, listening carefully.

"What is it, my lord?" Arill asked quietly.

"The king. He is mobilizing his troops."

"His troops? How many? What will he do?"

"Shh." Mowat held up one finger. "Listen." He motioned toward the orb.

"… and I want reinforcements to quarter upon the town of Toten, to lie in reserve until they are called forth," King Jebhadsen commanded to his battalion of guards.

"It shall be done," General Morim hailed him salute.

Telius stepped forward. "Sire. Shouldn't we send more forces? If they were to come across any… abnormalities … wouldn't being a little more precautious give us the upper hand?" He held the king's gaze imploringly.

"Oh, er, Right, then," the king agreed, somewhat scattered. He called out to the departing general, "I say take four armies!"

Telius stood back as the general gave salute, smug and proud.

"To the Deep Forest, my lord?"

"To the Deep Forest," the king confirmed.

Mowat frowned at this vision. What would this mean?

"Why are they going into the Unknown World?" the Dolphin asked with great consternation.

"Relant wants it all," Mowat said with the heaviness of the ocean depths. He closed his eyes and the moon moved in front of the sun in an eclipse. "He has manipulated the armies of Man... He wants the whole world."

"Is this why you let those children soil your robes?" Arill asked with a twinkle in his eyes. "Because of Relant?"

Mowat gave him one exasperated glance. "It is because I am testing the one I have chosen. She already has one tool."

"It is dangerous to give her the Rune so soon, my lord. You know as well as I what happened last time the Rune fell into unstable hands."

"I wouldn't do it if I wasn't sure of her potential."

"And what if she is not the One?"

"Then I shall have to get my sword back, won't I?" Mowat quipped.

A heavy fog began to move in over the land as the moon uncovered the sun once again. A fog from the sea, bearing uncertainty and instability. And the tides moved, the weak slept, and the world felt of fear.

Mount Odel

The following afternoon Deiji was bent in hard labor, using a long hoe on the newly planted seed and daydreaming about that man's incredible eyes.

Unable to locate the man, she brought his staff home and stashed it in the corner of the barn. Upon closer inspection, she found it wasn't even a staff at all – it hid a sword of folded steel, with a Dragon etched into its long silvery blade, and dragon stone on the hilt. One of the stones had an odd circular symbol that she did not recognize.

Not even the blacksmith from the village could produce such a wondrous work; it was such a show of craftsmanship. She longed to finish her chores so she could look it over again in secret.

She straightened her back slowly and wiped the sweat and dirt from her brow. She mildly entertained the thought of drawing herself a drink of water from the well and headed toward the house.

Suddenly, someone roughly grabbed her arm and threw her violently to the ground.

"You stupid, stupid girl!" her aunt Micid screamed at her.

She was back.

Deiji glanced at her scraped elbow and made to stand. Micid pushed her back to the ground. "Idiot!" she cried in moral outrage. "I passed through the village this morning, and do you *know* what Pav told me?!" Her voice was so high it began to crack. Micid swallowed, spat once, and began to yell again.

Deiji closed her eyes.

"She said that you came into the village unwashed, with un-brushed hair, no shoes, no stockings, your clothes in shambles, and that you fought – rolled in the mud and *fought* – with a village rat! Such a poor excuse for a bride! What am I to DO with you?" She kicked the hoe and it clattered onto the ground several feet away.

"And you've been playing with that dirty animal again!" she threw in for good measure.

Deiji froze and looked up at her aunt. "Did Maia tell you that?" she asked quietly.

"Tell me what? That you were consorting with that bird? Indeed."

Deiji could scarcely breathe in her anger. She felt cold in the pit of her stomach, as if she had swallowed a stone from the pond. She closed her eyes and tried to steady her breathing. Deiji twisted her legs so that they remained beneath her, and she fell forward on her palms.

"I am sorry, aunt Micid. I will never do such a thing again."

Micid grunted and turned toward the house.

Deiji jumped to her feet and picked up the hoe, hurrying after her. "Aunt Micid?" she called out timidly, "how was the court, and your journey? Was anything, I mean, what has been decided?" Her heart was pounding in her ears. Something like fire flooded her veins and she bit her lip as she waited.

"I have been to the Nigh Court," Micid began, her eyes glittering. "I spoke to the king himself. His new vizier will send for you within the week. By the next, you shall be married." She laughed a little, and sighed in satisfaction.

Then seeing the look on Deiji's face, she added hastily, "we have made a contract! It cannot be broken. It is a promise that he shall have his new bride before the next moon. It's not all bad," she offered as an afterthought. "He is but twice married, and you will be well taken care of. Such riches that I could only dream of…" She seemed to fake a look of compassion, but had difficulty suppressing her grin, as well as the look of greed that was radiating from her eyes.

"No," Deiji said, loudly and firmly. "I will not."

Micid's nostrils flared. "You do not have that right."

"No."

"The vizier Telius will be sending for you soon. I suggest

you pack your things and start acting appropriately. He will be expecting a lady."

"You marry him then!" Deiji cried in desperation and fear.

Micid's jaw was set and she said nothing. They stood glaring at one another.

"I have chores to do," Deiji spat nastily, and she turned away, swinging the hoe up and over her shoulder.

Micid rushed after her and wrestled the hoe away, shoving Deiji to the dirt once again. She leaned over and grabbed the girl's neck roughly and hissed at her with years of built-up resentment, "listen to me, you clod. Are you a fool? How else do we provide your mother with what she needs in her condition? How else do we pay the taxes on this land? It is time to let go of your petty childish fantasies and grow up! Now, you will listen to me and do as I say, or you shall be hanged for disobedience!"

She stood back and swung the hoe, and struck Deiji in the ribs. She threw it down and stormed off toward the hut.

Deiji groaned and rolled up onto her side, her eyes dry and burning. She caught her breath and looked at her aunt's retreating figure.

"How much?" she called out with challenge.

Micid came to a dead stop, but did not turn. "What?"

"How much was I sold for? What was my running price?"

Her aunt turned and smiled slyly, then walked inside without uttering a single word.

For the next hour Deiji stood beside the pond, throwing stones into the murky green water, her mind turning over options to escape, each more unlikely than the next.

"*I'm not going to do this,*" she said to herself with conviction, again and again.

She knew her aunt watched all that she did from the window, and this was unbearable.

"*Maybe it would be good,*" she thought finally, trying to

convince herself. "*Mother would be well, I would be taken care of, and I wouldn't even be compelled to labor! I might even get to see new parts. We may even take our wedding trip to the Trinity Islands, as do all the wealthy, and I could see the ocean for the first time...*"

She tried to smile but could not.

She was filled with a sudden desire to flee and leave all behind. "Oh!" she cried out in her longing. "*What if I do leave? I could run away, join the separatists on the other side of the Longest River, and be free of this! I could venture into the Unknown World. It would be so... beautiful. Though my mother will surely die...*"

She tossed a stone in lightly and watched until the ripples faded. As the water became still, her eyes caught the slight shine of silver and a dot of red.

She peered closer, her heart caught in her throat.

Silver? And was that a Ruby? A single Ruby was worth well over two hundred white Pearls! Her thoughts turned over rapidly as she considered. To care for her mother, she might be able to gather the courage to turn the silver bit over to her aunt and then run for it. She could take the sword from the barn, gather her cloak and basket and find a way to journey to Toten Town. She could ford the river there.

She untied her apron with quick fingers.

"Deiji?" Micid disappeared from the window.

Deiji took a deep breath and jumped feet first into the pond without hesitation. The initial shock of the water was not bad, no; it was more the realization that the silver bit was farther down than she had anticipated. In any case, it felt good to be underwater, and she swam deeper.

"*It must have been a trick of the water,*" Deiji thought, as the journey down seemed endless. She fought the urge to surface to breathe and dive again; it was clear that aunt Micid was waiting for her at the top. She could almost see her standing there at the pond's edge, hands on her chubby hips, waiting to punish her the moment she came up.

"I'm already going to be in trouble for getting messy as it is," she thought.

Straining and paddling farther down she felt around for the metal. Her fingers touched slimy rock and moss, then something smooth and cold to the touch. She had it! Grasping it firmly, she pried it from the crack into which it was wedged and swam to the surface, the plan becoming set in her mind.

Suddenly, something slapped against her leg so hard she could not at first feel it, and then it began to burn. It was hot, and it stung as it snatched her leg and began to drag her down.

Deiji knew an incredible mixture of terror and amazement in that moment, for she knew what it was, but had no idea one actually lived in her pond! Or really existed, for that matter.

It was a Balla, a creature from the tales of old. A large benthic creature that used its long suctioned tentacles to drag prey into its small, toothed-lined mouth. Alive.

As it pulled her to the pond's depths, Deiji cursed herself as she struggled. She saw the murky green fade to black and knew she must be near the bottom.

Kicking and thrashing about, she was incredibly desperate for air, and had to deny herself as her mind commanded her to breathe.

"So this is the end," she told herself with bitterness. *"Maybe it is better this way."*

She knew that Pav would be recounting tales of her willful suicide, at least for a few weeks, or until another drama unfolded. Micid would moan of her polluting the pond with her rotting corpse. And then stories of her would fade into the background, remembered only in a pitiful simple sentence or two.

Deiji felt like she was going to cry. She hadn't cried since she was six years old, two days before her father died, the day they realized he was going to die.

Back in the first days of the fever, before anyone discovered that it was not contagious, quarantine was a standard practice in homes of those plagued by the sickness, and they separated those who were ill.

Her father lay dying and Deiji had not been allowed to be near him, to hold his hand or say good-bye. She had cried.

J took a hold of her hands and knelt down. She told her not to cry, that everything would be alright.

"Do not remember your father through your tears," her mother had said, wiping Deiji's tears away with her thumb, "but let him rest in your happy memories of the both of you."

Deiji saw the pained look on J's face and realized what a strong person her mother was. She hadn't cried since that day. Now, as she felt the hotness welling up behind her eyes, she swallowed the lump in her throat. She would not cry. For her father she would not cry.

Deiji felt her foot scrape against a sharp edge, an edge she felt sure was the Balla's hungry mouth. A distant idea surfaced and she realized that this creature was real! And if it was real, then the stories were true! She was suddenly filled with life at this thought, and she screamed bubbles and threw her body to the end of its energy in her struggle.

But nothing came, no teeth, no pain.

There was a swift tug on the creature's end, and she was pulled through the water quickly, her legs and arms flying loosely behind her.

And then, miraculously, she broke the surface!

She floundered, gasping for air, and realized she was not

on the surface of her pond. She seemed to be in an underwater cave, a little pocket of air large enough to admit her head, shoulders and a little more.

She gripped the sides of the rock frantically, the pads of her fingers digging into the grooves. She was aching and exhausted, but happy to have air. Astoundingly, the Balla had let her go.

It was dark here, but strangely enough a dim light shone from the necklace she clutched in her hand. It grew steadily brighter and she frowned, then looked up to the tiny cave that surrounded her form.

Trying to ignore the pangs of claustrophobia, she focused on breathing steadily. She glanced around herself and above. *What am I to do?* She debated silently with herself whether to go back under again and try to seek out the surface, but she was severely disoriented.

What if this was her holding place? What if the Balla was harvesting her for its hibernation, and had one tentacle standing guard, ready to strike her if she should move? That is how it was always described in the stories.

Terror knotted her gut and she vomited a little water.

She took a deep breath and leaned her head against the rock. Then, *something brushed her leg.*

Deiji gasped and frantically tried to pull herself from the water, her head banging against the rock, her fingers scraping raw with the effort.

Suddenly, it – the thing that had touched her – surfaced, sending up a watery spray. She screamed and choked on water as she floundered. When she sank under water, she got a good look at what it was. It was gray, with a long body that ended in fins. Its domed head had a long and narrow snout.

"A Dolphin," she sputtered, lifting her head for air, both relived and amazed. She had only heard of these creatures described in the stories of the elders, and she had seen the little pictures they sometimes drew.

Protectors, they were called, guardians of the seas and rivers. Known to rescue those who couldn't find their way through the waters, she found comfort in the knowledge that this creature wouldn't hurt her.

Then again, exactly how accurate were the stories?

It neared its head toward hers. She backed away, afraid, but it chattered persistently.

It moved toward her again, and Deiji closed her eyes and shivered.

When they touched foreheads, she felt herself being pulled into the Dolphin's very mind, and she could hear it speak; a voice distinctly male and soothing.

"I am Arill, Keeper of the Sea," it said. "Please do not be afraid, for fear is the end of reason."

Deiji bobbed there in the water, bewildered. Fear seemed to be a perfectly reasonable thing to her.

"I am not here to harm, detain or obligate you in any way. I have been sent on behalf of Mowat, the Teacher of Life. If you so wish it, I will return you home. But, if you care to listen to me, Mowat has requested an audience with you, and it is of great import. He may be willing to take you on as a student of sorts. He has much he would like to share with you; there is much that you can learn from him. You have paid him a great service recently, and he is not one who easily forgets."

"Well," Deiji began, astounded. Her mind was a flurry as she was desperately trying to absorb all the Dolphin was saying.

Arill sensed her doubt.

"*Biggeriones Omino*, Deiji," he whispered.

She looked up sharply.

"Come with me," he urged. Deiji hesitated, then gave a short nod. Arill swam under, exposing his dorsal fin. She figured that he meant for her to take it.

She took a deep breath and held onto his fin tightly, and they went under. It was a moment she would never forget, as they sank into the blackness, a moment between doors to a future of despair, or a future unknown. It was all a moment of mystery.

It was not long before they surfaced in a large dome of a cave, its ceiling and sides glittering a million stars against a deep black. They shone their reflections across the surface of the water, like Diamonds in sunlight.

As she took in yet another marvel, she realized she was suddenly alone.

"Arill?" she called out in panic. She hadn't noticed his disappearance. It was strange, but she felt such a tight-knit kinship to this creature of the sea when they spoke. His very presence was a comfort.

She splashed about in the semi-darkness and then, without warning, was lifted from the water.

Deiji watched, alarmed and amazed as she found herself hovering in mid-air and the cave around her began to spin, so that the stars became solid silver lines against the endless black.

A sharp blue light cut into the star patterns. An elderly man carried by the ice-blue light walked out across the emptiness of space toward her.

Deiji looked him in the eye and knew exactly who he was.

"You! I saw you at the gate the other day! I have your sword! You -"

"I am Mowat, Teacher and Keeper of Life," he cut in. "That is all you need to know for now. We have much to discuss."

"How do you know me? I have never seen you in the Odel Village."

"I have had my eye on you for quite some time, my friend.

I have found you to be bright, intuitive, alert, and to bear great certainty in the mysteries of the world beyond."

Deiji stared at him, uncomprehending.

"Furthermore," he continued, "you are reluctant to follow the path chosen for you by others. And you are right. It is not the path for you. And through your kind and immediate assistance in the village, I saw something in you that carries the potential to defeat the evil against this world."

"In me?" Deiji asked, certain he was mistaken.

"Yes. It was a test I had prepared in the village. I have considered you fairly and carefully for many days. And you came to my aid when no one else would. There is a nature about you, a powerful caring nature with a definitive historical link to the sea. It is something we certainly lack in this corrupting world of ours."

"But anyone could have come to your aid, sir. Only there was no one else around!"

"Do not let your pride overcome you, Deiji," Mowat said sternly. "I know the hearts of people. I know what people will and will not do."

"But how do you know?"

"Will you not trust?!" he roared, and the cave rumbled, as though an earthquake. "Will you not believe that I know what I know? How dare you question me!"

"My apologies," she muttered. The quake stopped immediately.

"We need your help," he said quietly.

"Well you seem powerful enough sir," Deiji said stiffly, with great respect. "Why do you need someone like me? Why not take care of the world yourself?"

Mowat sighed and a rush of wind blew through the cave. "What did I say about questioning me? I am the Keeper of Life for this earth. I am bound by the Code, which presents limitations to how much action I can take directly. This halts us Keepers from tending to our flocks with bias, from twisting things to fit our personal plans. We are to manage our jurisdiction, not bend it to our will. There is an evil creature by the name of Relant, the Keeper of Fire. He has abandoned his post and now moves through the mystical, magical people of the world. He has forsaken the Code and manipulates as he wishes."

"So there are creatures like those in the stories!"

"Yes. Like Arill, and there are many others. Your world is divided, Deiji. It must be reunited, for man and mystic must face each other at last and join together to fight. But not all can make the sacrifice to join the world together. Not all can make such amends. That is why you have been chosen to mediate through all elements. Relant has instituted a fever, a spell cast on the four elements of Nigh. I believe you are familiar with it." He eyed her heavily.

Deiji's jaw trembled slightly.

"Relant takes the greatest pleasure in his killing, holding the souls of his victims within him. It is important that this fever be quelled, for the good of the whole world. If there was even the slightest chance... Well, I put my assurances in you."

"Well," she said carefully, crossing her arms, "what's in it for you?"

Mowat smiled an age-old smile. His eyes shone with the glow of the sun on the ocean, and the ancient, migrating Whales.

"I must protect what is innocent and good, both humans and magical creatures alike. I am bound to pure goodness. If they are destroyed, so shall my spirit be. Relant is a rebel of all things good. He aims to upset a careful balance I put in place long ago. I seek help because I am bound to certain 'rules,' if you will, and it was in you, in your goodness that I saw that which could save us all."

"Okay," Deiji said, tilting her head to one side, "what's in it for *me*?"

Mowat laughed. A ray of sunlight burst from behind him, turning all the stars around them into millions of crystals. A million tiny rainbows shivered across their faces.

"Aside from what it will teach you personally, for I say you have much to learn and space to grow, if you break each spell by facing Relant's Guardians then the world and everyone in it will be rid of this fever. If you face what the rest of us cannot, then the world can be reunited. A new era will begin."

Deiji drew her eyebrows together in consternation. "Are you saying this plague is because of this Relant creature?"

"That is what I said," he nodded gravely. "If you do this, and succeed, all those affected by this illness will be restored to full health, as well as those who have lost their lives to it."

There was a long silence. Her jaw dropped.

"My... My mother. My *father*!" she gasped. She could not say it aloud. She thought of her beloved father in his grave, of her ailing mother and she was filled with a vengeance toward that which could now be in her control.

"On top of these things," he continued, "I will grant you your personal freedom, free of all social obligations. Once you have seen the world, and understand your place in it, you may choose any life you please and I will send you there. And no one, nay, not a single soul will judge you harshly for your decisions."

"And am I to see the world?"

"If you accept this. Can you accept these courses of action I present to you? Furthermore, will you?"

Deiji nodded, fighting tears again. This was it! *Biggeriones Omino.* The way. She felt a swell of pride and fear as she realized what her life might be, and with what purpose. Many innocent people were relying on her choices.

"What must I do?" she asked with seriousness.

"You will reunite the world. I will move you to four spe-
cific locations around the world of Nigh where you must face
four of Relant's creatures, the Guardians of that element's spell.
With each passing day you will encounter hardships, struggle
through trials and accept new concepts that will further mold
your character and give you strength. You now know Arill?"

Deiji nodded shyly.

"Arill will come see you toward the end of each element
to give you further instruction. Just focus on the task at hand
once you have spoken to him. There will be many difficulties
and hardships ahead of you if you do this. It is quite likely
that you may die. This is not some fantasy I have conjured
up, it is quite real. You must remember that, it's important."
His expression was curious, questioning. Was it doubt? Deiji
couldn't be sure.

She shook it from her head and nodded, taking it all in.

"Do you see the medallion?"

Deiji looked down at her hand where she still clutched the
silver bit that she had pried from the rocks, so tightly that it
dug into her flesh. Drops of blood spilled into space, dissolving
into nothingness.

It was a silver amulet set into a large, circular bit with four
stones on the edges, and a larger one in the center, as black as
the space around her. One was a Ruby engulfed in engravings of
flames; an Emerald tangled in vines; a Sapphire in river waters;
and sparkling diamond amidst clouds.

"You will wear this pendant always, Deiji. When Arill is
near, it will... *remind* you." He gave a mysterious smile, then
his tone turned serious.

She remembered the pendant's glow and grinned.

"Are you sure you consent to this?"

Deiji nodded.

"Then I purge you through fire! *Deicio Ferula!*" Mowat commanded.

"What, *now?*"

The stars and the Teacher faded away, and Deiji found herself lying in ocean waves.

CHAPTER TWO

The Island

Day One – Fire

The first thing she noticed was that all her pains were gone – her ribs, her hand, her elbow where she had scraped it… All her wounds were mended. Then she realized the water she was lying in was pleasantly warm. Indeed, one had never felt water warm like this before! And somehow, incredibly, it was *moving*.

Deiji tried to focus and saw that she was half-submerged in waves that tumbled over her every few seconds before pulling out again. She lay in warm wet sand, and there was a peculiar roaring noise in the distance that bothered her on some level. The air was quite breezy and smelled strongly of salt.

She stood, disoriented, and took a look to see where all this water was coming from. Had a river dam broke?

She fell back in utter surprise with a splash. She had never seen so much water in one place before! It stretched out and out until it met the sky, far in the distance.

The scorching sun was setting and the sky was streaked with burning oranges and yellows, reflecting across the water, blinding her eyes.

Even with the breeze the heat astounded her. It was hot, very humid, and nothing at all like the cool mountain air she was used to. Being thick and muggy, it was difficult to breathe quite the same way.

Deiji still sat in the water, propping herself up on her arms. She held up a hand to shield her eyes, already wiping beads of sweat from her brow, and she could see that the water twisted all the way around both sides of the land she was on. Swells moved in on the shore, breaking on the sand again and again leaving foamy traces.

Curious, she dipped her hand into the water to sample its freshness. "Oh!" she cried, abruptly spitting it out, "it's salty!"

Only mildly disappointed, she stood up and stared out at the massive body of water, still captivated by the sheer majesty of it.

She stood for quite some time in awe, and then she realized what it was. "The sea!"

Deiji didn't feel too bad about her ignorance; she figured it wasn't a mark of stupidity if one had spent their life only hearing about the ocean by rough description. She had waited her whole life to see it – and here she was!

No tale of the village elders or returning visitors from the Trinity Islands could even compare to this. It was even more beautiful than her valley at Mount Odel.

As she stood there entranced, she finally began to notice that the sky was growing darker, and there was a slight chill in the air.

"I had better find a village to stay the night out," she thought, and with a pang of worry, for she had no money for an inn.

She wandered along the shoreline, and then saw a small trail winding into the trees. She followed it, figuring it would lead to the nearest settlement. It wasn't long before dark clouds began to drift over the island and soft raindrops fell.

She saw a mound of rocks and trees ahead through the brush and headed toward it, wrapping her arms around herself tightly.

By the time she was near enough to see it was a cave, the rain broke from the sky like an eager animal breaks from its leash, and Deiji was drenched.

Seeing a rather large opening, she hesitated. Could she sleep here for the night? She knelt on the ground and saw a few scattered, clawed animal tracks, not yet washed away by the rainstorm. They were quite large, so she was cautious.

Placing a hand inside one of the tracks, she carefully peered into the cave but saw nothing. Entering further, she could see the cave was very large, and there was a dark shadow of rocks in the back, so she sat fearfully near the entrance, only just out of the rain.

A trickle of rainwater dribbled across the rock and she drank eagerly, enjoying its coldness. It was a damp and chilled place to spend the night, and Deiji shivered, though grateful.

Settling in against the wall, she leaned against the rock and tried to sleep, somehow knowing there was no village here, that she was utterly alone.

She surprised herself when she smiled at the thought.

As she stared up at the bright sparkle of the jewel-like stones on the cave wall and ceiling, her eyelids grew heavy. They were covered in dragon stone, with that beautiful blue dazzle that never left, even in the dark.

"*How fantastic,*" she thought wearily, and so she slept.

The Necromancer

Mowat stood above the Southern Ocean, intently observing the Dragon Islands, on one of which he had placed Deiji. It was the smallest, most southern of the islands, all of which belonged to the uncharted, unexplored part of the world.

He turned to his advisor and most trusted friend as the clouds stirred around him. Arill was there lingering beside him, also watching the young girl seek her shelter.

"It is she, my Teacher," he said to Mowat. "I am sure of it. She is the One."

"Perhaps."

Arill swam through the clouds to Mowat's other side and peered down into the cave where Deiji would sleep this night.

"She fits the description of the Prophesy, my lord," he insisted. "Her curiosity, her longing to explore the world around her, her family, her age, the *mountain…*"

Mowat nodded silently. "She certainly does carry all of those qualities. However -"

Arill interjected, "see how she does in this place, my master. If she performs well, you may put more stock in her and in her abilities. Do not pass your judgment yet."

The clouds cracked and rain gushed forth.

"It is not faith I lack in this child. My doubt is in her experience."

Arill smiled. "Well, and my lord, that is what this element will bring her."

Day Two – Fire

The morning sun shone in, and she felt something hot lapping at her face. It was sticky and rough, and it smelled *horrible*. Deiji opened her eyes and saw two large green ones staring into hers. "AHHHHHHHHH!" she screamed, scrambling aside, groggy and stiff from her poor night's rest.

The thing whimpered and ran toward the back of the cave into the shadows. Deiji collected herself and quickly followed the thing to see what it was.

It was cowering behind the boulders in the far back, and as she approached it was clear that it wasn't a pile of boulders at all. It was hiding behind a large Dragon.

Her heart leapt with fear, and she nearly ran. It was as blue as the ocean, and had scales like shiny aqua pearls all down its flanks.

She peered closer and realized it wasn't breathing. She was almost certain it was dead.

Cautiously circling around the creature, she could see no sort of wound or other cause for the Dragon's death. Then she saw the tell-tale red scabs around its nose and mouth. Yet another victim of the fever. It was time to leave this place.

But first, she walked behind it to find the small animal that had startled her so. It was a baby Dragon, looking up at her with such an innocent expression on its face that Deiji had to smile.

She stared at the young creature, which seemed more like a little dog than a Dragon, in so many ways. It was a dark blue-green in color, and its eyes were as green as Emeralds. Never had Deiji seen such a thing.

She looked at the dead Dragon and realized with a start that it was the baby Dragon's mother.

"Oh, poor baby," she whispered. A sparkle near the Dragon's

feet caught her eye. Stepping closer, she saw a mound of gem stones – Pearls, Sapphires, Rubies and piles of that same peculiar clear sparkly stone that matched the odd one on her amulet. Objects of gold were scattered across the floor amidst carvings of jade and leather objects. A pile of riches lay at her feet.

She looked around the cave with wonder. The walls looked spectacular in the morning sunlight.

She looked at the baby Dragon, who stared right back at her. "I think I will call you Geo." She walked to the mouth of the cave and beckoned Geo to follow.

He leapt after her, then abruptly sneezed little puffs of smoke which knocked him off his clawed feet. He crossed his eyes and looked down at his nose with wonder.

"Well," Deiji said, "I think the first thing for us to do is to make some sort of shelter."

They were walking outside into the surprisingly hot morning sun. She knew they shouldn't stay in there with the Dragon, not after how it had died.

Geo looked up at her hopefully. She laughed and patted his head a little. "Come now," she said, encouraging him to follow.

He hopped after her, and even a little ahead, turning back every few seconds to see if she was still there.

The entire jungle was lit up. The plants and trees were all a bright and colorful green, with yellow and pink flowers spotting the greenery; blinding to someone who was accustomed to the dark earthy greens and browns of the valley.

Colorful insects and birds buzzed and fluttered everywhere about her. Lizards with strange exotic patterns of blue and red skipped across her path.

Deiji's stomach rumbled. Back on the mountain she would

have a bit of corn meal to sup in hot water, and bread for noon and supper. There were no oats or corn here, no mill to grind them upon, and no cauldron to boil water in.

She wondered how long she was meant to stay here.

"Geo," she said, "how does some food sound to you?" The Dragon sat back on his haunches and gave her a toothy grin, his little wings folding and unfolding again and again. They wandered through the underbrush, and she kept her eyes open for anything she might eat.

The sights she saw took her breath away. There were butter-flies with wings of bright yellow on black and incredible plants with purple flowers that wound up and around the trees like ivy. The sights were strange, striking and shocking. Her eyes vibrated from the colors.

But even the most shocking colors did not even compare to the sounds.

The entire forest was alive with noises. Reptiles and frogs croaked and rustled the leaves and grass as they ran about. Snakes hissed and mice squeaked. Birds screeched and squawked incessantly; a continuous chatter as they took flight and landed again and again.

Being more used to the mild silence of the mountains, these animal sounds with the perpetual roar of the salty water were almost too much for Deiji to bear.

She gritted her teeth.

Seeing a withered tree dotted with purple spheres, she hurried up to it. Staring into the branches she could see it was sporting a sort of plumb fruit, far out of reach.

"It's a good thing I've got good aim," she muttered, picking up a few rocks. She threw the stones, chasing a few of the fruits as they fell to the ground. Though bruised, she cautiously took a bite and decided it was fine.

"It tastes alright," she said, doubtfully offering some to Geo.

He sniffed them, licked one, and eagerly gulped them down whole.

"We'll have to find other things to eat as well," she said as she wiped each shiny plumb off on the hem of her skirt. She slipped them into her pocket.

As they walked, they searched the trees.

They found other odd fruits, some red, and some brown that had to be cracked open upon a rock. She gathered a small collection of these in her arms, and her skirt pocket was stained purple and red with the juices.

Geo led the way into a small clearing, not too far from the beach. "It's perfect, Geo!" Deiji cried out.

It was a fairly large clearing. Her two-room hut on Mount Odel could have easily fit there alongside the corral. In the center of the clearing was a large thick tree, with branches that grew strangely – straight up and out, as if reaching for the sky.

"What an odd tree," she whispered. It was the largest tree she had ever seen; the foothills of Mount Odel only grew saplings and shrubs.

A freshwater spring bubbled up from the edge of the clearing, and she smiled and set down the fruit she carried.

"I think this is it, Geo. It's perfect."

Building a shelter was more difficult than Deiji had anticipated. She sent Geo to collect sticks and palm leaves, a difficult task, as most of the lower trees were nothing more than gnarled branches.

"I sort of remember assisting my Aunt Micid in the repair of our hut after the earthquake we suffered last year," she remarked, trying to convince herself as much as Geo.

She spent a few moments tying sticks together with grass to

make a tall, flat-roofed hut, but the frame was flimsy, and had no balance. It fell over onto its side at once.

"Okay," Deiji said, on edge, but not ready to admit defeat, "why don't we try making the branches come to a point at the top? If they all lean against each other, it won't fall."

She made it high, with the longest sticks Geo could boast. Unfortunately, they were mostly all different lengths, and were hard to lean against one another. Over the course of some hours she made a triangular hut of sticks, and she stuffed the cracks with leaves and mud from the spring. She stood back in satisfaction.

"Okay, Geo!" She ducked to go inside it. Geo whimpered as he tried to follow. It was obvious that he would not fit. It was far too narrow and cramped for them both.

Deiji gave a sigh of frustration and stood up. She struck her head upon the roof, and the whole thing caved in.

"Okay," she said, suppressing her irritation, pulling leaves and twigs out of her hair, "let's start over. What if we made it a lean-to, using the tree? It can make a crescent shape around the tree's base, and we can make it sturdier at the bottom. What do you think?"

Geo stared up at her with a blank look on his face.

"Okay, then."

And so she began sorting out the usable branches and grassy clods of clay. Deiji buried the ends of the sticks deep into the sand, so that even though they leaned at an angle they stood by themselves. She braced the buried ends with large rocks, and their tips barely touched the tree.

She stuck over three-dozen of these in the ground, making a half-circle around the tree, and added some forked branches to hold the tips, to give them more support. The roof and walls she made with branches and palm leaves, and followed in her own fashion in stuffing the cracks with mud and leaves and things.

She tied and double-tied the branches to each other and the trees with long grass and vines from the jungle.

Stepping back, she admired their work. The hut was large enough for them both to sleep in comfortably, and tall enough to stand in, if she hunched a little.

Nearby in the forest they gathered armfuls of leaves and made two separate piles for beds inside their new home. Geo proudly added his mouthful of leaves to his pile. Deiji laughed.

She went to the edge of the clearing and hunted around until she had found a sharp enough rock and she cut the thick stems of four palm leaves she selected. Slipping the jagged stone into her pocket, she dragged them back to her hut and placed the soft greenery over their leaf piles.

Looking out from the edge of the clearing, she felt strangely proud in the evening sun. What she had done this day, in making a home for herself, brought such an immense notion of satisfaction, for she had done all without instruction or direction for the first time in her life.

She was hot, sweaty and streaked with dirt.

She found the entire experience to be intoxicating.

Day Three — Fire

Deiji awoke yawning the next morning, enjoying the natural and consistent warmth of the sun.

After wincing at a smarting sunburn, she rolled onto her side and felt a persistent tug on her dress. Opening one eye she saw Geo tugging away on her skirt. She lay there quietly pretending to be asleep. He tugged harder.

"HEY!" she shouted out, sitting up quickly.

Geo stumbled backwards, letting out a squeak of surprise. He rolled into the dirt and out the doorway, hopped back and began nipping her toes.

"Oh, stop, Geo!" she laughed, pulling her feet away. He hopped backwards playfully, looking very pleased with himself.

"Let's go find breakfast, shall we?" As they stepped into the morning's strong humidity, Deiji instantly felt the need for water. After drinking their fill from the spring, they made their way into the jungle.

When they gathered their fruit, Deiji kept her eyes open for other possibilities. While fruit was good, it was not entirely filling. She had it in her mind to dry some in the sun, but she did not believe they could survive solely on fruit, dried or not.

They gathered and ate what they could hold as they walked. They went back to their hut and Deiji gathered a series of large flat stones and laid them out near the spring in a sunny spot, tearing fruit apart with her fingers and laying it out to dry.

"See?" She displayed her project for Geo. "We will have some for later."

They headed southward for a short hike, to seek out other options for food.

After a short ways they came to an extremely tall, skinny gnarled tree, with very slender branches and odd-shaped purple fruits at the top. Deiji snatched up a stone in confidence.

"Watch this, Geo!" she cried, throwing the stone. She missed.

She tried again, but the fruits were simply too far out of her throwing range.

"Hmm," she said, slightly embarrassed. "Well, I suppose I could climb it." She hiked up her skirt and clambered onto the lower branches. As she began to hoist herself up, the branch she was clinging to began to bend under her weight, and then it snapped.

She fell to the ground, landing on her back, and the branch smacked Geo in the head.

He shook his head abruptly, surprised and dazed. "Sorry, Geo," Deiji apologized sincerely, getting to her feet. They stared up at the fruits that they never tasted. The sudden failure gave her pause, and she stood for a moment, uncertain.

They collected other fruits and went back to the clearing where Deiji sat decidedly and fashioned a knife. With the sharp stone she had used the day before, she searched far and wide for a piece of wood thick enough to accommodate it. Neither was terribly flat or smooth, but they were good enough.

She tore the hem from her dress in one thin strip and soaked it in the spring, before binding it tightly around the wood and the stone, covering most of the wood handle. It was well bound, and it worked marvelously. She stabbed the air with it a few times and, satisfied, began to slice more fruit.

She spent the afternoon wandering through the jungle as Geo watched her curiously. She climbed trees and cut fruit for drying with her new knife. After laying all of the evenly cut pieces out to dry, Deiji couldn't help but feel that same sense of satisfaction, though it was much more level in terms of pride.

"Let's head down to the beach!" Deiji suggested after they ate. "Let's go, Geo!" she called back to him. He looked up and excitedly bounded after her.

Deiji had an idea. She found herself newly inspired at her attempts to survive by her own methods, however sloppy. She could not even explain to herself the new joy she found in the discoveries through trial and error, much less to anyone else. She marched purposefully toward the beach.

The ocean water was a bright blue, bluer than Deiji had ever seen. The early cool breeze was refreshing, and the sun was rising high and she could see the faded moon from the night still etched into the sky.

Looking out at the sea, she saw dozens of fish flapping in and out of the water as they leapt for insects. "Look, Geo!" she exclaimed. "I was right! This water *does* have fish!"

She watched a large bird swoop down, skim the water and take a fish into its large mouth. "See? He has the right idea!" Deiji whooped, and she began looking around eagerly for that which would craft a spear.

They ran into the tree line, and it took them a long time to find a stick both long and sturdy enough to pass as a spear. Deiji sang a soft tune as she snapped the twigs off as close to the stick as she could. She sharpened the stick against a rock until it was as pointed as a quill.

"Let's go, Geo!" she cried and she skipped jauntily down the beach, her Dragon hopping after her.

Deiji stood waist-deep in the ocean for the very first time, getting used to the swells and the current pushing against her. She stood with her spear over her shoulder, poised and ready to strike.

She saw a fish against the sand and thrust her spear. Yanking it out of the water, she was disappointed to find no fish on the end of it.

She stood quietly and let the waters settle around her. Seeing a few yellow fish swimming nearby, she threw her spear as hard as she could, but again to no avail.

The afternoon passed thus, and Deiji was miserable as all her attempts wholly failed. Frustrated, she slumped back to the beach and threw herself down next to Geo.

"What do I do now? I am hungry," she said sadly. She put her head in her hands, slightly disappointed in herself. Maybe she wasn't as well off as she'd imagined, she thought. After all, she couldn't even satisfy her own hunger.

Geo stared at her with concern for a moment then bounded off down the beach. She felt slightly abandoned until she saw him splash into the ocean and disappear. She stood.

Nothing. Not even a ripple. Deiji scanned the tides, but he was gone. Suddenly, Geo flew out of the water and onto land, water flying every which way, and he was holding five fish in his jaws.

"Geo!" she cried out with glee. He ran up to her and dropped his squirming prizes at her feet. Gathering them into her arms, she walked up the beach to make a fire. "This I can do," she thought with some satisfaction. "I made fires all the time on Mount Odel."

She sent Geo out to collect dried driftwood, grass and leaves while she made a circle of rocks in the sand. After his second trip, he came back to the fire pit to find Deiji sitting cross-legged, attempting to catch a spark to her fuel with two stones.

She was frowning in concentration. "I don't understand," she said, peering closely at her tools. "This stone is much different than the flint from the mountain. I cannot make a spark!"

Geo leaned over and opened his mouth. With a slight grunt, a stream of purple fire blew from his mouth, struck the pile of wood and a bronze flame caught. "Oh, Geo!"

As they roasted the fish on sticks above the crackling fire, Deiji's mouth watered at the smell and she thought about home. Back to Mount Odel, where she lived a simple, predictable life day in and day out.

She struggled with the same labors every day for no reward above or beyond daily living, material or personal. Daily life meant to walk in place.

But this place, which she figured was a part of untouched land, was different. She felt honored to be there in a new part of the world, honored to be presented with such a chance to make such mistakes and learn from experience.

This was everything and more that Deiji had ever dreamed was out there. And the newfound wisdoms that were just beginning to bloom within her, the insight that was gained from failure, the elation that came from success... it was all worth it.

It was freedom.

The Necromancer

Mowat stood on his perch in the clouds, looking down upon the ocean below. The sea was spotted with a series of islands, and he focused on one in particular, one farther south than the rest.

He was watching the progress of his chosen human, the one on which rested the hopes and survival of the people. He enjoyed getting to know this one from afar.

She was learning, that was sure. Nothing enlightening or intensifying – that would come later – but the personal gain from this trial would bring her perspective and confidence.

"The prophesy," he muttered, distracted.

He knew that Relant would send an enemy soon, a definitive challenge. And for the first time in her life, Deiji would have to stand against pure evil. He knew it would be an important lesson for her. He firmly believed that when things are consistently too good, one is ill equipped to deal with hardship when it comes. A little diversity in circumstance is valuable.

"I wonder how she shall handle it?"

He knew the Guardian of Fire would be called forth, the

Guardian placed to oversee the death and destruction of the Dragons and all others in the fire element. With a grim face and a steady hand, Mowat worked Relant's plan into his own, and knew that if the girl survived it, she would be forever changed.

"How long can we keep him off, my lord?" Arill asked Mowat urgently.

Mowat jumped. He'd forgotten Arill was nearby.

"Two days, maybe three, if she can hold out that long."

The Teacher of Life felt cold as he heard the darkness laugh and he watched the weather change.

Day Four — Fire

The next morning Deiji overslept, and when she did awaken, she was mildly surprised to find the sky dark, cloudy and overcast. It was still warm out, but not as strongly.

She wandered over to her dried fruit stores and frowned. Were they really moving, or was it her imagination? She peered closer.

"We have an ant problem, Geo," she announced. Geo lifted his head from where he lay dozing. She brushed a few ants away.

"Well, we have to do something. All of our fruit is ruined!"

She knelt and began to dig in the dirt near the spring. Geo showed up at her side, yawning. "Here, help me make a ditch."

She continued to dig with her hands, scratching away at the dirt. Geo snorted in disgust and ushered her aside. With one swipe of his spiked tail he cleared the earth to reveal one long, shallow ditch.

"Wow, Geo! Thank you!" she cried, delighted. He snorted again and raised his head high in satisfaction.

Deiji took a smooth palm bough and cupped it to fit the length of the ditch. She rinsed her drying rocks in the spring and set them on top of the leaf. "Come here," Deiji motioned Geo toward the spring. He followed, curious. "Now, fill your mouth, but don't swallow the water."

He stared at her.

"Go on, do it!"

He tentatively did as he was told, his cheeks bulging.

"Now spit it into the ditch," she directed.

He looked at her, confused.

"Go on, spit!"

Geo spat noisily.

"And again!" she said, pleased. Twice over Geo filled the ditch with water around the stones. They stood, berry-stained, like small, red-splotched islands in a puddle.

"Now the ants won't be able to get to our fruit. We'll have to add fresh water every day, but I think this will work." She smiled. *We can solve any problem,* she added silently to herself.

"So what do you think about exploring some today, Geo?" Deiji asked aloud. Geo looked at her curiously.

"Well, it's not very hot out, and we can see what lies beyond the beach. I mean, we're here together, for a while, and if I am the first of Man to set foot on these lands… a little exploring just seems exciting," she finished.

Before heading out, they went to the beach to catch their lunch first. Geo was a far more efficient fisher than she. As they walked down the beach after, Geo meandered behind her, absolutely fascinated by a butterfly that was circling his head.

They rounded the shore's curve and saw nothing significant beyond. Just more beach and rocky outcrops. It was a leisurely walk, and Deiji tried to keep a mental note of how far they had come, and when it might be wise to turn back.

Deiji paused at some tide pools where she could see watery

crevices. Spotting little cups clinging to the water-stained areas, she pried them away from the rocks, and was thrilled to find the meat inside them. She decided to take them back to her fire for cooking. Her pockets were full to bursting, juicy and very sandy.

The day wore on as they walked, and Deiji threw a few sticks far and wide for Geo to chase, idly thinking that Geo had grown some since even yesterday, and she finally decided they should stop to rest. Seeing a piece of driftwood on the sand ahead, they marched toward it.

As she got closer, she could almost make out a face and a body. Was it a person? She quickened her step. "Geo?" she called over her shoulder, her heart pounding, and she broke into a run. She stopped breathlessly as she came upon the thing, which was not a person, per se, at all.

Stretched out gloriously before her was a Mermaid, dead in the sand. Perhaps it washed up early that morning.

She knelt before the sad creature, which retained a beauty so bold it nearly brought tears to her eyes.

She had hair as red as Maia's and a long silvery-blue fish tail. And she, like the Dragon in the cave, had the raw chapped skin of the fever on her face. She looked almost peaceful lying there, as if sleeping.

Peering closer, she saw a little bag of woven seaweed clutched in her hand. Deiji pried it from her fingertips, and a mess of Sapphires fell into her palm, twinkling as they caught the evening sun.

She glanced at her Dragon friend.

Geo paced restlessly, keeping a distance away, and finally sat back into the sand and let out one single howl toward the sky.

Only after the Mermaid was far behind them did Deiji stop to rest. She couldn't bury her; it seemed a travesty to take such a beautiful jewel of the sea and trap her within the earth. No, she was to have a Mermaid's burial, out with the evening tide.

They clung to the perimeter of the shore as they made their way along. This made everything so much more real to Deiji. Mermaids were real. There were parts of the world that held undiscovered creatures. Fanciful, awesome creatures that roamed these lands and oceans, as real as she.

She glanced back at Geo. Even he was walking with his head down, deep in some contemplative thought. She imagined the tide pulling the lost Mermaid back into the sea forevermore and she sighed a little. It was getting dark.

Just when she was considering mentioning that they stop and camp there for the night, she saw something out of place in the sand ahead of them, something unnatural…

It was her fire pit! They were back.

It suddenly made sense to Deiji. "This is an island! Like the Trinity Islands of the Southern Gale! Oh my goodness!" She was suddenly very excited and tired.

Only the very wealthy had the luxury of visiting, much less inhabiting such a place. "Back to camp, Geo?" she asked pleasantly.

They went home.

Day Five — Fire

Deiji woke up yearning for a bath. Sitting up, she looked herself over, noticing that her sunburn was quickly deepening into a tan. She was covered with more bug bites, bee stings, sweat, sand and sticky sap than ever.

Grinning, she looked over at her Dragon friend, who rolled over and stretched. "Morning, Geo."

He grunted in reply, and rolled onto his side, his eyes still closed.

"Oh, come now! Today is going to be fun!"

Geo turned his head away and tucked it under his arm.

"Okay," she said teasingly, "I guess I'll have to eat all of today's fruit by myself!" She made a move toward the door.

Geo scrambled to his feet and ran out into the clearing, tripping all over himself.

"Wow," Deiji remarked as she followed him outside, "things have really cooled down. It's foggy." She looked up at the sky, which was gray and muggy and overcast.

Goosebumps prickled in a wave across her arms. She felt the chill in the air, but shrugged it off.

"Let's get some breakfast," she called out with optimism. They gathered fresh fruit for the day, and some to shred and dry for the next. They went fishing off the beach and played fetch with a stick.

As Geo again leapt into the air to catch the stick, his wings unfolded and slowed his decent. Deiji noticed quietly how rapidly he was growing and she mused for a bit.

A lizard skittered its way into the grass, and Geo chased after it. It froze, and Geo held it down with his claw. He poked at it a little, and backed off as Deiji came up behind him.

"Geo?" She looked down at the limp lizard, which had turned green and gangrenous where he had scratched it. "Poison," she muttered. She looked at his claws with curiosity, inspecting them. The tips were dark green – so dark they were nearly black.

"Interesting."

They fished some more and relaxed on the beach after lunch, watching the frothy waves tumble in again and again. The sky was a muddy gray, the sea was a chalky blue, and the waters that stretched out before them were spotted with whitecaps. It began to drizzle.

Deiji's mind wandered back to the mountains. They stood so high above everything else in the world, and she could see for miles from Mount Odel.

The mountain air was thin and cool and wholesome. A single breath breathed for the soul. Everything was lusciously green, the same green all around. The hills, the knolls, the dark distant forests, the cool trails that led down into the valley…

Here on the island the air was thick and humid, and filled with the sweet decay of rotting foliage. Here in this jungle, Deiji was sure she could pick out a dozen shades of green, as well as any other color.

What did she prefer? She asked herself this as she looked out over the cloudy sea. She did not yet have an answer to that question.

The sea churned and roared restlessly, and Deiji could almost sense the calm before the storm.

After finishing the day's tasks, she sat in the strained sunlight beside the hut and watched Geo wrestle with a stick. She finally made a remark. "You've really grown a lot, Geo."

It was true. When she had first found him, he had been about the size of an average village dog. Now he was quickly on his way to gaining the bulk of a small horse. And whenever he stretched, she saw that he had an impressive nine-foot wingspan.

"I guess Dragons grow quickly," she mused. Geo ignored her comment playfully, but she could tell that he was pleased.

Deiji looked up as she leaned back on her hands. Her eyes wandered to the tree overhead; the fruitless tree that was the main support of their hut. She took a long look at those odd branches, the ones that grew outwards and upwards.

Standing up, she found herself drawn to the tree, as if it were calling to her. It was as though it almost whispered... The breeze rustled through the leaves and she felt a chill on the nape of her neck.

Deiji walked around to the back end of the hut so she could look at its lowest branches. They started far above her head; too far to touch.

"Geo, come here," Deiji called without tearing her eyes away. Geo poked his head around the corner quizzically, and walked over to her.

"Boost me up!"

She stepped precariously onto his scaly back. Geo stood on his hind legs, straining to reach his full length, wobbling back and forth as he tried to keep a steady footing.

Deiji grasped the lowest branches and hoisted herself up. She wove her body through the thickly grown wood and leaves until they had thinned out; indeed, the branches became sparse near the top.

On the trunk she saw an odd circular carving that looked very similar to her amulet. It was round, with four circular points. She touched her thumb to the grooves and found the wood smooth.

"Where else have I seen this symbol?" she wondered.

She wrapped her arms around the tree trunk and rested against it for one moment. Suddenly...

"Build a home within my highest branches. It will save you when the light comes," a voice whispered in her head, seemingly from the tree!

"Oh!" Deiji cried out in surprise, losing her footing. She fell off to the side, her leg snagging against a branch. She caught a glimpse of the sky beneath her feet as she dangled. The branch snapped with surprisingly little noise.

Just before she hit the ground, Geo scrambled to break her fall. "Ugh," she said, sprawled on top of her friend. Are you okay?" She rolled onto the ground and Geo came to his feet, nodding his spiked head.

Deiji felt something wet on her leg and she looked down to see a nasty scrape along her calf. She hobbled over to the spring and washed it clean. Tearing a large strip from the hem of her tattered dress, she folded it over twice and bound it around the wound.

She glanced down, and was scandalized to see how short she had made her skirt! It was uneven, and for the most part came to just above her knees. She shrugged inwardly. There was no one to see her, to reprimand her. Besides, the dress was so torn and dirty it didn't really matter.

Deiji tore another thin strip and pulled back her matted hair with it, and glanced up at the tree. Putting her hands against its trunk, she waited for it to speak again. She heard nothing, but there was a definite presence coming from deep within. "Are you there?" she whispered.

Geo looked at her like she was crazy. Deiji hesitated. Was it a voice she should trust? What if it was something sinister, what if it were an enemy that worked for Relant? How was she to know for sure?

She looked up through the jumble of branches and smiled.

"Okay," she said with excitement, "we are going to put together some places to sit in up high." She patted the trunk of the unique tree, trusting the presence she knew was there. "Six of them."

Using grass, clay and leaves, they gathered the largest,

longest sticks they could find to make six thick platforms, large enough for both of them to sit upon.

Geo helped Deiji haul these high into the tree, halfway to the top, one by one. Since Geo couldn't climb up between the tightly knit branches, Deiji climbed through them and had him nudge them up until she could pull them over.

This tree was perfect for it, Deiji saw as she bound them to the branches. They sat up against the trunk, and were supported by the high-reaching limbs.

She tied three platforms down and climbed higher and put the last three above the others. They were done.

She couldn't help but feel satisfied, as if the tree were happy with her for complying with its wishes. Because of her aching leg, they wandered to the beach for the remainder of the day to rest.

Sitting down in the late afternoon sun-warmed sand, Deiji sighed contentedly. "We're going to find a different way for you to get up there, Geo," she said dreamily, her voice carried away on the soft breeze.

Geo looked at her sharply out of the corner of his eyes from where he lay. They sat in the soft and steady wind of the evening in silence, watching the waves.

"I really love it here," she finally said. "*I wish it could last forever,*" she added in her heart. Geo snorted agreeably and rolled onto his back in the sand.

She smiled peacefully, enjoying the beauty of her world, her island.

Day Six – Fire

Deiji sat up in her hut the next morning with a yawn, fresh from a dream of her cornhusk mat and her woolen cloak. But within her heart she carried the truth that this island had somehow become her true home. She nodded her head to Mowat in silent thanks. She was calm in her elation, for she had carried her thoughts with her into her dreams and had awoken to discover that she loved this island dearly.

"Geo," she said, nudging the young Dragon with her foot, "get up!" He opened one eye and stared blearily, still half-asleep.

"Come on, Geo! You're going to learn how to fly today!" Geo's head snapped up, fully awake, with a stricken look on his face. He thrust his head into his pile of leaves and burrowed, whimpering all the while.

"Oh, come now!" she scolded him, forcibly tugging on his leg. He refused to budge.

"Geo," she said with exasperation, and surprising disappointment, "please? At least try?"

Silence.

"You don't want to be a sorry excuse for a Dragon, do you?" she taunted with a hint of a smile.

He stood up slowly, ruffling his back with dignity, not quite looking her in the eye.

Once they had eaten and were on the beach, Deiji suggested that he stretch his wings to prepare them.

"Go on," she prompted, "open your wings."

He cautiously crouched down to the ground and leaned forward, spreading his wings to their full length. He looked at the leathery things over his shoulder, completely uncertain about what to do next. He looked at Deiji for help.

"Um…" she was pained to admit she knew only as much

about flying as Geo himself. But she had a few ideas. "Just try flapping them for starters," she suggested, "that's right, up and down!"

Geo winced and closed his eyes, moving his wings up and down, again and again. The air that caught beneath them made a wonderful WOOSH sound.

He opened one eye and glanced back. He then had his full attention fixated on his wings, wide-eyed and amazed at his own wit. He flapped harder and harder still, and with growing confidence. As his flapping grew steadier, he began to lift from the ground!

"Geo!" Deiji cried, laughing. "Look at you!"

Geo looked down and saw that he was several feet off the ground and gaining. His elation turning to panic, he stopped flapping and tumbled to the sand. He stood up instantly, fresh determination in his eyes, and he flapped as hard as he was able, pushing off from the ground with his clawed feet.

He flew high into the air, quickly attaining and embracing the Dragon's instincts. He zoomed around, doing little stunts and flips in the air, and he came to rest next to Deiji, who was jumping up and down excitedly in the sand, hands clasped together.

"Oh, wow!" she cried, throwing her arms around his scaly neck. "That was magnificent!"

Geo looked down modestly, digging a little with his claw in the sand. Deiji laughed with delight, clasping her hands together.

He looked at her slyly, shifted his wings and lowered himself to the ground. He looked back at her expectantly.

Deiji J Cu eagerly climbed onto the Dragon's back, laughing all the while. She situated herself between his wings, her legs hooked in front of them. "Let's go, Geo!" she shouted.

All at once they lifted off, flapping hard into the open sky.

With the wind rushing from his wings on either side, her hair and face were blown straight back. She grinned as they rose into the air, high and above the island and the ocean, her arms wrapped tightly around his neck.

She looked down and saw a fantastic view of the island below, a circle of green on a blue sheet of glass. She focused on the exhilarating pleasure of flying. Geo did flips and dives while Deiji hung on for dear life. It entered into her mind that perhaps she shouldn't have eaten breakfast that morning, but she was laughing the whole time.

Geo flew higher and higher until the island was nothing more than a dot, a black spot in the vast blue. Farther north she could make out the shapes of more islands; other islands, and strange, airborne shapes that took her a few moments to realize were other Dragons.

"I have seen the world!" she exalted to the sky.

"You have seen nothing yet," a husky voice on the wind carried to her ears.

"*What?*" Deiji looked around, startled, but Geo bucked her off his back in play, and with a jolt she was tumbling through the open air! She fell many, many feet toward the ocean, screaming and laughing, and Geo swooped beneath her and caught her on his back!

He folded his wings into a dive, and they free fell. He opened his wings to catch the air only tree lengths from the water, Deiji laughing from the fun and from the fear. Tears were drawn from her eyes involuntarily as they fell. They made a sharp turn toward the sky and she was nearly torn from his back. Giddy with laughter, they made their way back toward the beach.

Her heart pounding, Deiji flopped down on the cold evening sand. Geo slumped next to her, out of breath. She laughed again, trying to steady her shaking hands. They lay back and breathed.

After dinner that night, she took a walk alone on the beach and up the bluffs. A stronger, colder wind blew, and she kept her gaze on the sunset. She ignored the chill as well a deep, unsettling feeling that something wrong.

Who was the voice that had spoken to her above the clouds? Could it have been Mowat? Her spirits darkened. Relant, maybe?

Flying had been everything she dreamed of and more. It was freedom. This new life was freedom.

She watched the sun set, lost in her thoughts. Beautiful streaks of pastels, purples, blues and yellows all blended into a shocking, burning orange.

The ocean waves poured in and receded over and again. The roar was almost musical. Dark clouds loomed on the horizon, an unsettling omen.

"A storm is coming," she said aloud to no one. She could only wonder how great a storm.

CHAPTER THREE

The Tiger

Day Seven — Fire

Deiji and Geo, accustomed to their simple new life with few worries or frowns, devoted their day to play. On this particular morning the two were playing in the ocean, splashing about in the waves, when Deiji noticed a glow emitting from beneath her.

Looking down, she saw the medallion. The Ruby surrounded by the silver engravings of flames had lit up a fiery red, and its glow cast an orange glare into the water.

"What on earth…" Deiji wondered in shock, snatching up the medal. Her mind seemed strangely blank. Then she remembered!

"Arill!" she cried, frantically searching the waters around her. "Arill, where are you!?" She plunged her head underwater and span around in hasty circles. She lifted her head from the water and searched the shoreline.

"Mowat said there would be a signal of Arill's coming!" she cried. Geo looked around skyward, clearly confused.

Then, Deiji heard the distinct whoosh of a blowhole. She whirled about in the water, and there he was!

"Arill!" she cried with joy. She hugged him as best one can hug a dolphin and brought her head to his.

Once they touched she felt herself being pulled into his mind and space.

"I am here," he said in her head. "I have come as Mowat promised, and I bring a message." Deiji's heart filled fit to burst! It was so lovely to hear a real voice.

"Deiji, my friend, I am in urgent need to tell you of this thing. It has been a week in this selection of time and space for you."

A week? It felt more like a year.

"Moreover," Arill continued, "it is a turning point in time. The decisions you make now will forever mold the future. The challenges you face..." his voice trailed off and she felt a twinge of worry from his end. "An enemy is coming."

Yet another chill ran down her spine.

"You must be prepared to face this enemy of fire. He is a servant and a tool of Relant's, and he will guard this element with his very life."

Deiji drew her breath in sharply. She had quite forgotten the point of this project, of this whole experience! She felt a shift of change in the way of the wind and the future.

Oh, but no! She desperately wanted to hold on to these times of joy and freedom. She wanted nothing more than what she had now. Here, on this island, with Geo...

"Mowat may take what is good and bring forth what is better, Deiji," Arill said quietly.

She did not answer.

"This life will not be lost forever."

She closed her eyes and nodded, feeling the beginnings of blind acceptance flood through her veins.

"The edge of fear has left you," Arill said suddenly in admiration. "That is well. Fear is the weakened knees of all that can be good."

"What must I do?" she asked heavily.

"You will face Adar, the orange tiger. He is brutal, mighty and merciless. He has arrived to clear the way ahead for Relant, whose journey keeps him three days away. Can you feel it? He is coming. If Adar wins, Relant will arrive here to join him in the killing of the entire colony of Dragons. You will be discovered and slaughtered. But if you defeat this evil, Mowat will come for you in that moment. If you die…" He let the warning hang in the air.

"But how, then?" she asked earnestly.

She felt a wave of genuine sorrow and concern from him. "I cannot tell you how," he admitted. "I do not know. But I can say he has a power within him; a power that can control all things fire."

"Well, what do I do, then? I do not know how to do this! What power does he have?" Her voice rose to a higher pitch.

"Be calm! You will use what is available to you. You will use caution. And ultimately, hope."

Deiji swallowed hard.

"I may, however, offer a verse of comfort."

"Go on."

He paused. When he spoke again it was with the song of the Dolphin, and Deiji could feel the pressures of life lift away, and the soul of the ocean bringing light to her heart.

"Look inside the dragon stone, I see the lost of me.
The strength and pride the Dragon holds, his humble majesty.
Cast away the dragon stone, losing all I've sought,
The time of rocks and all the Runes, now what have I forgot?"

The lymric echoed with song in Deiji's head, the words transfixed in her memory.

"Now then, my friend, I must go."

He sank beneath the waves, and with a splash of his tail he was gone.

"Wait!" she cried frantically, trudging through the waters after him. One glance at her amulet, however, confirmed with its dullness that she was truly alone.

Well, not entirely. She turned toward her truest friend. "Geo…"

His eyes were fixated on the shoreline. "Geo?"

Following his terrified gaze she saw a large, muscular tiger with black stripes and a white mane standing on the beach. Smoke was misting from his nostrils, and his eyes reflected in dancing orange flames against black. His tail was twitching like a dancing serpent.

"Adar," Deiji whispered.

Adar leapt, springing toward the surf! Deiji hurriedly sloshed through the waters toward Geo.

"Fly fly FLY!" she screamed, wrenching herself heavily out of the water and onto his back. She was suddenly seized with fear.

Geo flapped quickly and they rose from the churning waters. What to do? Oh, she was so lost!

"Geo!" she shouted down to him through the rushing wind as they glided over the jungle, "go to the tree! Our little planks are high enough, and he won't be able to get through the lower branches!" *We hope*, she added silently as Geo changed his direction.

They landed in their clearing and Deiji frantically gathered up the dried fruit and the knife she had crafted, bundling it all into her arms.

She leapt onto the Dragon's back and they were airborne just as Adar leapt into the clearing.

They took refuge on their lower platforms, using the second set of planks above them for shelter against the rain that started to fall.

The roof was leaky.

Geo flitted from treetop to treetop, gathering large palm leaves to keep the water off, as Deiji shivered behind in the tree. Adar had seemingly vanished into the foliage.

Deciding there was nothing more they could do that night, they fell asleep in discomfort, lulled by the sound of the pounding rain.

Day Eight – Fire

When they awoke, Deiji knew immediately where they were and why they were. She'd hardly slept the night through, only dozed. She woke Geo with a gentle nudge.

They wolfed down their wetted dried fruit from the day before and took but a brief moment to dart down to the spring to drink.

Deiji was standing near the water, urging Geo to drink and be done with, when she caught the smell of smoke on the air.

She paused and looked about the trees for the source of the smell. Was the forest on fire? She stared at the bushes to the left of her. She had a sense that something was wrong. Evil flooded her senses, as she stood frozen, unable to think or move.

"Geo…" her voice carried warning. He looked up abruptly and Deiji still stood transfixed.

Then from the bushes came Adar! He leapt at them with a

mighty bellowing roar. Smoke was wafting from his nostrils is great clouds, and the flames in his eyes danced with rage.

Geo flew into the air faster than Deiji could see. He caught her around the shoulders with his mighty talons and carried her off just as the orange tiger came falling through the air after them, claws outstretched.

He missed them by mere inches as they flew up to their treetop. They watched him land on the ground effortlessly, with liquid grace.

Adar circled around their camp clearing, pacing restlessly. Pausing before her hut thoughtfully, he opened his mouth and blew a gust of red-hot flames. Their hut caught fire and burned to the ground in seconds, right before her eyes.

"My home," she whispered.

Adar sauntered around the camp, pausing periodically to burn out parts of the clearing. He marked his scent on the base of their tree, and kicked his hind legs to fill the spring with dirt. He looked up at her smugly.

His message was clear: "This is not your home."

Deiji's eyes stung as she looked at the clearing that was now nothing more than a big, black smudge. She felt awful. Her carefully constructed world had been pulled from beneath her feet in a matter of moments. She placed her hands against the tree and closed her eyes in sorrow.

"*Acceptance will make you strong,*" the words of Mowat echoed in her mind. She opened her eyes. Had Mowat ever said that?

Geo nudged her arm and she released the tree to hug him. For the afternoon they glided from tree to tree, Geo hovering while Deiji picked fruit and gathered it into what remained of her skirt.

There was no chance for them to fish or cook; for Adar was always near, stalking, waiting.

"What do I do?" Deiji lamented. "I have three days! One girl and one young Dragon against a full-grown tiger? A tiger who breathes fire, nonetheless! What does Mowat expect of me?"

They sat on their treetop, waiting and thinking. Deiji knew she needed to explore what she was up against; needed to really know her enemy before she could make any decision or action. What other secret powers might he posses? She sighed.

Deiji kept her eyes on the tree line. She figured if she kept a careful eye on him, he couldn't pull anything sneaky. A sudden movement in the bushes caught her watchful gaze.

"He's back," she hissed. Geo's ears flattened back, and Deiji spat, infuriated that she was under siege on her own island.

Adar grinned, baring his teeth and the flames in his eyes began to dance with excitement.

He strutted up to the tree with the utmost confidence, his tail twitching eagerly. The wispy smoke emanating from his nostrils began to billow into darker clouds.

He blew a large, crackling fire from his open mouth to ignite the tree and Deiji braced herself to flee.

But the tree did not catch flame.

Adar tried again, his eyes moving quickly, losing a bit of his cocky swagger. Again and again he tried, but it was in vain. The tree would not burn.

He leapt into the branches, but he could not make it over the tightly grown limbs.

He turned away and burned down the nearest sapling in anger, and stalked off into the jungle in a piteous rage.

Deiji sat there dumbfounded. Geo, a Dragon of insight and of action, quickly gobbled down his fruit.

She sat back in near-shock. "Geo," she said with wonder, "this tree is special. There must be a magical quality about it. I am so glad we set our home here. I am so glad he cannot touch us here."

They watched the sunset that night in bitter silence, skipping dinner. And when the sun was gone and the sky was once again a cloudy black, they nestled under their palm leaves with the hope of sleep.

The smell of smoke was wet in the air. Rolling onto her side, Deiji opened her eyes and frowned. The night air was eerily cold, and the wind was howling shrilly.

Disoriented, it took her but a moment to realize that the earth beneath her was moving.

No, not moving… The tree they were perched in was swaying. She pulled the leaves from her face and looked to the ground.

As she suspected, Adar was sitting near the base of the tree, waiting patiently, his tail twitching.

"Geo, get up!" Deiji said sharply. He lifted his head at her urgent tone. It was raining hard and their platform was hideously wet.

Suddenly and fully awake, she saw that the tree was swaying too heavily in the raging wind, and it groaned under the strong gusts. The world around them was almost completely dark. There was no moon.

Thunder and lightning flashed in the distance and lit up the ocean waves, which wildly tore at the beach, an angry vengeance in motion.

"Up, Geo!" she called out again calmly. He was rigid, alert and ready to fly. "Hold on!" she called out against the wind and rain.

Deiji needed to see what Adar would do, and they held on desperately as the tree was rocked violently back and forth in the harsh wind.

A flash of lightning nearby and Deiji's and Adar's eyes met. Those flames in his eyes flickered and danced with confidence. She suddenly knew his plan…

"Geo!" she screamed, "he's using the storm to drive us away from the tree! He's going to use light -" No sooner had she said it than lightning flashed, striking the top of their tree.

The wood cracked and groaned, sparks flew into the night, and the tree snapped right down the middle, straight to the ground!

Geo became safely airborne at once, but Deiji found herself plummeting headfirst toward the dirt.

"Geo!" she choked out against the storm, but the wind tore her words away.

The Dragon swooped down, catching her shoulder in his talons just before she hit the ground. They dug into her flesh, not quite breaking the skin, and though it smarted, she did not care.

He flapped hard against the wind, the gales of rainwater beating him down, his scaly brow set in firm determination.

"Higher, Geo!" she cried, though she knew he did all he could. She screamed in terror, seeing a flash of orange leaping toward them. Geo fought the storm with all his strength, lifting her higher and not an inch too low, for Adar caught her lingering left leg with his outstretched claws. At first she felt nothing, and then a blinding pain shot through her body. Her leg felt as though it were on *fire*.

As they headed higher into the storm, Geo tumbled around, fighting desperately to keep them upright as he was tossed around.

"Geo!" Deiji shouted suddenly, thinking of Arill's riddle, "Dragon stone! The CAVE, Geo!" She felt blood and rainwater running down her leg.

She needed to stop, needed to rest. She was cold and scared

and hurt, and knew that it would end soon. They needed a place with few exits, where Adar couldn't get behind her, couldn't trick her...

Geo shifted his direction and flapped hurriedly through the torrent of rain toward the dragon stone cave where they had first met. When the lightning flashed Deiji could see the jungle trees rushing by beneath them as they flew.

Geo swooped straight into the cave, dropping her straight away. They both tumbled and rolled, coming to a stop on the cave's cold stone floor.

They stood to collect themselves. Deiji glanced at her leg and had to look away. It had four long, blackened bloody scratches running down it. Her throbbing leg issued more blood with each pulse, and felt as though she had burned it badly.

Tearing the sleeves from her dress, Deiji sat and gritted her teeth to the pain as she wrapped the gashes tight and applied pressure. Securing the dressings with a knot, she laid her head back against the cave wall and listened to the rain pattering outside.

She rolled her head to the side to look at her Dragon friend. He was sitting close, catching his breath, and licking at a bloodied scrape on his shoulder from their sudden landing.

"Adar is coming," she told him calmly. Geo nodded in silent acceptance.

"I wish I had your strength, Geo." She closed her eyes. "What do we do now? The tree is down... Adar is hunting us as I speak..."

Geo looked at her for a long while as she rested, then looked at his mother's skeleton in the rear of the cave. Something had picked her flesh nearly clean. He walked quickly over to the cache of treasure and plucked a Ruby from the pile with his teeth and carried it back to her.

Deiji accepted it into her palm. "Is this good luck?"

He nodded.

She smiled.

She smelled cinder and ash and her smile faded. She jumped to her feet. Geo growled toward the cave's opening.

Lightning flashed, lighting up the cave's entrance. There, amidst the pouring rain, stood Adar. Deiji and the tiger stared at one another for a moment, and then Adar sprang!

Geo leapt, overshooting Adar's jump, landing behind him. He doubled back and swiped at the tiger with his bladed tail before he could reach Deiji, who had ducked to the ground.

Adar was flung forwards by the blow, right over Deiji's head, and he tumbled across the cave floor. He rolled, landed upright on all four paws, suddenly positioned and ready to strike. Geo landed next to Deiji, tail poised, prepared to fight.

Adar sneered at the Dragon. He sprung right against the wall, and used his momentum to fire himself straight at Geo. He caught him under the chin with his muscular paws, knocking the wind out of him.

The tiger landed gracefully, and kicked his hind leg at the recovering Dragon's head, sending his spiked head into the cave wall. Geo crumpled to the ground, unmoving.

"Geo!" Deiji cried in fear.

Adar turned toward her, snarling. She backed away, her mind desperately searching for a way out of this, or something she could do to save them. For the second time in her life she felt death tapping on her shoulder. And this time it would not be an easy death. She wondered distantly how long the pain would last.

The tiger was approaching her. She felt wave after wave of blind panic and adrenaline course through her body, and she suddenly turned and *ran*.

She squeezed through the rib bones of the Dragon skeleton

and threw herself against the opposite rock wall. Adar could not fit through the bones, nor could he jump over them.

The tiger snarled and she shuddered at his blackened teeth. He stuck a paw through to swipe at her in frustration, but he could not reach. Deiji snatched up a long piece of splintered bone from the ground and held it tightly.

Adar opened his mouth wide to scorch her, and Deiji ducked and rolled. She hurried to her feet and slipped through the ribs again, just in time. The skeleton charred behind her and crumbled to ashes.

She used the splintered bone in her hand and jabbed at Adar's head harshly as he turned, but his thick mane protected his neck.

He breathed fire at her once again. She rolled onto her back again, and to her feet, dodging the flames.

She held the bone out in front of her as one would hold a sword and snarled at him.

Adar gave a loud roar of indignation and darted forward, slashing her good leg with his outstretched claws.

Deiji cried out and grabbed her leg, falling to one knee. With another swipe of his paw, he knocked her to the ground.

Using one hand she backed herself up against the cave wall. *"I only have one shot at this,"* she thought, her heart pounding in her ears. Though bruised and bleeding, her mind was surprisingly clear through the pain.

Adar approached her slowly, proud of his work. It was clear as he circled her that he was making a show of it. Smoke billowed from his nostrils and clouded the air around his face, and Deiji coughed a little.

He let out a growl and shook his mane, and as the smoke cleared, she saw the flames in his eyes become more distinct.

Deiji tightened her grip on the Dragon bone. He moved closer and leaned back as if to pounce, and she thrust it through his right eye with all her might as he came at her! The tiger let out a howl so terrible her heart caught in her throat, and she leaned to the side as he fell back writhing in pain. She jumped to her feet, stumbling away as quickly as her injuries allowed.

Adar screamed like a wildcat in his pain and his rage, bringing his paws to his face, trying to get the bone out of his eye. He used his paws to grip it, and it he pulled it and shook his head until he was free of it, and it clattered to the ground.

He turned one murderous eye toward her, the other gushing blood and already beginning to swell.

Deiji was staggering, limping with her injuries. She glanced back and saw him charging toward her, blood streaming from his torn eye socket. She stumbled and fell.

Adar approached her, ready to kill. Her fingers found a rock and she threw it in cold defiance. "Get away!" she screamed shrilly. It all seemed strangely muffled.

Deiji felt as though it were an image from a dream – the kind of dream she hated, a dream where she had to get moving, had to run from where she stood, but was absolutely frozen in place.

She glared at her conqueror from where she lay, angry to be robbed of her life by such a fate, and she spat forth through gritted teeth and with as much courage as she could muster, "I will not cry."

Adar opened his mouth and Deiji closed her eyes…

And then Geo landed between them! "Geo!" she cried out with joy and surprise.

The Dragon's wings flared out, shielding the girl as he faced the tiger, and he let out a low growl. Adar roared back at him, and Geo lunged forward, forcing him to back away.

Deiji pushed herself back against the wall as the two foes circled one another, occasionally lashing out, paw for claw and gnashing teeth.

Adar opened his mouth and blew his fire at the Dragon. Geo rose into the air, circled behind him, and nicked him in the back with his great poisonous talons. Adar twisted around and saw the open wound on his shoulder and he gave a mighty roar of outrage.

All at once they both leapt into the air! They jumped to strike, blowing fire at one another. Adar's flame was a crackling, sparking orange and white-hot red. Geo's fire was a soft purple, imbued with silver and white rays of light.

Deiji watched in awe as the two jets of flame collided in a shower of sparks. Time seemed to stand still as the two creatures remained in mid-air. Geo lifted his claws and shot his poison at Adar, squirting the dark green stuff into his remaining eye. The tiger fell back to grab at his blinded eye. Geo jumped forward and struck him with a swipe of his spiked tail. A splash of blood and Adar tumbled backwards.

There was a blinding white light, and Deiji found herself staring into the face of Mowat.

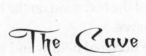

The Cave

"You made it," he said, pride and sunlight beaming from his eyes.

"What? I – what?" Deiji sputtered in shock. It was over.

"Yes," Mowat said encouragingly, "you did it. You survived. You did all to the best of your abilities, and you have won."

Deiji closed her eyes, relief flooding her body. It was over.

"What does this mean?" she asked carefully.

"By defeating the enemy of the fire element, you have restored those sick in that region to full health. Relant will arrive to the islands to find that not only has Adar failed to begin his work, but that he has perished. He has lost one of his servants."

"Then it is done." The beginnings of a smile tugged on the corners of her lips.

"Unfortunately, no," Mowat said with obvious patience. Her smile faded.

"You have liberated a mere one fourth of all who are in need," he said simply. "Three of his henchmen remain as well as those who follow him, and they need to be stopped."

She sighed. "Go on."

"There are four main elements. I believe I told you that you had four tasks to complete?" His eyes twinkled, and he continued. "And each allotment of time you spend it the different elements will be different. Some may be shorter, others longer."

"Ah. So what has happened, then? What does it mean that they are liberated?"

"All damages to that part of the world have been repaired. Relant's hold on the fire element has been loosened. Mind, if you are not victorious for the duration of the next three elements, everything will go back to as it was."

Deiji remembered the Mermaid on the beach and wondered if her life had been saved.

"I will do it," she declared boldly, and with passion.

"That is well. Now, you must rest for a time before you continue in your trials."

"But…" Deiji couldn't find the words. "Geo!" she finally choked out, feeling a wave of gratitude for her brave friend who was no longer beside her. Geo, who had ultimately fought and won her battle.

Mowat smiled. "Geo is well. But his part in this is over. I have placed him under the care of Docin the Dragon Keeper on the northernmost of the Dragon Islands."

"Docin." Deiji nodded, accepting this as a positive. "And Adar... He is dead," she confirmed.

Mowat nodded. "The fight between Adar and Geo became so imbalanced that I even dropped my scales. Dragon stone and tiger's eye all over the floor..." He winked.

"You will have a day to rest before you move onto the next element. Arill will be by tomorrow to visit with you. Sleep here. Oh, and there's a hot bath waiting for you behind that curtain," he nodded toward the wall.

It was then that she first noticed the room she was in. It seemed to be in a cave of sorts, Mowat's cave, though somewhat different than when she had first seen it. It had a high, rocky ceiling, which was the only confirmation that it was a cave. It still had a slight slope that led down to a pool of water, and she knew that this was where she would find Arill later.

She was on a large bed with two silk green coverlets. Deiji was pleased to find she was propped up against two great, fluffy green pillows, and dressed in an equally luxurious robe. She looked up to thank Mowat, but he had gone.

Behind the curtain in the left corner, as promised, was a large wooden tub, filled to the brim with hot, sudsy water. Ornate and decorative soaps lined the rim, and she laughed, for never had she seen such things.

Exploring further, she found a fresh dress, robe and cloak hanging on hooks on the wall. Below them sat a pair of shoes with stockings folded neatly underneath.

As she sank into her steamy bath, she laughed again at the clean and perfumed scents. It was so strange to be so clean, and she relaxed a little. Deiji understood that this was to be her save haven; a place of respite between battles.

She looked at the pretty array of scented soaps and wondered if she was meant to use them. She decided Mowat wouldn't mind.

After drying off, she put on her fresh robe and it suddenly hit her – all of her wounds from the previous day's hardships were mended. She was surprised to see that her legs carried scars, but there was no pain.

There was a table set near the entrance of the cave, and a hot meal of meat and potato sat waiting for her on ceramic dishes. She ate heartily and drank hot tea from the mug and found herself overcome by exhaustion.

She clambered onto the bed and snuggled into its softness and in minutes was lost to the world of dreams.

The Necromancer

Mowat was relieved. And proud. Never had he been so proud. His pupil had not failed him. She had shown great courage and strength. She had done what no one else could do.

He watched from above as the girl slept, safe and silent in her dreams. He knew Deiji was inexperienced to the things of the world, only a child, but he now held an undying faith in her, which filled his heart fit to burst. He could sense Relant's outrage from afar and he smiled again.

"Do you think she can do it?" Arill asked his master and lifelong friend. "Do you believe she can handle the pressures of water?"

Mowat stepped to the edge of space, observing the rotations of the planets and stars, distracted.

"I believe she can," he said at last. "She has shown that she is capable. And you have heard of the legend. If it is indeed she, then she will do so much more than what I am asking of her." He looked to Arill. "And you?"

"The moment our minds touched I knew that there was something unique about this human," Arill confided. "She carries the essence of the ocean in her soul, and I believe she is the One they speak of."

The last individual Mowat had chosen for a task had failed him greatly, many years ago. For a long time he had been very skeptical of any student he had taken on, lest one disappoint and humiliate him again. And so much more was at stake this time around, even if he did have the assurances of the Prophesy, aside. Still, he did not know.

Mowat turned away again, adding a Sapphire to his scales and he gazed at the sleeping child for a long time. Finally he spoke.

"We shall see."

The Cave

Deiji stirred where she lay. She rolled over, pleased and comfortable in the gradual awakening of her mind, basking in the sweet warmth and relaxation she found in this large, fluffy bed.

"Comfortable," she grunted from between the silken sheets.

She opened her eyes slowly and tried to pull things into focus. Feeling a bout of anxiety, she frowned, not remembering all at once where she was. She sat up, staring at the spacious cave around her and sighed as it all came back to her.

Moving the soft covers aside, she swung her feet over the edge of the bed. A bright light caught her eye from below, and glancing down she saw the edges of her medallion glowing like the sun, piercing the cave's dim lighting.

"Arill!" she cried, leaping to her feet and throwing herself down at the water's edge. Sure enough, Arill surfaced in front of her. Kneeling by the water and touching heads, they excitedly engaged in conversation.

"It is so good to see you!"

"And you, Deiji."

"When you suddenly left me alone on the island to face Adar, I almost panicked!" she laughed.

Arill's tone turned serious. "I sincerely beg your forgiveness, Deiji. I hope you have a full understanding of the reasons behind my actions?"

"Of course I do."

"My congratulations on your recent success, by the way. Very impressive."

Deiji beamed.

Arill continued. "Soon Mowat will assign you to your next task. I have the honor of escorting you there myself."

"I am rested."

"Then why don't you dress and prepare. I will summon Mowat within the hour."

Deiji smiled nervously. "Thank you, my friend. I will see you there."

She spent a lost moment sitting back and staring into the watery void. She found this place to be eerily quiet, without the constant roar of the ocean, but she was relieved to have a chance to catch her breath, and she was overly glad that at least a portion of this project was over.

She longed for Geo, that was sure. She had grown used to having him at her side, protecting her, walking through things as her friend and companion. He had helped her fish...

She got to her feet and realized she was quite hungry.

After eating the porridge and warmed bread and tea that were laid out upon the table, Deiji donned the fresh dress that was hanging near the tub. As she reached for the cloak, a sudden burst of water came from the pool behind her.

She turned and saw the wave twist up into the air, a brilliant blue color, with thousands of tiny radiant Pearls spinning around the swell. It parted and hung in midair and never fell.

In the middle of the parted waves stood Mowat, looking strangely noble. The cave around her began to dim, and millions of silver pinpricks slowly came into focus; stunningly bright stars emerged into the night sky all around her. Mowat still hovered in front of her, looking as wise as ever. He spoke.

"For the deeds you have done, and for your willingness to move forward with these tasks, I will bequeath to you a valued gift: the gift of magic."

Deiji was stunned. "Magic? Of what sort?"

"If you can say these words, '*Ferula Imperio*,' you will be impervious to fire and flame. It will not be of much use for this next trial, but it will useful in the future. Even smoke will not harm you. If you say '*Ferula Debeo*,' you will shoot flames from your fingertips. You have the power of fire within you now, until the end of your time. Use it well."

Deiji could hardly breathe. Magic.

"Does this mean you do not have these powers within yourself anymore?" she asked with concern. Mowat smiled sadly and did not answer.

"This next task is quite different than the one you have just experienced. It involves a sort of … transformation … to adapt to this element. Your goals to keep in mind are for the liberation of all those lost to some imbalance or injustice. Arill will take you there. And you will not need that cloak," he added.

The cloak she held in hand slowly disappeared into space. "That dress will be modified as well," Mowat said mysteriously.

Deiji looked around nervously, not knowing what to expect. "Um, thank you," she mustered. She wanted him to know that she was grateful for her new powers. He was looking hard into her eyes and began chanting.

"The ocean moves; the sea, it sings,
Her heart is ailed by many things.
Heal her now, forevermore,
And she will live in tales of lore.
Mystics of the deep, come forth, unite!
One has come to fight your fight.
To kill the creature of the night,
The reason you have fled in fright.
She is from above,
Not of your kin.
So for this task, to maybe win,
I might just have
to give her fins!"

CHAPTER FOUR

The Mermaid

Day One – Water

Deiji blinked. When she opened her eyes, she began to panic. *Water! Pressing in from every side!* Instinctively she kicked, thrashing about.

"My legs!" she cried in horror, discovering three things at once: she could speak! And breathe! And she had a *tail*. Her legs seemed to have melted together, surrounded by green flesh and scales.

"Fins?" she asked herself aloud, disbelieving. Turning about in the water, she saw a Dolphin.

"Arill!" she cried out. She moved toward him to speak, but her movements were clumsy and she turned about in the water helplessly.

Right away she discovered she could speak to him without making contact, because he answered her as he swam. "Hello, Deiji!" he called out cheerfully.

"Arill! My legs! What did Mowat do to me? I can talk and breathe! *Under water!*" She was astounded.

Arill gave her a funny Dolphin grin. "You are a Mermaid now, my friend. You can now live and breathe underwater. You can speak to others in the sea, and they will understand you."

"This is so amazing!" Her eyes widened.

"Welcome to my world!" He swam a few circles around her happily, and she laughed at his graceful movements, cheered to be with a friend.

"Your world is lovely," she smiled.

"It is," Arill agreed, "but it is also a dangerous place."

"Dangerous?" She felt the slightest bit of fear at his tone.

"The ocean is as vast as the heavens. Not in size, perhaps, but in its mysteries. You must be very careful, my friend. The stories of predator and prey here are never-ending."

She nodded.

"My world is also in danger. The continents are shifting, the Merpeople are ever dwindling in number, and the Whales... oh, the *Whales*..." If ever a Dolphin could look sorrowful, somehow Arill managed it.

"You see, my friend," he continued sadly, "many years ago a creature known as the Balla was killing off the Merpeople to such an extent that a council was held by the creatures of the Deep, and many actions were made to preserve the species. They were rash decisions, made in the hopes that one day the Balla would be defeated, and the Merpeople could come back to the water. To this day the creatures prey upon them still, and in a few short years this hope to restore their numbers to the sea will be lost. Coupled with the spread of the fever, the situation is dire."

"What must I do?" Deiji asked earnestly.

"Save my world, if you can. If ever you did a more important thing... You are my friend, Deiji, and this is my greatest hope."

"I will do what I can, my friend."

"I know you will. Now, I must go. Keep your eyes on your Sapphire."

She looked to her amulet, the portion where the teardrop stone sat among the engravings of water. "Please don't go," she pleaded softly, knowing it was useless.

"I must. But I will see you soon, when the time is right." He slid around her like a silk ribbon and swam away.

She moved to swim after him but her movements failed her. She thrashed about, turning upside-down and sideways, completely disoriented. She watched helplessly as Arill faded into the blueness.

Deiji took a moment to look at herself. She was wearing the top of her dress, but it was sleeveless. The stone knife sat in a leather holster at her waist, its strap draped across one shoulder. Her tailfins were long, sparkling and green. Her long hair was loose and floated about her in the water.

She tried to swim, but could not paddle individual legs as she was used as a human. This new form required her to paddle her tail up and down, as if it were one big leg. She felt quite awkward, but found she was getting better at it.

And so Deiji began steering herself around, mimicking the Dolphin, and she relaxed a little. "Okay," she said. "Okay." She paddled more quickly, and more still, and she began to move with speed.

She laughed, the water flying by her as swiftly as air. "Okay! I think I have this! I can swim!" After twirling around weightlessly, she took notice of the scenery surrounding her.

It appeared to be a shallow coral reef. It was alight with brilliantly colored fish, all changing directions in synchronized movements. The beautiful pink coral was twisted into millions of branches, with hundreds of the tiny fish weaving in and out of its forest.

The ocean was a beautiful sky blue, and the sun dappled waters reflected off the sandy floor, sending the silver lines wavering across everything Deiji saw. Seeing all these wonderful colors and shapes, she laughed, pleased with this new corner of the world that Mowat presented her with.

She allowed herself to sink, and lay down on the warm sand, watching it cloud and settle around her. Staring up at the surface, the little jewel-like fish could be seen flickering overhead; glossy colors flipping shades all at once with every change of direction. Deiji laughed again and moved toward them.

"The surface!" Air... Sky... As she swam upwards an instinctive fear struck her. She felt suddenly intimidated, and she hesitated. No... She had to see.

She swam with speed and propelled herself through the clear, cool waters toward the sky. Deiji flew up, up and out of the water, the warm air whipping her hair around, and she did a flip. She saw a landmass in the distance while she turned. An island, perhaps, but not her island.

Deiji fell like a rock and splashed into the warm, bubbly comfort of the ocean. She was startled by the natural-bred uneasiness the surface brought to her. She could see, as she treaded water with her long tail that the reef had grown off the shore of some unknown land. Turning away from the land and reef all that could be seen was an endless blue that faded to nothingness.

Popping her head out of the water she was surprised to see that the pale afternoon sun was farther on than she'd thought. She turned tail to sky, searching along the bottom for what might be a safe place to stay the night. Being out in the open made her, as both Human and Mermaid, uneasy.

She saw several caves about, both small and large tucked beneath the reef. Something inside her objected strongly to venturing there, and Deiji decided to go with that feeling.

A shadow crossing above caught her eye. There were seven Dolphins swimming overhead, chasing each other in play. "Arill?" she called out desperately, but none of them were he.

One larger Dolphin swam down to her and chattered with welcome. "Hello there, little one! I am Hael!"

"It is lovely to meet you! I am Deiji J Cu," she answered with pleasure, and Hael grinned.

"Are you searching for one like you?" he asked her enthusiastically.

"One... like me?" Deiji echoed, confused.

"Yes! A little Fin, just like you! I saw her not too long ago. Her name is Elail, and the poor Fin's family is lost. Ah, she is alone."

"Wait," Deiji said, holding up one hand. "I am a 'Fin?'"

The Dolphin Hael stared silently for a moment, obviously confused. Deiji continued on, "and Elail, this one you speak of, she is a 'Fin' as well?"

Hael jerked his head through the water, peering at her closely.

"Um," Deiji said cautiously, sidestepping the awkwardness, "where might I find shelter this night?"

"Why, in the lagoon, little one. It is called Safe Bay." He continued to eye her with curiosity.

"I am a bit unfamiliar with these surroundings," she explained quickly. "I am new to this sea. I do not even know where I am."

"Ah!" the Dolphin cried cheerfully, doing a little flip in the water. "Why, you are in the Southern Gale, little Fin! By the Trinity Islands!"

"Really? That's incredible!"

All her life she had heard of the cities and villages on these tropical islands. The blacksmith's map was quite detailed of this coveted place. Only the most wealthy and adventurous prospered here. These weren't quite the circumstances she had expected for her first visit, but it was still wonderful.

No, it was better!

"Yes, this is the place," Hael confirmed. "And if you so wish it, I could take you to Safe Bay this night."

"That would be wonderful!"

He turned to let her take hold of his dorsal fin, but hesitated. "There is but one thing, my friend." He seemed to have grown very solemn.

"And what is that?" she asked, perplexed.

"In this sea, at least, it is customary for all to swear to the Code."

"The Code?"

"The Code is for the lasting preservation of creatures of the ocean everywhere. It is known that all are in danger, and each and every one of us must go out of their way to protect one another. These are the acts that were instituted to assist the triumph of Man's safe return to the sea.

"Furthermore, each and every act of kindness one performs must be from the heart, not perfunctory. There is a beauty to making the water a safer place, where there is the assurance of kindness repaid with ultimate sincerity. You must take this kindness with you, and through consistent acts of selflessness we will all spread it to the whole ocean! It is our way of fighting for life."

"Then I swear to it," Deiji said easily, for she was of a kind heart. She reached for his dorsal fin.

As he towed her through the waters toward the bay, she stared down below at all the eventide sea life ending and starting their days. As the waters grew eerily darker and night came on, the creatures of the night emerged to go about their part of life.

Deiji was lost in her thoughts as they swam. What did Hael

mean when he said Man would return to the sea? The thought struck her. Was Man from the ocean? It sure made a lot of sense, after all.

Hael brought her to a nearby island, entering a small bay on the northern side. The entrance was quite shallow and they both had to jump over the rocks into the pool on the other side.

"Here you are, little Fin! You may stay here as long as you wish, and you will be safe. And remember the Code!"

"Thank you, my friend." She paused. "Might I request a second act of kindness? I will pledge to take your Code and walk the world with it."

"That you may!" he cried, though she knew he did not fully understand her meaning.

"In the morning will you come here and escort me to this Fin you spoke of, the one called Elail? I believe she will help me in my purpose a great deal."

"Of course we will," Hael said kindly. "I will see you in the sun."

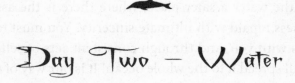

Day Two — Water

Deiji awoke squinting into the sunlight, groggy and considerably hungry. She would have to ask Elail what was appropriate for a Mermaid to eat.

She found herself pleased with this element, as she smiled to the morning sun. Living underwater was like something from a dream, or a fantasy from an early imaginative youth.

Deiji yawned indulgently and noticed that Hael and his family were already in the bay, waiting. "Oh, my," she said swimming up to them. "Are you ready to go? I hope I have not kept you long."

Not a single Dolphin acknowledged her presence and she frowned. Every one of them were staring, alert with fear, out into the open ocean.

"What is happening?" Deiji asked quickly; keen to sense the Dolphin's perceptions. Her eyes searched wildly over the rocky entrance into Safe Bay.

There was a shark's fin, just visible on the water line. It was a very large shark, with many rows of jagged teeth and black, soulless eyes. He looked to be five times the size of a single Dolphin and Deiji shivered instinctively with fear.

"It is a very good thing he cannot get in here!" she declared in relief, but as she spoke, she saw the creature was circling around something small in the water. She peered closer and saw a baby Dolphin. The shark was preparing to lunge for it.

"Who...?"

"It is Crosso, my son," Hael said hastily and nervously. "We came for you, and when we were near, we saw the creature... We leapt here to safely, one after the other, and in the confusion, my son was left behind." His voice rose in panic, but there was no accusation in his voice.

Still, Deiji felt a wave of guilt roll across her. "It is my fault!" she wailed, putting her hands to her head. "I asked you to come! I am so sorry!"

"No one is blaming you," he answered distantly. He swam ahead, trying to get a better view of his son. The shark circled and snapped at the young Dolphin, missing his flesh by mere inches. It wouldn't be long now.

"Crosso!" Hael called out, leaping forward, but his family cut in front of him, holding him back, saying nothing.

Deiji charged ahead before it was even a solid thought in her mind. She flew through the water and leapt into the air, high over the rocky wall. She could see the shark and Crosso below. As she passed over them and dove under, a plan began to form in her mind. She hit the waters behind them with a splash.

Turning quickly, she began to yell at the shark, desperate to gain his attention.

"You! Over here!" she called out as she thrashed about wildly in the water. The shark paid her no heed.

Swimming angrily at him, she pounded him on the head with her fists and swore, for the skin along his body was as sharp as if he were coated in broken glass and her hands began to bleed heavily.

Once her blood clouded the water, the shark turned suddenly toward her. He charged at her, his mouth peeled back to reveal his teeth, and Deiji turned tail and fled, leading him far away from the little Dolphin.

"Swim, Crosso!" she screamed back to him as she swam, "into Safe Bay!" She paddled her tail quickly, but she could tell the shark was gaining. Deiji swam for all she was worth.

"Height," Deiji thought to herself, in a mixture in logic of Mermaid and Man. Determined, her heart pounding, she dove deep and the shark moved after her.

Nearly scraping the bottom, she suddenly fired herself straight up toward the sky, and threw herself backwards as she broke the surface. She flew marvelously through the air, facing the lightly clouded blue sky above, her body in a perfect arc.

She sliced through the waters headfirst, twisted around and raced for the bay. Deiji was grinning, somehow knowing that sharks couldn't jump.

He turned, but all too slowly, and with a small leap, Deiji landed safely among the pod. Hael and his family gathered around her with cries of gratitude. Many pleasant voices saying and singing "thank you! Thank you!" again and again as they embraced her, one after another.

Hael shouted, "My thanks, friend! You have truly shown yourself to be true to the Code. I feel I am now in *your* debt!" Deiji could say nothing for exhaustion.

After all excitement had trickled down, and it was confirmed by a scout that the shark had left, Hael agreed to take Deiji to find Elail the Fin.

"Come," he said, as she bound her palms in scraps from her shirt. He and his brother Lolanel offered their fins and she put a hand on each and was escorted as an honored guest between the islands.

"We have just left the Rock of Rint. This is the Large Rock," Hael explained as they approached the island Deiji had seen the evening before. "I saw the Fin Elail here yesterday. We spend most of our time between these two islands, though there is another pod that lives beyond Rainbow Reef," he continued. "We will bring you to Low Lagoon. You enter there just as you do in Safe Bay."

Deiji saw an outcropping of rocks on the shoreline and knew it was the entrance.

"Please be cautious, Deiji J Cu. I cannot go any farther than this."

"What is the danger?" Deiji asked, alarmed.

"My mate sought refuge once from a pair of sharks. She leapt into the lagoon and waited there, trapped, even past the time when the tides went out. She was beached, and she died in the afternoon sun. This is why we no longer use the lagoon for safety; we use Safe Bay, which is considerably deeper."

"I am sorry."

"There is so much that is wrong with our ocean. Too many predators remain while the rest of us fade. Crosso is the last of the Dolphin young in the whole Southern Gale. We are loathe to make a migration to Whale Waters to escape this place, for there may be larger, fiercer predators there that only the great ones may pass by unscathed."

"What has happened? Has it always been dangerous like this?"

"There has always been a certain amount of danger," Hael admitted, "but in these last few hundred years the danger has grown, thus the Mermaid's desertion. And in these last ten, a sickness has spread among us. We do not know why, or even how. All we know to do is to keep living, spread our Code, and wait for the water to be safe once more. Our last hope lies in this lost generation of the sea." He motioned toward Crosso.

Deiji touched his face. "The world will be better."

"One day, perhaps. Now go, my little Fin. Live by the Code. We thank you for what you have done."

"Farewell, my friends," she said, and she swam the rest of the way to the lagoon. When she made it to the rocks she dove a little and launched herself lightly over the barrier. She landed with a splash, thumping onto the low-lying sand bed inside the lagoon. Deiji instantly saw that Hael was right; this water was not deep at all.

She floated around, her head exposed from the water to get a better view of the enclosed area. It was actually quite large. Wide, but shallow. All sorts of little creatures lived in these tide pools. She could see anemones, crabs, tiny fish and sea slugs. Deiji watched them, interested, and realized she was terribly hungry. The day's events had worn her out.

"But what does a Mermaid eat?" she asked herself.

As she looked around curiously, she saw a blur of purple and gold pass her in the water. She tried to follow it, twisting all the way around, but saw nothing. She froze, and turned a full, slow circle and was suddenly staring into a brightly tanned face.

"Oh!" she cried out, and the face screamed back at her. They both propelled backwards in the water. Now, at a distance, Deiji saw the creature at a whole. A Mermaid! They stared at one another. This Mermaid had bright golden hair swept back by a sea star. She had very large blue eyes; eyes that captured the motion of the sea itself. Her tailfin was a shiny, dark purple, faded lightly down the center. She wore no tunic.

Deiji blushed and looked away, embarrassed.

"Who are you?" the Mermaid asked plainly.

"I am Deiji. I was brought here by the Dolphin Hael. Are you Elail?"

The girl did not answer, but began to circle Deiji, looking at her curiously and closely from every angle. Deiji followed her movements and her piercing stare. She suddenly felt very uncomfortable.

Satisfied, the Mermaid sat back at a more respectful distance and spoke. "I am. And you are new to the Gale, yes?"

"Yes!" Deiji said, relieved. "How do you know?"

"There are few Mermaids in these waters," Elail said wanly, looking her from head to tail in one last, skeptical consideration. "Have you any word from my family?"

"Your family?"

Elail looked very disappointed.

"Well," Deiji said quickly, trying to be of some comfort, "what of your family? Maybe I can help."

"They were taken," Elail said sourly.

"By whom?"

"The mother Balla, Ahava."

Deiji's blood ran cold. "When?"

"Days ago."

"Why?"

"Do you not know?" The Mermaid scowled at Deiji. "When a Balla hibernates for a season, they capture and cage food for when they awaken. Those who are not eaten straight away starve."

"Yes, I do know of this," Deiji replied quickly, blushing.

Elail continued, "I fear my family to be dead, and I must

go to them, but I am too afraid to leave the Gale." She looked rather ashamed at this.

"Where are they?" Deiji asked intently. She remembered with frankness her skin-deep fear of the small Balla she had encountered in her pond, and she grieved for this Mermaid.

"They are near Hei Village," Elail confirmed. "Ahava's cave is around there, or so it is rumored. I do not know the exact location."

"That far north? Then we will go to Hei Village at once," Deiji promised, only hesitating slightly. This town was around the northern isle, past the peninsula of the northernmost point of the Nigh continent, over three hundred miles away.

"Will you?" Pure, joyous light spread across the Mermaid's face.

"I need help with my problem as much as you need help with yours. I believe we can assist each other."

"What must I do for you?" Elail's eyes narrowed suspiciously.

"I need a guide of sorts. I am new to this, er, area. I need someone to show me where to sleep, what to eat... Things like that. I am from a colder sea," she added hastily.

"Easy!" Elail cried with excitement.

"Then I will help you find your family."

"Oh, you have answered my plea to the heart of the sea!" The Mermaid was smiling brightly.

Deiji smiled in return, remembering Mowat's words. She cleared her throat. "Will you help me now, then? I am extremely hungry."

"Then we shall eat!" Elail declared cheerfully. "Come with me." She swam to the tide pools in the lagoon.

Although Deiji pretended not to, she watched carefully all that the Mermaid did. Sharp stones were used to pry two shelled mussels loose from the rock; a generous handful of sea slugs were drawn from beneath the base. Elail plucked a few tiny crabs from the sand and hauled herself out of the water and onto the rock, her arms full.

"Come," she beckoned with her tailfin. She spread her collection out on the rock as Deiji joined her.

"Do we build a fire now?" Deiji asked, with the beginnings of an idea. She was beside herself at the idea of her new and magical gifts.

"A f-fire?" Elail asked, confused, sounding out the word.

"Never mind," she answered hastily.

Elail picked the flesh from the mussel shells with a stone and dropped them onto the pile of slugs, which writhed about in a small pool of water that dripped from her arm. She smashed the crabs up delicately inside their shells and handed two to Deiji.

"Here! Eat!" she cried happily, her mouth already brimming with the squirming slugs.

Deiji looked upon the raw, living food in horror and disgust. She tried to mask it, so as not to offend her, but the Mermaid caught some of the surprise on Deiji's face.

"Do you not like these foods?" Elail cried incredulously. "Where exactly are you from?"

"Um, the islands… With the Dragons," Deiji mumbled lamely.

"Ah, the Dragon Islands of the west." Elail seemed to accept this.

Deiji took the food she was offered, for she was quite hungry, though doubtful. She tentatively took a bite. A strong, fresh pleasure filled her mouth. Surprisingly, it was very good, even if she wasn't entirely pleased with the idea. She sampled all the different foods and found herself enjoying them soundly.

They ate their food and spoke of many things that night, of sea, of sky, of rain and wind. Deiji had forgotten the marvels of conversing, having been devoid of a verbal companion since Maia's crossing, and she enjoyed herself immensely.

"Oh, my," Elail exclaimed, "it has been a long while this day. Evening has set upon us."

Deiji saw that it was true. The sky was a musky blue and a star or two already shone in the sky.

"We will sleep now, Deiji."

"And tomorrow we will set out North to search for your family," Deiji finished.

"Yes." She led the girl to a shallow corner of the lagoon and they lay in the sand. Deiji was excited to see a myriad of bright blue sparks sparkling all around her in the water, and found that her movements made them shine more brightly.

She stared up through the clear surface and could see the stars emerging out and above. She watched the currents and the movement of the water swells, and fell asleep smiling.

Day Three — Water

Deiji awoke slowly. Something was tugging on her neck. Opening her eyes, she saw Elail hovering above her in the water, holding her medallion and peering closely at it.

"What is this thing, Deiji?"

She scowled and tucked it back inside her shirt. "It was a gift from a friend," she said crossly.

"Ah. Wonderful. And may I ask what this thing is?" She fingered the hem of Deiji's shirt, yanking it close to her face.

"My, you are rather over-bearing, aren't you," she said, pulling away from the Mermaid with a scowl.

"I'm what?" Elail asked, following closely behind her.

"Never mind."

As they ate more food that morn, Elail nimbly wove a

small basket out of seaweed to hang across her shoulder. She swam to the bottom and filled her little bag with bits of food to carry. "Let us go," she proclaimed boldly, and they left Low Lagoon. They swam between the two islands for the first part of their journey, heading north toward the mainland.

Down below Deiji could see a stone fortress covered in mossy algae. It was a whole castle and many courts, obviously deserted. The waters were still and quiet.

"What place is that?"

"That is the old court of the Mer King. It is an old city of the Merpeople, long since abandoned. We could not survive in a large community there, and have since scattered our numbers across the sea."

"It is beautiful."

"Yes. It was."

As they swam beyond the reefs and the slope, Deiji found some delight in the open waters. She was overcome by a pure instinctual love of the sea, untainted by the years of slaughter that Elail had witnessed.

Laughter filled her whole body and she shouted, "the whole sea is my home!" She darted ahead through the water, wanting to touch every drop.

Elail glanced at her, but said nothing.

After an hour or so of swimming, the Trinity Islands far behind them, Elail grew nervous and restless and began to speak of the reef she had grown up in.

"It is in the small bay of Sartica, about halfway along between here and Hei," she said happily. "There is a town there, and we have always concealed our presence well. But every now and then a human sees one of us, and they tell tales of it – especially fishermen."

They swam on.

"Come," she said abruptly turning toward the surface. "Fly with me and turn your eyes to the west!"

They breached high into the air and landed with a double splash.

"Did you see that land there yonder?" Elail asked.

"Yes, I saw a castle of sorts on the shore."

"That is the court of Nigh, where a Man fancies himself a king," Elail laughed. "Isn't it quaint?"

"Wow, I had no idea we were so close! I have never seen the court before."

"Yes, they have many humorous laws and customs. Now, we must be careful ahead," Elail's tone changed drastically, and Deiji could sense the warning in her voice. "Many creatures of the sea are caught and lost in the kelp forests that lie beyond. Do not let yourself be tangled; in fact, do not touch any of the plants at all. Please follow my instructions carefully. There are many dangerous miles ahead of us."

"Can we go around it?"

"It is far too wide. We would lose too much time."

They ventured into the deeper waters and could see a moving mass of murky green ahead. Deiji followed closely behind Elail as they entered into the forest. The long, stringy kelp bobbed on the surface, reaching to the sunlight, and its trailing seaweed hung to the ocean floor, out of sight.

They moved about carefully, dodging and gliding between the kelp. Here and there Deiji noticed the decayed body of a seal or Dolphin, still wrapped tightly in the weeds.

Suddenly, Deiji saw a flash of gray behind her. Pointed fins and cold, soulless eyes… "Shark!" she choked out and Elail didn't even look back.

"Swim quickly, Deiji!" she called back to her, and the Mermaid sped through the kelp, disappearing from sight.

Deiji followed in her direction, pumping her tail through

the water with force. She bounded up and around, left, right, UP! Eluding every branch that would hold her down.

She was out of breath and her blood was pumping hot in her veins. She knew she could not leap clear of the water this time; the forest would surely snag her once she landed again.

It was like a maze. Deiji swam faster and moved around and through the kelp at a speed higher than she would have ever thought possible, her reflexes and responses as quick as lightning. She dared to glance back. The shark had given up. She had lost him! Elated, she slowed slightly to look for Elail.

Suddenly, she felt a tug on her tail. She was caught! A string of kelp was wrapped around her fins. "Elail!" she screamed in fear, "help me!"

She struggled to free herself and, as she reached for her knife, found one of her arms winding itself into the plants. "Oh no!" she cried.

A flash of purple among the plants and Elail was hurrying toward her. "Be still," she hissed, and Deiji froze. Elail floated up to her and hesitated. She tugged on the ropes but could not untangle them. Deiji felt herself sink into a mass of seaweed.

Elail looked scared. "I think you are stuck, my friend."

"No!" Deiji wailed, her heart pounding in fear. She twisted about as the mess of plants coiled further about her body.

Elail backed away, not wanting to get tangled. "I am sorry," she offered with finality.

"You can't just leave me!"

"But there is nothing I can do!"

"Mowat!" Deiji screamed. "Help me!" But there was no answer.

She was afraid. But then… a single thought struck her mind.

"*Ferula Debeo!*" she called out and the water around her hands began to boil. "*Ferula Debeo!*" she screamed again. Blue flames twisted out from her whole body and the seaweed dissolved and unraveled from around her.

"Yes!" she cried as she swam free. "Let us get out of this forest!" she shouted, leading the way, and Elail quickly followed. They swam on into deeper, emptier waters where the only plant life was the endless specks of floating material.

Deiji saw a great Whale nearby, but she felt no fear. She knew it was a peaceable creature to them.

"What was that thing you did?" Elail finally asked. She had been very quiet.

"Magic," Deiji answered firmly, honestly.

"Magic? I did not know Mermaids could possess such a power."

"It was a gift. A reward of sorts, from a friend."

"Was it from Mowat?"

Deiji stopped. "How do you know Mowat?"

"You called out his name when you were trapped."

"Ah. Yes, it was a gift from him."

Elail suddenly fell silent. Glancing back at her, Deiji could see she was terrified.

"Elail? What ..?"

The Mermaid shushed her and pointed out into the blue. In the distance Deiji could see a group of black and white Whales – not as big as the great one they had seen this day, but much bigger than a Dolphin.

Elail motioned for her to follow. "They're hunting," she mouthed. They allowed themselves to sink slowly to the ocean floor, so as not to attract attention through movement. Once on the bottom they lay flat behind a small collection of rocks and plants.

This day was almost too much for Deiji to handle. She had never realized how many dangers filled the sea, even with all of Arill's warnings. The continual urge to draw her knife was quite stressful.

The small Whales continued on their way and faded into the distant blue. The danger had passed.

"What were those?" Deiji asked as they headed out on their way again, still hugging close to the sandy floor.

"Those were killers," Elail said, giving Deiji a strange look. "Where exactly are you from?"

Deiji dodged the question. "Would they have eaten us?"

"Well, no one really knows. My only memory is of times where a Mermaid or a human have been mistaken for a seal or a Dolphin. We assume that they would not deliberately eat one of us. But even then you would not want to risk such an encounter. We shall rest soon. Much worse things venture out at night." She jetted ahead, pumping her tailfin.

"They eat *Dolphins?*" Deiji called after her.

CHAPTER FIVE

The Great Whale

Day Four — Water

They awoke the next morning feeling quite stiff and tired. Deiji felt very exposed, as they had slept in the open ocean that eve and she had hardly dozed.

They ate what was left in Elail's seaweed bag before going on their way.

The pair navigated the seas as they headed through Whale Waters. Deiji discovered that being a Mermaid meant she had a natural-bred navigation sense, and she was only just becoming accustomed to it. No matter which way she swam, she always knew which way was north.

She enjoyed the certainty.

"We should pass by Hinward City this day," Elail said, "we will stick to the shoreline to avoid further encounters with killers."

"Good idea," Deiji credited. She knew of Hin City, as many referred to it. They were still many miles from Hei Village.

"By afternoon we should reach my home in Sartica. Maybe my family will have escaped. Maybe they will be there." She sounded wistful, hopeful, and Deiji would not deny her that.

"I would like to see your home," Deiji said carefully.

The ocean floor was mostly bare, with the scarcest of plant shrubs in the sand. The water temperature was changing as well, and the currents were rougher, cooler. Warm enough to her Mermaid's body, but certainly no longer tropical. The subtle change felt familiar.

By mid-day Deiji was hungry enough to eat the bag, and so she expressed to Elail.

Laughing nervously, Elail said to wait; they would be nearing a cove soon. Her face became wrenched from some inner agony, and finally she spoke. "We are near the bay of Sartica. We are near my home." Her voice sounded strangely muffled.

Deiji slowed her pace and let Elail lead her.

"This is the bay."

They came around a slight bend and Deiji saw a lovely arc of water against land; smooth hand-sized rocks covered the sand and sea flowers bloomed, woven abundantly between them. It was a sweet spot for sunlight, and the waters were very still.

"It is beautiful."

"It's empty." Elail's jaw was set firmly.

"Why did you go all the way to the Southern Gale when you left this place? Will you tell me what happened?" Deiji asked softly. She plucked a bright pink flower from among the stones and tucked it behind Elail's ear.

The Mermaid swam on into the open sea, her back to the bay.

"I am only a young Mermaid," she began with a deep breath. "Being the only two of three Maids in Whale Waters, my older sister and I rival each other in every instance…"

One Week Ago:

"Elail!"

The young Mermaid looked up to see her older sister Ornilia swimming toward her gracefully.

"Mother says not to venture too far, little sister," Ornilia said haughtily. She flashed her bright blue fins as she moved through the water. "You may be seen by a fisherman."

Elail frowned. She knew her sister goaded her.

Ornilia pushed back her ebony hair vainly. "Come. Tyl has asked me to bask in the pool with him and I must find a sea star for my hair." She twisted about in the water showing off her delicate figure.

Elail followed behind sluggishly.

"Now what might be a good color?" Ornilia wondered absently. "It has to be catchy. Maybe he and I will luxuriate this night." The slightest blush rose to her fair cheeks.

Elail began to shake ever so slightly in anger. She almost spoke, but saw her orange-tailed friend in the distance.

"Ange!" she called out cheerfully, grateful for an excuse to be gone.

Two Merfamilies shared the bay by Sartica. Elail's family lived on the south side with her sister Ornilia and their parents. The family on the northern edge consisted of Elail's best friend Ange, her older brother Tyl, and their parents.

Now, Elail had had her eye on Tyl since they were very small Fins who could barely swim. Tyl grew to be strong in mind and body and had always treated her kindly. She admired him greatly, and always held a strong hope that one day her unspoken affections would be returned.

"It is time to eat," Ange said to her, glancing at Ornilia, who raced ahead. "What is the matter?" she asked Elail once Ornilia was out of earshot.

"She is going to kiss Tyl," she answered bitterly. "He has asked her to sit in the pool with him this night."

Ange touched her arm. "Tyl does not even like her," she assured. "He is only polite."

"Really?" Elail asked, clinging to a shred of hope, "does he like me?"

"That I do not know. But you do know this is the week of harvest for the Balla, so it would be well for you to remain silent and hidden. No matter what unfolds, do not make a scene. It would be a tragedy to attract attention to ourselves at this time."

That was Ange – firm and practical, always.

They swam on to join their families, who would eat together on this night, cheerfully and harmoniously. Elail couldn't help but feel the weight of sorrow lifted from her heart; family life was her favorite part of life.

The personal boundaries of her kind were small – almost invincible. To a Merperson, everything is social, and tonight Elail was full of that same ecstatic energy that came with the gathering together of Merpeople.

After the meal she and Ange played with the seals just beyond the. "Shh!" her friend cried, pulling her from the game. She pointed toward the tide pools.

Ornilia could be seen clinging onto Tyl's arm as they swam, as if in courtship. They disappeared behind the rocks.

"Let's follow them!" Elail whispered. They raced onward.

As they snuck up onto the basking pools they heard hushed voices enjoying the sunset. Elail gripped her fingers into the rock, her heart pounding, and they lifted their bodies out of the water and peeked over the rocky edge.

"Maybe this isn't such a good idea," Ange warned, but it was too late.

Ornilia and Tyl were kissing passionately, their tail fins entwined. They did not see the pair of Mermaids peering out at them.

Elail dropped back into the sea, defeated. Ange plunged in after her. "Are you alright, my friend?"

Elail did not answer her.

And she did not sleep that night.

The next morning Elail was quite dejected. She did not appear for the morning meal. Her fear and anger turned quickly to a tightly wound hatred. A plan, an immature, mean-spirited plan began to form in her mind.

"Elail!" Ornilia called out into the water in a chipper smug voice, "Mother says I am to watch you today." Elail jetted into a sheltered cove.

Ornilia caught sight of her tailfin disappearing around the bend and rolled her eyes. "I swear, little sister, you are as pesky as sea lice." She tossed her hair and called out, "come on now!"

Elail held back. She darted behind a rock and waited until Ornilia was close enough...

"Ornilia!" she screamed suddenly, shrilly, "help! A killer Whale! Oh, help!" She ducked down behind a rock and snickered.

"Somebody help me!" Ornilia called out to their family and friends in real fear, "Elail is in danger!" She raced in Elail's direction.

Elail scowled. Now she was going to get it! She did not know why she had done this. She had planned to leap out of her hiding spot when Ornilia came by, and laugh loudly at her. Make her feel as much of a fool as she did now. It really did not make much sense, she admitted.

But her childish revenge took a sudden, serious turn.

As Ornilia rushed to her alleged rescue, Elail noticed a disturbance in the water. It was long and large, a thick brown tentacle. It took her but a moment to realize what it was.

"Ornilia!" she screamed, leaning out from her hiding spot. "SWIM! It is Ahava!"

Ornilia turned to flee but it was too late. The Balla snatched her up, wrapping one of its many arms around her waist. She screamed.

From her vantage point, Elail saw Tyl and his father rushing toward them from the bay. More tentacles flew through the water and they were caught!

His mother came after them, moving to save her husband and son, and she was taken as well...

Elail's head was spinning as the rest of them began to turn tail and swim back, but were caught by the creature. All were taken.

She saw a flash of orange, and Ange was trying to escape. Mustering as much courage as she was able, Elail flew at the creature, dodging the tentacles, narrowly slipping this way and that as she made her way to her friend...

And then one struck her. She tumbled about in the water. "Ange!" But her friend was caught in its grasp, and began to pull them all out to sea...

One or two tentacles lingered, and they swiped at her like long, living snakes! She swam just beyond its reach, knowing she was done for... She breached.

She flew through the air, landed hard on the rocks, and rolled with an "umpf!"

The tentacles squirmed and writhed about on the surface of the water then disappeared.

Elail sobbed, but not from any physical injury, beyond a few cuts and bruises. She knew it was her own fault. There was no misconceived blame here.

In shock and in blind sorrow she leapt into the waters ... She *swam as far South as she could, as if the Balla was on her tail the whole time. She swam until she lay still and exhausted in the water... dazed and disoriented, the ocean currents carried her far ... She found herself in the Trinity Islands and spent two days succumbed to her grief, desperately wanting to take action ... And then she met Deiji.*

Present Day

"I am sorry," Deiji said softly.

"Now you understand my shame," Elail said, avoiding eye contact.

"Then you do not deny that it was your own fault."

"No. I do not."

"Then there is freedom in that, at least."

They had left the Bay of Sartica, and Elail recounted the story as they traveled. "Let us stop and rest a while," she suggested. "It is difficult to think about what is past. Besides, I am not sure which way to go from here," she added.

Elail swam down to the sand to rest and Deiji flopped down next to her. Staring skyward through the watery ceiling, she noticed that the birds in the air seemed rather excited about something.

Small things were dropping from the shoreline into the surf with a plop! plop! plop! Overly curious, she swam up to have a look.

All across the beach little piles of sand were shaking and moving. "Elail! Look at this!" Deiji called, motioning her over.

As she watched, a baby turtle, newly hatched, emerged from her little shell and crawled slowly toward the water. "Look!" she whispered, "oh, she's cute!"

One of the seagulls swooped down, and to Deiji's horror, it caught the little turtle in its beak. It dangled there for a moment, then the seagull wolfed it down whole!

"Ahhhhh!" Deiji cried in shock, and she made for the beach.

"Deiji! What in the name of the ocean are you doing?" Elail popped up from the waves.

"Come on! Help me keep these birds away! They have to make it to the water!"

"That is a waste of our time, Deiji."

"Just help me, okay?"

Never had Deiji seen such a murderous event. Innocent baby turtles, their skin still soft, snatched up and torn apart by seabirds in their first hour. It was an injustice in her eyes.

She clambered onto land and flopped like a seal up the beach, making noise and waving her arms about.

"Go away! Get!"

"This is very dangerous, Deiji," Elail called from the waves. "Very foolish indeed."

Deiji leaned back on her arms. "Elail, I need your help. I cannot guide all of these little ones to the sea by myself; they are too spread out! If you do not help me they will die."

And so Elail gave a great sigh and proceeded to pull herself out of the water. They rescued many sea turtles that day, carefully shielding them until they were blanketed by the waves. Deiji saw each one to safety and she slept soundly that night.

Day Five – Water

She awoke early the next morning to greet Elail who was just returning with their breakfast.

"The ocean feeds us scantily these days," she apologized. "It is the best I could find." She held out her bag, which held a handful of stringy seaweed and two oysters.

Deiji accepted her share gratefully and pried open her oyster. She was surprised to find a small Pearl inside it. It wasn't a very nice Pearl, a gray-black in color and not altogether round, but a Pearl nonetheless.

"Elail," she said, holding it up, "look at this."

"A Pearl," she responded matter-of-factly.

"That's incredible." She held it up to the sun and squinted at it.

"It's a jewel, of course, much like those on Mowat's gift to you." She motioned toward Deiji's pendant. "It is the same."

"What is?"

"See that jewel there?" Elail asked, motioning to the Sapphire on the amulet between bites, "that is a Mermaid tear."

"What?" Deiji was entirely surprised.

"When an oyster is agitated by sand it will produce a Pearl after a time. When a Merperson is taken by sadness, her tears harden as Sapphire. I suppose you have never cried."

"Incredible," Deiji said again. She thought of the bag of Sapphires she had found on the island, and decided not to mention it.

They ate in silence.

"Do you think those baby turtles made it?" she asked quietly.

"Many of them, perhaps. The sea is an ocean of danger, Deiji. You have known this since you first entered into our waters of the Eastern side of the world. Very few survive, and the water has become a wasteland of sorts. Were your waters by the Dragon Islands calmer?"

"Quite," Deiji said. It was true. Since she had arrived here she had seen nothing but danger in every current. Nothing but moments that threatened to take her life away.

"What is that?" Deiji suddenly asked, pointing to the shore. Something gray was thrashing on the very shore where they had rescued the turtles.

"Let us see what it is!" she cried, and she pulled herself onto the beach once more.

"Deiji!"

"Oh, look!" There on the beach lay a great Whale. It was stranded, beached, lost at the mercy of the tide. The waves tumbled freely over his flukes, but it was not enough to save him.

"We have to help him!"

"Deiji!" Elail cried sharply, "we have not moved in nearly two days! We are out of time! We don't even know where Ahava lies, and there is much to be done! Leave the great one to rest."

"No!" Deiji yelled angrily. "I made a promise!"

"To what? To interfere with the natural order of things? To upset the balance of what is natural and normal? Forget the Code you have sworn to! I do not believe in such a thing! No one will help my family. No one is watching out for us! Why would we do the same for others?"

"The Balla took your family!" Deiji shot back. "And I came to help you because the Code compelled me to. Not enough turtles would have made it to bring more of them around next season. There are more sharks and killers than anything else! Your ocean is dying for these very reasons! We aren't upsetting the balance, we are restoring it!"

She pointed one strong finger at the great Whale. "Does he deserve to die? When we are the only ones who could prevent it? We will preserve what we can. We owe the world that much." And she continued up the beach, using her arms. She came to the Whale's head.

His skin was dry and cracked from being in the sun for so many hours. "*He must have washed up while we were still sleeping,*" she thought. Unsure of what to do, she finally decided to touch foreheads, as she would a Dolphin, if she were still human.

But this, in whole, was different.

When they touched the universe caved in around them and Deiji was thrown into a deep green sea, entranced by visions of the ocean as he knew it. He was old. Older than the Dolphin Code. She saw the long years of his life… Hundreds of great Whales swam about him singing in a harmonious chorus… A longing as deep and as ancient as the sea itself…

She was inside the great one's mind.

"Hello, little Fin," he said heavily, his voice weighing down her very soul. "I am Sych of the Northern Tide Pools."

"I am Deiji."

He nodded.

"And how are things," she asked respectfully.

"A little worse for the wear, my child."

"You seem to be in some need of assistance, my lord."

"I am landed," he admitted. "And I fear this last hour's wait for the tide, as I will be pressed to the death by the weight of this world."

"Sych, I will do all I am able to spare you from such a fate. I have taken great pleasure in the promise set forth by the Dolphin Code of the Southern Gale."

"I too have sworn to the Code, many years ago." His smile was pure at the memory. "What action, what method of assistance shall you require in turn, my friend?"

The question was an unexpected one. "Oh," Deiji stammered, "well, there is one such thing. We are searching for my friend's family. They were taken by the mother Balla Ahava, and we need to find her cave."

She felt an overpowering wave of compassion from the Whale. "I do know of this creature and where she might be found."

All at once her head was full of flashy, colorful visuals of the sea and of the cave's coordinates. They were to go north for a day and pass the Northern Tide pools and turn west. Not a day after that they would find a lone rock, Treehorn Island. At its southern base they would find the entrance to a large, underwater cave.

She thanked him. "I know you will try to help me, little one," Sych said slowly, "but there is no harm if you should fail."

"I will save you," she whispered, and she pulled away.

She was once again sitting in the bright sun on the sand, staring at this wondrous creature. She stared into his wise, deep eye and Deiji knew what had to be done. Flopping around in the sand, Deiji began to dig around his enormous bulk with her arms, making a moat all around him.

"Elail!" she called out to the Mermaid. Elail hesitated, then begrudgingly pulled herself onto the beach to help dig. As the moat was dug around and underneath the Whale, the waves rolled in and began to fill it with water.

"Quick!" instructed Deiji, "take that conch shell and keep him wet!"

Elail did as she was told, spooning water from the waves and pouring it again and again onto the whale's skin until it glistened.

They worked for the whole hour, digging wide and deep around the whale as the waves poured in, softening the sand. Elail dug between the shore and his flukes, making a wide path between him and the ocean.

Inch by inch the succession of waves pulled him off the beach. The girls crawled up to his great head and pushed him in tune with the tides, straining and groaning as the water called him home.

"There he goes!" Elail cried as the waves receded and took Sych with them. But he was only moved into the shallow waters, still stuck. They dove into the surf, digging and pushing themselves to exhaustion until finally he was freed.

Once submerged, they could speak to him.

"Thank you, my loyal and beloved friends," Sych gasped in relief.

"How did it happen?" Deiji asked gently, placing one hand on his side.

"I was scouting the way ahead for the great migration south. I see with my eyes, and I see all that is around me without using my eyes," Sych explained. "I can see things that are far away in my head when I wish, but I cannot see land. The broken continent of Nigh has been shifting further into our waters these last ten years and more. I did not remember the land being so close beyond the reef, and I made a mistake by venturing into such shallow waters."

"It must be the Longest River has grown wide," Elail interjected.

"Then the world is forever divided," Deiji confirmed heavily.

"Soon the Longest River will be wide enough that even I may swim between the two lands of Man and Mystical," said Sych. "It is doubtful that they will ever reunite."

The three fell silent, absorbing such thoughts.

"I must go now, my little Fins," Sych interrupted. "My mate and my young one will be grieving heavily for their loss. I must hurry north to meet them, then continue on in escorting them to the Southern Gale, and so complete our Migration. May you make it to Ahava safely."

"Farewell, friend," Elail said, and Deiji smiled.

Sych swam into the open ocean and lifted his great tail in one final wave. And with a hearty splash, he was gone.

"We will get to the tide pools by morning if we hurry," Elail said, grabbing her bag.

They left immediately, swimming hurriedly and in silence, for both were too out of breath to speak at all. They rushed against time.

Deiji saw many miles of reef and coastline. They passed the occasional Dolphin, none of which were Arill. She was getting hungry. Elail seemed to be driven, pushing onward for something she could not touch. Deiji could scarcely keep up.

Suddenly, Deiji came to a dead stop. "Elail! Look! Killers!" She pointed at the two black and white whales that were swimming nearby in the opposite direction. Deiji could see what they headed toward so intently. There were two gray whales, like Sych – a large one and a young calf.

"Let's get out of here!" Elail cried. "We should swim away while they're distracted! And don't you dare -"

"We have to help them!"

"Us? Against them? Are you disoriented?"

"Let's go!"

Though she spoke with much bravado, Deiji felt entirely helpless. The killer Whales were much bigger than they were. And those teeth! The girls watched as the killers surrounded the mother and calf; they were superb and expert hunters.

The great Whale lifted her baby out of the water using her flukes, keeping him out of reach. The killers breached again and again, landing on her blowhole, suffocating her. She cried out songs and pleas for help, and Deiji could understand her.

"They're calling for Sych!"

Deiji began to race around the water like a crazed animal, making a racket of Dolphin noises like she'd never made before.

"SYCH!" she called out at the top of her lungs. Elail followed in her fashion.

Deiji stopped and concentrated on that deep connection

she'd experienced when the great one had touched his forehead to hers. She tried to draw that space of mind into focus, and she called out his name with all her heart. *"Sych..."*

... It echoed across the depths of the ocean... In the distance, a shadow... She peered closely and saw the silhouette of a great Whale. Sych!

Out of the blue murkiness he swam, swiftly and powerfully. He charged at the two killers, three times the size of each, and Elail clasped Deiji's hand in delight.

They watched as he weighed down on them with his magnificent body, charging and thrashing will all of his strength. His mate ushered the little one to safety with the Mermaids and joined in on the fight and they quickly drove the killers away.

Their little family was soon reunited in a lovely dance of fin and tail. They breached fantastically, Deiji and Elail applauding with enthusiasm.

The three whales came up to them, and Sych swam underneath them and rose until both Mermaids were on his back.

"I will take you north!" he declared. And so Sych and his family turned from their migration to escort the two to their final destination.

Deiji grinned. It was quite magnificent, really.

They rested and rode forth on the back of the great one, rising and falling with the waves, all through the night. They did not sleep a wink, what with the constant movement, but they clung to Sych's back gratefully. It was a journey of hope.

With every swish of Sych's tail Ahava's cave came closer and Elail began to look apprehensive.

"Are you alright?" Deiji asked her over the rush of the water.

"Yes. No. I think so," she stammered. "My family… It will be hard to see that. I do not know what lies ahead."

Deiji touched her shoulder.

"None of us do, my friend."

Day Six – Water

"Here you are, my little Fins!" Sych exclaimed with joy.

Deiji shook her head out of a light doze and blinked into the heavy fog. Elail too was looking about blearily. The Northern Tide Pools. They were all the way around the peninsula. It would be a straight shot from here.

"Thank you," Deiji breathed as they slid off Sych's back into the welcoming water.

"No, my dear friends, it is I who thank you! Thanks are not always due to those who are great, but to those who dwell in the small, who have large purpose."

Deiji bowed and they parted ways.

"I suppose we continue west from here," Elail said nervously. They hugged the shoreline as they swam.

"What village is that?" Deiji asked as they swam past a quiet but large town. She had never been so far north.

"The Village of Hei, presumably," Elail said with slight interest. "That means we are close."

They saw a lone Dolphin in the distance. This was not at all unusual. They had seen many a Dolphin on their journey, but Elail stopped altogether and stared at Deiji.

"Your stone! It is glowing!"

Sure enough, the carvings of rivers around the Sapphire

were glowing a bright blue. The stone, lit from within, cast a lovely twinkle in the waters around them.

"Oh!" Deiji laughed with excitement. "It is my friend, Arill! The stone does this whenever he is near me," she hastily explained, and she swam as fast as she could to the approaching Dolphin.

"Arill! Arill!" she cried. They met, nearly colliding, swirling around each other in the water, in a sort of Dolphin hug.

"You have fared well!" he said joyously. They laughed together. "Oh, I am surprised in you!" Arill cried out.

"Is that a good thing?"

"Oh, indeed, my friend!" They both grinned. "But do not take too much pleasure yet, Deiji," he warned. "You are about to face an ancient, dangerous creature in possible battle."

"Yes," Deiji said with all seriousness. "We are on our way to the Balla now. We must save Elail's family," she motioned toward the Mermaid who had drifted up beside her.

"Hello, little Fin," he said in quick acknowledgement.

"What must we do?" Elail asked forcibly.

Arill looked saddened. "That I do not know. But remember – you have an advantage in your speed," he said steadily.

They both nodded.

"Mowat sends his luck to both of you. I bring my presence here merely as a token to inspire bravery and confidence, whatever that may offer you in such a time." They touched foreheads in anguish and affection.

"Good luck, my friend."

He nuzzled her briefly and left in haste.

"Does he often do that?" Elail asked mildly.

"Yup." Deiji smiled.

CHAPTER SIX

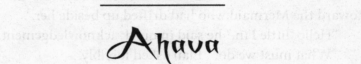

When they finally saw Treehorn Island it had to be noted how still and cold the waters around them were. It was unusually murky, and all the vegetation on the ocean floor was rotted and wilted.

They swam to its southern end, keeping low to the ground, searching for the cave's entrance beneath the eerily quiet waters.

They came across a very large, low hollowed out tunnel of rock. Broken fragments of stone and bits of algae and rotted seaweed were scattered across the tunnel floor as far as they could see.

They hung about the entrance warily.

"Well?" Deiji asked, looking to Elail. For once she wasn't ready to lead the way.

The Mermaid took a deep breath and Deiji knew why she was reluctant. The water smelled of death.

"Let's go."

They ventured in cautiously, moving around the bends slowly, as if expecting a sudden attack. But nothing came.

After several turns, Elail put her finger to her lips. "Listen? Do you hear that?"

Deiji trained her ears and heard a faint cry. No, many cries!

Begging, pleading cries of despair. Elail shot forward and Deiji went right after her. Her Mermaid's intuition insisted she swim away from here, and it was a great test of will to ignore the urge.

As they rounded the last corner they were suddenly thrust into a large, open cavern, and they doubled back into the tunnel. It was the lair of the great mother Balla, Ahava. Elail leaned forward in the water and vomited out of fear.

Ahava had over a dozen suctioned tentacles, all of them waving around her. She had but a single eye, placed above an enormous mouth lined with hundreds of teeth. Ahava was bigger than any other creature Deiji had ever seen.

And the Merpeople...

Along the rocky overhangs that lined the wall were several Mermaids and Mermen – all caged about by large ribs bones from some unfortunate dead animal, or bound tightly with seaweed, guarded by a ready tentacle or two.

The bottom of the cavern was littered with the decaying remains of the dead; half-eaten pieces of Dolphins, Merpeople and even other, smaller Ballas.

Deiji quickly ducked back around a rocky outcrop. She glanced out and saw Elail still floating there in the mouth of the tunnel and she leaned forward. Locking her fingers around her wrist, she yanked the stunned Mermaid into hiding.

"Do you see your family?" she whispered to Elail urgently. She peeked over the rock.

"My mother! I see her!" She scanned the rock face hopefully. "Tyl... And Ange, oh thank the water! Their parents are there... I see others I do not know... Where is my father? Oh, I see him... And -" Suddenly she stopped.

Deiji touched her arm. "Elail?"

Her voice rose in a panic. "Ornilia! My sister! She is gone."

"Well maybe you just do not see her."

"She is gone, Deiji!" She began to wail. "Oh, my sister!"

Deiji grabbed both of her shoulders firmly. "Elail, listen to me!"

The Mermaid looked down miserably.

"Look at me."

She lifted her sorrowful eyes into the face of a friend.

"We have to focus on the others right now. We must save them. We will find your sister when we can. Do you understand me?"

Elail nodded miserably, her worst fears confirmed, blue tears hardening into Sapphires on her cheeks and slipping to the ocean floor.

Deiji peeked out at the massive, tentacle-laden beast, in both awe and in fear. She stared at its mouth thoughtfully, then she peered at its small, single eye.

"Elail," she said, something occurring to her, "does the Balla have good vision?"

"Yes. She depends on her acute sense of sight to hunt. Other than her brute force and tentacles, it is all she has."

"So if she were, per se, blinded, she would not be able to guard her captives as well?"

"Sure."

"How does she even capture them?" she wondered. "Doesn't she mostly stay in one spot?"

"Well," Elail began, "she caught my family herself on her annual migratory hunt. But she is a very powerful creature in the sea. All Ballas and most sharks bring food to her. It is not really a balanced power at all; she is like a queen. She sometimes eats the offerings as well as those who bring them."

"So it is by this power that the ocean lives in constant danger."

"That is a just accusation."

"Then it will end here." Deiji leaned in close to Elail. "I have a plan. You will focus on the cages. Whatever you do, don't let up for one second. Free them all." She handed Elail her knife.

"What are you going to do?"

"Arill said my speed was my advantage. I'm going to take his word on it."

"His word. You mean the word of a Dolphin who repeatedly abandons you after bringing you some foul news of some horrific thing to face?"

"One and the same."

"Okay, then. Just tell me when."

"Let's go."

She swam off into the shadows while Elail crept against the cavern wall toward the Balla. Deiji kept to the left, watching Ahava and her friend carefully. The timing had to be perfect, she knew.

"This is going to be quick, no matter what the turn out," Deiji thought. She could only hope it would be in their favor. She crept silently, waiting to distract Ahava the second Elail was noticed.

Elail swam swiftly, albeit silently to the first cage. She began to cut the seaweed that bound a pair of Merpeople. Deiji stared on, apprehensive. Soon the Balla would notice the strange vibrations in the otherwise still water. Soon Elail and the others would be found out and caught if Deiji could not distract the creature.

She breathed herself steady, and then bolted into sight, yelling as loud as she could. Immediately she saw several tentacles whipping through the water toward her. She dodged, weaving in and out between the curling, twisting things.

She saw a flash of purple and green movement out of the corner of her eye; Elail had freed the two Merpeople, and they spread out to rescue the others.

"Good," Deiji thought distantly as she eluded the Balla's hungry grasp. She shifted her direction and suddenly aimed her course at Ahava's large body, which held her large, indistinguishable head. And her eye.

She could feel the drafts of water on her tail from the tentacles, only inches away. With a determined look on her face, she aimed straight for its eye. Looking back at the arm that trailed after her she saw the stingers on the tentacle open, poised and ready to strike her flesh.

Just when she thought she would hit the Balla's face, she suddenly banked to the right, and the bulky and less maneuverable tentacle followed through. Ahava's large stingers slapped into her own eye and skull and the cave was filled with her hideous screeching.

"Yes!" she cried, elated.

As blood began to cloud the water, Deiji swam hurriedly to the top to assist Elail and the others. The water was filled with a chaotic jumble of writhing tentacles amidst the blood, and a great rumbling filled the cave. Great rocks and pieces of the ceiling began to fall around them.

"We've got to get out of here!" she cried to Elail.

"Go!" the Mermaid shouted to her kin. They all rushed toward the tunnel.

The world was rumbling all around them, and they could hardly swim straight. Deiji fell back to see them all to safety, and Elail turned around. "We have to find Ornilia!" she shouted above the roar and rumble of the collapsing cavern.

"No!" Deiji pushed her on. "Just go!"

Elail opened her mouth to speak, but Deiji snatched her arm and forcibly yanked her into the tunnel. As the Mermaids and Deiji rushed into the open sea, there was a great crashing sound and the tunnel caved in.

The Balla behind them gave one last shudder and was dead.

The Cave

All at once Deiji opened her eyes, not remembering having ever closed them.

She was staring into the face of Mowat once more, still motoring her legs as if swimming. *Legs?*

"Mowat!" she cried, sitting up abruptly. There was no water around her at all. Just the dry air of Mowat's cave. She swung her legs out of the bed and stared at her toes as if greeting an old friend. She stood, wobbling a little, and steadied herself on the headboard.

"I pray I did not fail," she said to the wise Teacher, who smiled his quiet smile. A beam of sunlight burst from behind him, illuminating the cave, giving him a sharp, shadowed silhouette.

"You did very well."

"Oh!" she breathed. "I did not even know what you wanted of me! When I met Elail I just went along with it. I did not know if there was a plan set for me, for sure."

"There is never a plan, my dear. Only your choices and the impacts of such decisions made."

"Then it was well."

"And wonderful," he added. "You did a very good thing today, Deiji. Many good things, in fact. Hael's son, the turtles, Sych and his family… Because of you these creatures live! As do all of the ocean who have been lost to death in these times. Though you were not one of their world, you expressed such a loyalty and compassion to the sea that no family there will soon forget!"

"That is good."

"That is noble."

She looked at him as if he were teasing her. "I only did what was to be done. Why is that so different?"

"Because you had a choice. Turning a blind eye is quite a normal thing to do. Not a trait that you possess, thankfully. In fact, it was that particular way about you which persuaded me to approach you in the first place."

"Well I could not leave such things undone," she said, almost defensively.

"That," Mowat said, "is precisely why you are noble." He smiled. "Now, we must discuss the long term repercussions of your actions. I will give you a full briefing immediately."

Deiji stood up straight, ready for a serious exchange of words. Mowat cleared his throat. "Come with me." He walked to the water's edge and they stared down at their reflections.

"Ahava was a beast who spread her lordship throughout the sea. For over three hundred years she terrorized the Merpeople communities to the point where half abandoned their home in the ocean and ventured onto the shore. But she was not omnipotent. She remained on the edge of starvation for quite some time until recently, when Relant offered her eternal feedings in exchange for the extermination of the Merpeople. It was in this way he was to guarantee the permanent separation of the world," he explained.

He gestured toward the pool.

Amidst their reflections an aerial vision appeared. Deiji saw the whole world of Nigh in the water. The continents collided into one and the world was rejoined. A young boy lay on the shore and a grown Centaur stood on the other side. They were staring at one another.

"The world must be rejoined," Mowat continued. "But Man and Mystical are not ready to meet. Neither fully grasps the concept of what lies on the other shore and what it means. Toten Town is the first point on the map where Man and Mystic will collide. We will start there.

"King Jebhadson has sent a legion of four hundred men into

the shadow of the Deep Forest with the intention of war. We must avoid bloodshed at all costs. The world will be reunited whether they are ready for it or otherwise.

"What you have done is great, but I must ask you to complete your work. Stop the battle before it begins. Relant has his fingertips in the land of Man and the courts of Nigh. It is time for you to connect with the main ground of the Mystical peoples, and make the knowledge of the world known to Man."

"Do you mean to send me to the Deep Forest?"

"I do."

"Then I will go," she answered bravely.

"I will not send you unequipped. This may be the most important element you face, for the world has not been rejoined yet."

"But you just showed me…"

Mowat smiled. "I work outside of Time, my dear."

"Then you have seen it. I will succeed."

Mowat's eyes narrowed. "That future is pure speculation, Deiji. Nothing is set in stone."

She bowed her head. "Yes, my lord."

His expression softened and he looked upon her fondly.

"Remember the magic you carry within. As an additional gift, you will retain your natural compass you held as a Mermaid, enabling you to a sure sense a direction, always."

Deiji smiled, very pleased with this.

"Furthermore, an equipment of magic. You need only to cry 'Cascata!' to summon the waters of the rivers to you."

"My thanks."

"My pleasure," he smiled. "Now, I have many affairs to tend to this hour. Bathe. Eat. Rest. Arill will be by to see you shortly." The sunlight flickered as he turned to go, and faded when he left.

She took his advice heartily and hurriedly dressed in her

green silken robe, eager to see Arill. She lay back on the bed and drank in the cool stillness of the cave until the edges of her pendant gave forth a white light, signifying Arill's arrival.

"Hello, my friend!" she cried out as he lifted his head out of the water. Then she realized – she wasn't a Mermaid anymore! She laughed aloud and knelt at the water's edge to speak.

The Necromancer

Mowat met Relant atop the mountains of the Eastern Ranges.

The dark Keeper's voice was choked with rage, and Mowat tried exceedingly not to gloat.

"You have defied me," Relant hissed at the Teacher.

"We can end it here. If you forfeit this war and call the king and his vizier off, you may still retain a fraction of your dignity when this is over."

"I will forfeit nothing," Relant growled.

"Then the bloodshed will continue, ending with yours," Mowat shot back. "I am already halfway to your demise. The world is only days short of reuniting, and when these halves come to term with one another, you will never be able to separate them again."

"It will never be whole!" Relant lashed out.

Mowat said nothing, only smiled.

"Do not ridicule me, dear Teacher! When I discover your advocate, I will stop this entire timeline!"

"You know nothing."

"That may be the case, but it is only a slight matter. The sure location of your little student will come to me in due time. I have eyes everywhere."

"Then that is only a slight matter," Mowat snapped, and he raised his new staff. *"Ciechi!"* A haze of stone and flint shot from his staff toward the dark Keeper, who was startled and did not deflect the assault.

It struck his face, and he was instantly blinded. He screamed in pain and clutched his talons to his face.

"Mowat, you fool," he spat, "I do not need only my eyes to see."

He opened his mouth and fired off several clicks, reading the flashing images that returned to him. Images of Mowat standing atop his mountain, and of the mountain between them.

"Your student will surely die. And I have an idea of where to look." He turned his sights to the lone mountain that stood parallel to theirs, and he spread his wings.

"Mount Odel," he growled, blood streaming from his eye sockets. He caught the brief look of worry that crossed Mowat's face and he laughed. "And there we are," he said with satisfaction.

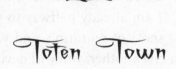

Toten Town

Zechi hugged the ground outside the stables. The world rocked and swayed beneath him and he was crying. Soaked to the bone, he shivered. After all that had happened these last few years, how could things become worse? Someone had promised once that things would be better…

He cowered, facing the river as a wave of earth rolled beneath him. Then, incredibly, the opposite river bank surged with force and collided against the shore of Toten Town. There was a great groan, and Zechi dug his fingers into the dirt to keep from being tossed around.

The shores had joined.

The earthquake stopped, as suddenly as it had begun. Buildings had fallen all around the village. Even the few soldiers that were left emerged from their hiding places looking shaken.

Zechi stared across the waterway, which was nothing more than a trickling stream now. The girl had gone. The two shores of the Known World of Nigh had always touched – just barely – at the southernmost end, at Toten Town. Now they were joined, thrust sloppily over one another, sending a whirlwind of questions throughout the boy's mind.

He thought he saw movement on the opposite bank. A Centaur? He looked again but it was gone. He shook his head as if to free his thoughts to clarity. His entire world was askew.

Some weeks ago he had been tending the water buckets for the crops in the village. He was a simple stable boy with a heavy heart, very young... Over the hill rise outside of town a messenger had come, fear on his face, out of breath, bearing news of terror.

Soldiers. Soldiers were upon them, a number of four hundred. And so they came. And they took what they would of food and of women. Those who would protest any action paid with their lives. Zechi himself was a newly made orphan. He slept in a straw-pile in the corral, as the soldiers had taken his house for their own.

As Zechi stared at the shifted landmasses, a soldier walked up behind him. "I saw you sniveling, boy," he said gruffly. He reeked of his liquor.

Zechi kept his eyes downcast, and his shoulders quivered.

"This world is not for the weak," the soldier growled. He lifted his dirtied hand and the last thing Zechi saw was blackness.

Mount Odel

Micid was working the garden on her hands and knees on a chilly, overcast afternoon. As she weeded the vegetable beds she cursed.

The day for Telius to collect his bride had come and gone, and Micid had no sound explanation for the girl's disappearance. Admitting the girl's suicide was a great shame to their family, but she had done it.

The day she had returned from her summons, Deiji had instigated a quarrel. Then Micid had seen her facing the pond... She had run from the house, but she had already heard the splash. All there was to be found was Deiji's apron on the ground. The girl had drowned herself.

The only curious thing was the pond, which the animals continued to drink from as if nothing was amiss. In Micid's experience, if water tasted of death the animals would refuse to drink, even to death. There was no way to know.

So Micid went about the region telling J and Pav and anyone who would listen that the girl had run away from her duty on into the next world. Micid remained exceedingly sore in her loss; one hundred Emeralds!

She brushed the dirt from her hands and groaned again at the thought. She headed into the hut, frowning as she walked. Her only possession of value had been that girl. And it was gone. She groaned again.

As she stepped into the house, she heard a slight shuffling from the bedroom she shared with her sister-in-law.

"J?" she called out to the pallet where the woman lay ill and bedridden. J hadn't taken well to the news of Deiji's death. Her condition had worsened by far. Micid was glad for this. The sooner she was free of this obligation the better. She had bitterly let go of the promise of wealth to come, and all that filled her heart was hate.

"J," she called out again, hurriedly walking into the room. She stood there, stunned and dumbfounded, fear clutching her entire body. There was something in the room! A *Dragon?* It was black, as black as a midnight with no moon. Its enormous leathery wings were folded back, and its entire bulk filled the room.

Its murderous talons were still wrapped around J's limp and lifeless body. There was blood everywhere.

Micid stumbled backwards, and then fled.

Pav the baker stood outside her hut, sweeping dirt and flour from her threshold. She glanced to the mountain, and then looked again.

There was a figure running down the mountainside, falling and tumbling all the while. Pav waddled over to the trail and met the person as they burst from the underbrush.

"Micid?" she exclaimed. The woman was as white as if she'd seen a ghost.

"A creature," she gasped, "killed J."

"A what?"

"I swear it was a black Dragon – a demon!" She nearly collapsed.

Pav supported her back to her own hut. "Calm down, honey, we'll take you home."

"I cannot go back!" Micid gasped as Pav poured coffee and handed her a heel of bread.

"Maybe it is gone," Pav suggested soothingly.

"Or maybe it is waiting for me," Micid whispered. They

both looked up at the mountain. A storm was on its way. It was a bad omen.

"Maybe it is."

The Nigh Court

Telius stood in the entrance hall beside the king, bored with the days' audiences and proceedings. He yawned and mused a bit on ruling the entire world from the throne that would soon be his. He glanced at King Jebhadsen and stifled the urge to roll his eyes. The blubbering peasant before them couldn't stop stuttering, and the king's patience exceeded his own by far.

A shadow fell over the stained glass window for a moment, and his eyes widened. "Er, excuse me, my king," he said hastily, bowing and backing away toward the door behind the dais. Once outside, he broke into a run and headed for the royal stables.

A large Dragon Bat swooped down into the Nigh court, his blackened shadow sending the king's horses rearing and running in all directions. Telius ran onto the open pasture, racing to meet the dark creature as he arrived. Breathing heavily, he bowed.

"My one and true majesty," he panted, touching one hand to the ground in his honor. He was truly surprised at his master's visit; this was a highly unusual occasion.

"Indeed," Relant growled, waving him away carelessly with one bloody claw. "Now, down to business."

"Yes, go on," Telius said eagerly, standing up straighter.

"The information Micid gave you was of great use, and Mowat's student is now dead. What you have done for me is well, and I will reward you greatly one day. Someday we must find you a new bride as well, since I have destroyed yours," he added with a nasty grin. "The important thing is that we have undone the work that Mowat has so precariously molded."

"Then Mowat has nothing on us," Telius gloated. "He is as well as dead already."

"Oh, he most certainly will be once I have released my army upon his earth. He is not expecting this. I am wholly unstoppable, even if I had not murdered his student."

"Indeed you are, my lord," Telius said, bowing once more. "And is your army ready to make battle?"

"Absolutely. You must make sure the soldiers strike at the perfect moment. Contact the general and remind him – it must be on the morning after the sixth full moon of the year. That is the surest way to destroy all of them."

"How will you do this?" Telius was more than curious – he was driven to find the source of his master's power.

"There is a creature," Relant mused. "My pet Djin. A servant of mine from long ago. She will hand me the girl."

"Very good, sir."

"Just be sure it is on that particular morning, are we clear?"

"It will be done."

"Good."

Relant spread his leathery wings and flew back to his mountain.

The Necromancer

"Relant!" Mowat boomed on the mountaintop. "You are a *fool!*"

The dark Keeper laughed richly, licking the blood from his

talons, assured of his own power and victory. "I have slain your apprentice as she slept," he gloated. "Of course you are upset! I would expect nothing less from someone who had just lost his entire victory."

Mowat's eyes flashed as fire, and lightning struck the mountain behind them. "You have not taken my student," he growled. "You have taken an innocent! A bed-ridden woman, sick from your fever on her deathbed."

Startled, Relant frowned. He touched his wounded eyes. Trying to save face, he forced a grin. "Then she is the first of many." He tried to mask the disappointment in his voice. "I DO have another weapon, a weapon so great that your world will lose its life in waves!"

Mowat shook his head slowly. "They can never be raised," he said defiantly.

"They will!"

Mowat glowered. "One day you will know what you have done. One day soon the innocent will rise against you and you will be forced to pay for your crimes. And on that day I swear I will be there to witness the fear on your face."

PART TWO

Deiji woke to a warm breakfast of gruel and milk. She ate slowly, trying to not think of what lay ahead. She glanced over at her shelf that held the items she had collected thus far; her stone knife, Mowat's sword and the bag of Sapphires from the beach. Before preparing for the day, she went to the water for a swim with Arill.

As she looked into the pool, she thought she felt a taint of the Mermaid's instinctual love of the sea. She jumped in. Once completely submerged she transformed! Deiji looked to her long green tail and smiled.

Arill sided up to her. "Hello, my friend!"

"Arill! Look at me! I'm a Mermaid again." she grinned, and took hold of her Dolphin friend's fin.

"Yes, you will become so when you are completely immersed in water from this point on, unless you will yourself not to be. It is a gift he has allowed you to retain."

"Oh, thank you, Mowat!" she called out, and she kissed the top of Arill's head. They played the morning away, then Deiji pulled herself out of the water. She stood there, on legs again, dripping wet as Mowat walked in. He was as tall and withered as an old oak tree.

"Are you ready, Deiji?"

"I need to dry off and dress." She reached for the cloak that hung on the wall.

"There is no need." He raised his hand passively and Deiji found she was fully dry and clothed; the cloak already around her shoulders. She fastened the clasp firmly at her throat. Glancing down, she saw that she wore trousers, men's trousers. She delighted in the flexible and clingy feel of them.

"Remember all I have taught you," Mowat whispered, handing her the sword. She caught a look of sadness in his eyes and for a moment thought she spied a tear.

She cocked her head sideways. "Mowat?"

"It is time," he said heavily. "No matter what pain or sorrow you encounter, do not lose your demeanor. It is all that will keep you steady."

Deiji nodded, though not appeased.

"Close your eyes a moment," he said softly. She obeyed.

"Now go!"

When she opened them again, she found herself in a different land.

CHAPTER SEVEN

The Dryad

Day One — Earth

Deiji looked around her and immediately noticed the clamminess of the air clinging to her exposed face. She pulled her heavy black cloak tighter around her shoulders and pushed the hood up. She felt more lost than ever, and even a bit emotional over this last few week's happenings.

She was indeed in the depths of the Deep Forest. The trees pressed in from all sides, blotting out the sky. The heavy fog that loomed over the distant brush sunk so eerily in and out of the trees with such a ghostly presence that Deiji felt the hairs on her arms and the back of her neck prick up.

She remembered the trees she had seen all her life in the distance when she had lived on Mount Odel. Such a forest was continually damp. Deiji could feel the heavy, chilly air nipping at her skin, and was heartily thankful for the shoes and cloak that Mowat had supplied her.

It began to rain.

Feeling as though she could cry, she began to walk. She knew not where she was, and it was becoming to be an old feeling she was quite familiar with. Every tree looked the same. It seemed she would never find a clearing, or a settlement or even Toten Town. She was, indeed, alone.

Looking ahead, she noticed a little brown rabbit in the brush.

"*Human?*" it cried out in a teeny little voice.

Alarmed, Deiji peered down at the little animal. "You can talk?"

"Well, yes," it said, a little confused. "And you are a Human."

"Well, yes," Deiji mirrored the little rabbit.

"And you are *here*. What is a Human doing in the Deep Forest? I have never seen one before." Its little heart-shaped nose twitched eagerly.

"I am here visiting. I would like to meet the creatures of this wood before I go on to Toten Town."

"Ah. Well, have a nice evening, Human. Thank you for letting me see you."

"Um, you're very welcome?"

And without another word, the little bunny hopped into the trees and out of sight.

Darkness began to fall in the already dim forest. Deiji could only see a vague outline of the trees she passed now. She began to walk faster, using her inner compass to sense where she might be headed. Thinking back to the blacksmith's maps, she found she couldn't recall anything in this area beyond Toten Town.

Turning quickly to a sudden splash of movement and ruddy color, Deiji saw two Centaurs stepping lightly beyond a grove of trees.

"Oh, hello!" she called out, surprised and cheered. The

Centaurs stared at her for a brief moment, startled, then bounded back into the trees and out of sight.

"That's okay," she muttered to herself with bravado. "Skittish creatures. I can stand being alone."

She turned and tried a new path through some brambles. With every step the forest seemed to dim more and more and soon it was very black, and the rain fell harder. She wandered aimlessly for quite a time, seeking out a cave or something in which to spend the night.

"I can figure things out in the morning," she said to no one. The trees were creaking in the wind, and Deiji felt like she was being watched. Remembering the magical tree on the island, she eyed them all suspiciously.

She suddenly spotted a single tree with a hollowed opening at its base. It was large enough to admit her whole body, if she tucked herself inside tightly.

Pushing the sword ahead of her, Deiji crawled inside and huddled there, desperate to keep a bit of warmth. Looking down at her hands, she muttered, *"Ferula!"* and a little spot of flame hovered there. She cupped her hands to her chest to warm herself, and fell into a light sleep, dreaming of the soft feather bed she had left behind in Mowat's cave.

Day Two — Earth

Deiji stirred slightly the next morning to the sounds of chirping birds and rustling as the forest awakened. Opening her eyes she saw the sun piercing through the many treetops, allowing strained spots of light to seep through to the layers of leaves and pine needles on the forest floor.

She pulled herself from the tree trunk, cramped and tired from the night. As she stood and stretched, Deiji noticed something interesting about this particular tree.

From where she stood all she could see was a straight, long tangle of ivy leaves traveling down its trunk. It was not a very tall tree, but it seemed to have almost a human presence.

Deiji propped her sword against the trunk and curiously circled around to the front of the tree to get a better understanding of it, and she nearly choked. For there, growing out of the tree trunk, from the waist up, was a woman. But it was like no woman that Deiji had ever seen.

Her features appeared to be carved out of oak, and she wore a sort of moss tunic across her shoulders. The ivy that trailed to the forest's floor was her hair. She grew quite gracefully out of her tree, her arms melting into branches, her legs into the trunk. The expression on her face was almost mournful.

"What a beautiful carving," Deiji breathed in awe.

"I am most certainly not a carving, I assure you," the tree suddenly reprimanded her in a clear, feminine voice.

Deiji screamed at the top of her lungs.

"Please, child, I do have ears." The carved woman shook her head a little, as if the shrillness really hurt her.

"I- I'm sorry," Deiji sputtered forth.

"It is quite alright."

Still shocked, Deiji attempted to speak to this wondrous creature. "Hello," she offered pleasantly. "I am Deiji J Cu of Mount Odel. I took shelter in your trunk last night. I – I wanted to say thank you."

The woman responded in a hollow, saddened tone. "You are very much welcome, my child, for I am the Mother of all things, and it is a care to me to nurture one of my own."

"What is your name, honored Mother?"

"I am Jayna, a Dryad, and I keep a watchful eye over all in

the forest. I was informed of your arrival last night and I am pleased I could shelter you with my boughs."

"So you said."

They stood there staring at one another. Deiji had never seen anything so beautiful be so sad. "Maybe you could help me," she asked. "I need to know where I am in respect to Toten Town. I know which way is north, but I am not quite used to the thickness of these trees..."

"You are well into the trees of the Deep Forest," Jayna answered promptly. "It is half a day's leisurely walk, maybe one, to the town of Toten. I will summon a guide for you. Yes, that would be for the best. I myself would lead you, but alas! I am bound to the earth."

"You mean you cannot move from place to place?" Deiji asked, startled.

Jayna smiled sadly. "My roots go deep into the earth. The trees speak to me through them. This is how I call upon those who serve me faithfully. There is nothing in this forest I do not know of; little in this forest I do not tell of."

"Jayna, I must be getting onto what I am obligated to do. Which way to Toten Town?"

"I will send for a guide, and he will take you there."

"I do not need a guide," Deiji insisted. "I am perfectly capable of finding my own way."

Jayna sighed and an invisible breeze ruffled the leaves around them. "Though I could tell you," she said lightly, "it would serve you better to be taught."

"That is not necessary. I have been doing this sort of thing for many days now, and I am confident that all I need is a prompt in the right direction. You see, I -"

"*No.*" Jayna interrupted her so forcefully that Deiji swallowed her words.

"No," she repeated softly. "Do not let your pride overcome

who you are. You have come far and learned much, it is true. But it is time to perfect that wisdom and fine-tune your knowledge. It is time that you are taught directly by a wizened mentor. I have just now summoned Mangiat, and he will be here tomorrow to meet you and lead you. A very resourceful creature, I might add."

"Fine," Deiji said, completely fed up. "Your *suggestions* have been taken well into account." There was no way Jayna could have missed her emphasis, but the Dryad continued on.

"Be here tomorrow after dawn to meet with Mangiat. He will teach you well. There is a cave set on higher grounds that may serve you for shelter this night, uphill." She pointed west with her boughs. "There is also the river just down the slope from here." She pointed east.

Deiji sniffed in irritation and turned to go, snatching up her sword and slinging it over her shoulder.

"Do not let your pride dictate your actions, Deiji!" Jayna called out after her. "There is so much more that lies ahead. Things you cannot possibly imagine. There is so much more to learn in this life, Deiji, and humility is the key…"

Deiji kept walking.

She set on up the slope, breathing hard as she searched for the promised cave. It was actually quite easy to keep track of her trail; the branches and bushes were so thick that she had to tear her way through them, leaving leaves and broken twigs in her wake.

Her cloak felt very heavy as she leaned into the incline, and she was slapped in the face by the branches as she plowed her way through. She felt blood and sweat trickling down her face and she knew there were cuts and welts on her cheeks and forehead.

Deiji looked about herself as she walked and bore witness to many of the secluded forest's hidden secrets.

Fairies, whose small glow and dusty golden sprinkles were little bright spots among the trees of the remote forest. Dainty, strong Centaurs who leapt out of the way at the coming of her human presence. She saw a large bear pawing at a hole in a tree, paying her no heed. A pack of wolves warily watched her pass. She caught sight of a cougar slinking around the trees, avoiding her path but getting a peak.

She walked on, enjoying the incredibly ordinary plant life. The island and ocean that she had explored had vastly differed in their outstanding assortments. They had both been so colorful, full of alien animals and plants, in a myriad of brilliant shades. Here the earth tones of brown and green were so common place; it was almost more of a shock. There were some birds chirping and a light breeze rustling the trees, but it was a fairly quiet forest.

Deiji stopped to pick a handful of berries from a low-lying bush. She crumbled a handful of fungi mushrooms from a tree and stuffed her pockets with them.

Looking up she knew it was impossible to gauge a straight line between her path and Jayna's spot, but she was sure she could follow her own trail back to the Dryad. She wondered where the cave was. As she glanced forward, she noticed a dark shadow amongst the brush.

She approached it cautiously and saw that it was indeed a cluster of trees with a rocky cave in the middle of it. Behind it, a small clearing where the sun shone.

It was a slight, hidden opening, and she brushed aside some hanging branches carefully. Glancing in the mud, she saw no animal tracks, and she was almost certain it was uninhabited.

Squeezing inside the narrow opening, she was relieved to find it empty. It was almost completely dry as well, though quite small. She could see it was possible to lie down at full length in either direction and stand without striking her head, so she was satisfied.

She wondered about building a fire, and thought with a pang of heart of Geo and of times long passed. It felt like years ago that she had romped around with her Dragon friend. She wondered how the Dragon Keeper, Docin, was getting along with him.

"A fire inside a cave would be too smoky," she told herself sharply, focusing her thoughts. The fuel outdoors was too damp, anyhow. But if she were going to hunt fish, she would eventually need a fire. She stepped outside and began gathering short pieces of wood, tree branches and twigs to dry out inside her little cave, then restlessly tossed them aside.

Deiji decided to head back toward Jayna; the Dryad had said if she headed down the slope she would find the Longest River. Her sense of direction most assuredly noted which way south was. If she found the river she could follow it south until she found Toten Town. Forget the guide.

She went down the slope walking quickly, no longer fighting the incline. Shifting her sword to her other shoulder, she wondered vaguely if there was another route she might take; she did not feel much like crossing Jayna's path. Something about the saddened Dryad and the things she spoke of made all of Deiji's shields and appearances drop... As if her soul stood naked. It was not pleasant.

Then again, she thought, *encounters with the self seldom are.*

She leaned to the right as she made her way down the slope, keeping Jayna's back to her left. The river bank was clear of all the trees and the sun shone down on the waters brightly. It looked to be a pleasant place for drinking and washing.

Across the way she could see a mother doe and her fawn drinking in the sun and she smiled, somewhat cheered. The doe stared at the girl, her ears perked, as if considering the possibility of danger.

Ignoring them, Deiji plunged into the water and stood knee-deep and waited for the river to be still. When she saw a tiny fish circling her ankles, she rested her fingers near her feet, and then snatched it!

She carried the little guppy to the shore in her fist. Glancing at it she shook her head and tossed it back. It was too small for her liking.

Resting her hand on her head, she lay back on the muddy grass and thought for a while. She loathed feeling such indecisiveness. Finally she stood and had a quick drink before making her way back to the cave. Two little bunnies skipped ahead of her on the path, and Deiji knew they were interested in what she was doing.

Looking around she frowned. While her sense of direction was perfectly acute, it appeared to be very easy to overshoot her destination in this thick wood. She lifted her eyes to the sky. The sun was past its high point; the air was cooling down, settling into the afternoon hour. Deiji swallowed hard.

Then, an idea... She placed her hands upon a tree. "Jayna?" she called out cautiously, feeling a little silly. "I believe you can hear me, Jayna. Please tell me how to find my cave." She hesitated. "I am lost. Please show me the way."

Silence.

Then... A tree root raised itself from the earth! It rippled like a snake in and out of the dirt. Then, another! And another! Deiji followed the direction of moving roots as they made a trail for her to follow. In this strange fashion it was not long before her cave came into focus beyond the trees.

Deiji sighed in some relief. It was difficult to consider oneself lost when one hardly had a destination. She knew she had wanted an alternative route to the first one she had known. It looked like she had found it.

She tore the lining from her cloak away and wrapped the thin cloth around a bundle of leaves for a pillow. A brisk walk into the trees found her several pine boughs to chop down with her sword. She dragged them inside and made up a bed. Settling into the furthermost corner of her cave she pulled her cloak around her shoulders tightly.

The late afternoon sun still shone, but all she wanted was to sleep for this time. She stared at the cave's ceiling as the day began to dim, thinking an adventurer's thoughts, until those thoughts melted into dreams.

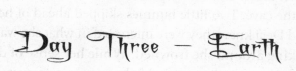

Day Three — Earth

She woke early the next morning with the sun feeling quite hungry. She stood to stretch, drawing her cloak around her quickly, for the morning's air was bitterly cold and the dampness had seeped into her clothes. Shrugging off the clamminess she set out for the river, aiming to find her way to Toten Town, pausing only to pluck berries from the occasional bush.

Deiji walked down the slope easily, deliberately sidestepping a possible confrontation with Jayna. But as she walked it seemed that the force of the trail pushed her in the Dryad's direction. She had to plant her feet steadily and resist, and as she set out on a different path, she came right back to where she had started. She was walking in circles!

"Fine!" she threw up her hands. "What do you want?"

"Her honored Mother requests a word with you," a sweet voice rang out from the trees.

"Who is there?"

She found herself not surprised at all when a little white

rabbit poked its head out of the bushes, its little whiskers twitching along with its nose. "It is I, a messenger of the woodland creatures. Jayna would like to see you now."

"What did Jayna want?"

"I do not know. That tree there yonder called me over, and I was told to tell you that Jayna requested your presence right away."

Deiji rolled her eyes. A bunny messenger. "Oh brother."

"You mean Mother," the rabbit corrected gently.

"Sure." The animal obviously missed her sarcasm.

Satisfied, the little fluffy tailed animal hopped back into the bushes. Deiji started to walk aimlessly, knowing that her steps would be directed to the Dryad.

Sure enough, she entered the little clearing and was standing in front of the beautiful woman herself.

"I take it you found food, water and shelter well enough?" Jayna asked coolly.

"Oh. Yes. Thank you," Deiji said, rather miffed at this whole business. Jayna nodded slightly in response.

"So," Deiji said, trying to fill the silence, "is he coming?"

"Yes. The trees say he is on his way."

It wasn't long at all before a young, muscular Centaur stepped delicately yet powerfully into view. Deiji stood in awe for several moments. Never had she found such a masculine figure to be so beautiful, for beautiful he was.

Mangiat had the glistening black body of a well-bred horse, large and impressive, with long hair fringing each hoof. He had a long, silken black tail, which he flickered in such a horse like manner that Deiji couldn't help but smile a little.

His upper body was that of a well-exercised man, bare, and he had a very kind face. World-weary, but kind. A large scar ran the length of his shoulder to the middle of his chest and Deiji wondered how he'd gotten it.

His eyes and hair were as black as midnight, his hair pulled back into a straight ponytail. He wore a diagonal leather strap that hooked a holster for a bow and arrows. Scraps of rope made of some woven plant material clung to his wrists and neck.

The Centaur stepped in front of Jayna without even acknowledging Deiji, sinking into a deep bow.

"Hello, my Mother, my Queen of the Forest, the trees and its people." He rose. "I stand to serve."

Jayna gave a warm nod while Deiji tried to contain her amusement. She was offended at the very idea of this creature, and she instantly detested and resented him.

"Mangiat," Jayna said loudly, drawing Deiji from her thoughts, "this is Deiji J Cu of Mount Odel. She requires much assistance in the areas of knowledge and skills to be acquired in the ways of the wood. I ask that you stay and teach her for a time, and thus fulfill your duty to the Forest. Teach her all that you are able, my son, for she is a stubborn thing."

Deiji glared at the Dryad, somewhat embarrassed, but Mangiat didn't even look twice.

"Yes, my Mother," he replied, giving a shallow bow. He stood and turned his face to the woods. "Deiji," he said with a curt nod, and he walked passed her.

She took this as a gesture to follow him. They walked through the trees, Mangiat making his way a lot faster than she, and she struggled to keep up.

"Um," she stammered, trying to find the speech in which to converse with such a formal creature, "how, sir, may I ask, is the length of your instruction that has been imposed upon me?"

Mangiat glanced back and started laughing. "There is no need for such formality, Ju Ju! I only talk like that around Jayna. You see, she is the queen of this wood. That sort of respect is granted naturally, nay, *required* of us forest folk. And as far as my time here to teach you? However long it takes." He looked at her directly for the first time, his face gaining a sort of bemused expression, and Deiji looked away, embarrassed.

She felt a pang of guilt. She had been so loose, so casual to the point of being rude with Jayna, this Queen of the Forest. For the first time in forever she felt ashamed. Deiji then paused, and considered the Dryad's tones and gestures toward her, toward anyone. She seemed so sullen and quiet a creature.

She called ahead to Mangiat. "How long has Jayna been in these woods?"

Mangiat laughed again as he stepped daintily through the bushes and trees, never touching so much as a leaf. Deiji hauled herself through the underbrush after him, stopping every now and then to untangle her cloak from the brambles.

"Well," he began, "for hundreds of years, I suppose. Let's just say that my father's mother's mother can remember when Jayna had been here for a long time."

"Oh." Deiji fell silent.

"Lead me to your temporary residence," the Centaur said suddenly.

"Oh, okay," she said, and she pushed ahead of him. She glanced at her surroundings a moment, then led him up the incline into her small clearing.

"This is where you stay?"

She nodded. "Yes, it is strange. Jayna said there was a cave and right when I thought about it, I found it. It's almost as if the forest shows me the way to what I need. It has been an odd day," she finished quickly.

Mangiat laughed again, loudly. It was a very pleasant laugh.

"Yes, that is nearly the way it works. The woods provide us with what we need, sometimes. The resource was there all along, but the Forest does tend to point the way."

"What?" Deiji was legitimately surprised. "Then what is the challenge in that?"

"Well, it is a bit more complicated and involved than simply acquiring what you have asked for," he chuckled. "The forest will give you what you need, not necessarily what you *want*," he added slyly. "And even in times of the most desperate need, it will provide only what is in your best interests."

He glanced around the small clearing. Satisfied, he continued. "I will stay here with you for now before we make our way to your destination. It is Jayna's will that I teach you the ways of the forest. I am to teach you to hunt, fish, make traps, weapons, fires and many other things."

"What?" Deiji cried out in indignation. "I already know how to do many of those things! I –"

Mangiat broke into her speech with a light touch on the arm. "I am the Keeper of the Forest. It is my sacred duty to take on such a responsibility."

"Duty." She stared at the young Centaur skeptically.

"Yes. My duties include many things. Many tasks and favors. Many hours devoted to my lady, my Mother..." He mused on this, brushing back his long black hair with one hand.

Without warning, he stepped swiftly into her cave, and Deiji rushed in after him.

"Hey!"

Mangiat knelt, and with skillful fingers tied up the corners of her pine boughs with bits of rope he had woven himself, and wore daily around his neck and wrists for such a purpose.

"Just what do you think you are doing?" she demanded angrily.

He didn't even glance at her as he worked. "I am making a better place for you to sleep. It will support your Human form more efficiently, and will offer more comfort for sure rest."

Deiji crossed her arms, greatly annoyed.

"And if you bring it over here," Mangiat continued, dragging the boughs to the western wall, "you are less likely to be rained upon when the wind blows the rain against the mouth of your cave."

She glared at him, the corners of her mouth twitching. She couldn't remember being as irritated as she was now, not even when Micid denied her freedom or demanded that she be wed. Here was this self-assured pompous Centaur – an absolute *stranger* – telling her that her methods were flawed and inefficient? How dare he!

"What is the point of making camp? We should make our way to Toten Town right away. I have much to do."

"You are wrong and you are right. We are not going to Toten Town yet because Jayna says you are not ready. You have much to do, yes, and it is in preparation for things to come. When you are ready, we will make our way there."

"So," she said with challenge, surprised at the bitterness in her own voice, "you always do what Jayna says, eh? Little errand boy?"

Mangiat looked at her, all traces of a smile gone from his face. "You are acting like a child, human. And yes, I do what Jayna tells me to do. Everyone needs a mentor, at some point or other in their lives. This happens to be your time. Deal with it." He snatched her bundled cloth and stepped out of the cave.

Deiji blushed and glanced away before following him outside. "How did you get that scar?" she blurted out, then blushed again.

He ignored the question. "Will you ever be serious enough to do as you are instructed, Deiji? Will you ever be open enough to learn something? I took this job because I was told to, not because I volunteered for it, or wanted to. Believe me, there are a hundred things I would rather be doing right now, than dealing with a willful brat."

They stared at one another.

"Yeah, okay," Deiji mumbled, looking down at his hooves.

"You will look me in the eye and address me as 'Teacher,'" Mangiat commanded. "I require your listening ear and complete openness to each and every thing I am to teach you. Try actually listening, and stop talking so much. I am as obligated in this as you are. Do not waste my time, for time is a non-renewable resource, and one of the utmost value to me, at that."

She opened her mouth in surprise, but closed it tightly. She swallowed hard and gave a slight bow. "Yes, my Teacher."

Mangiat smiled. "Good. Now that we've covered humility and obedience, we can move onto other things." He winked.

He shook the leaves out of her stuffed cloak lining and walked to the tree line, pausing here and there to peel moss from the trees.

"Humility and obedience are often difficult things to attain," he added with some afterthought. Deiji trailed behind him, defeated.

"There is a story of the wood that can show an example to this thought. Once a year the Rockman Taur emerges from beneath the ground. This happens at midnight of the sixth full moon in the forest. When I was ten years old he killed the Keeper of the Forest. He had been teaching a student, a student he was to mentor in all ways and secrets of the forest. The Keeper served under Jayna, grateful and reverent of the respect his position granted him."

Deiji wondered where this was going.

"Not even cougars would attack this Centaur," he continued. "The student that tutored under him was young, ignorant. This naivety would lead to the downfall of the revered Keeper." Mangiat closed his eyes for a moment.

"The student did not recognize the danger of Taur, though he had been warned many times. See, when the Rockman emerges, the people of this wood flee to the northern end of our side of the world, as far north of Toten Town as they can. The Rockman came this night on his usual mission: to commit six murders, six sacrifices to the moon before taking the life of Jayna. This is the oath the Rockman has taken before Relant – to compliment his murders with a great earthquake that further divides the continent.

"The forest's Keeper holds the honored task of holding off Taur and defending Jayna each year, while avoiding becoming a sacrifice himself. And so was the annual duty of this honored Keeper." He took a deep breath. Deiji was listening closely.

"Instead of fleeing with the others as the Keeper demanded of him, his student snuck into the forest, waiting for Taur. He didn't tail the Keeper himself, no, he would know if someone was following him. But the student did find the resting place of the Rockman, and he waited for him to rise from the earth, thinking he could claim glory and honor through such a heroic action.

"He found himself in a desperate situation, face to face with Taur himself, and he would have died if the Keeper had not saved him, sacrificing his own life. The student escaped and was reprimanded harshly by Jayna. He was pressed into years of servitude and tutelage under a great Teacher, to make amends before he could earn the title of Keeper of the Forest.

"Never think you can do anything yourself when you are not fully knowledgeable yet. Especially if your works contain raw motivations, such as pride. It is very important to listen to instruction, Deiji, and follow it carefully, even if it seems a hindrance at the time." He drew the corners of the cloth together, drew the strings expertly, tied them up and handed her the pillow.

"There is a certain amount of honor in wholesome pride, when appropriate. If you are living well, and it is not a lie, you may do well to be proud of yourself. Avoiding snobbery, of course." He winked again. He waited for her to put the pillow back into her cave.

She was silent for a time. Finally she spoke. "Who was the student the Keeper was teaching?"

"It was a long time ago," he said in a level voice, and he turned away. "Do you know how to make a fire?"

Deiji looked up, startled. "On Mount Odel I used flint and could make a fire."

"I mean with your hands and with sticks and stone."

"On the island I made fires… Well, it was a friend who really did most of the work." She thought of Geo and smiled. Her face brightened. "But I do not need to make a fire from scratch! Watch this! *Ferula Debeo!*" she cried, pointing her hands to a little patch of brush.

Yellow flames flew from her fingertips and ignited the grass instantly in a small blaze.

Mangiat was startled at this, and Deiji had to smile.

"Impressive," he grinned, stamping it out with a hoof. "But really, it is important to possess skills for life, skills that you might pass on to others in the future."

Deiji considered this, and could see the logic. "Alright then."

"Let us clear the ground of any and all grass, leaves and twigs. Here, help me find some larger stones like these." He nudged a large rock with a hoof.

"Always remember to toss dirt on a fire to put it out. Never leave a fire unattended, for fires can easily take the entire wood." He knelt with her to clear an area and make a circle of stones for the fire to rest within.

"And now we'll make the fire," Deiji said cheerfully. "By hand."

"Yes, Ju Ju." He looked her full in the face and smiled. "Now we will."

And he showed her how.

CHAPTER EIGHT

The Lessons

Mangiat continued to teach her things throughout that first day. He assisted her in gathering, stripping and drying wood and twigs for burning. He had her practice feints and stances with her sword, holding mock fights with her sword against his staff. Much to her enjoyment, he admired her steady aim in the throwing of stones and assisted her in the fashioning of a sling and a leather drawstring bag to hold stones in, girded at her waist. They visited the river together to hunt for stones. Mangiat seemed quite interested in the river, from the way he spoke of it.

"It is the lengthiest river in the whole world," he explained, even though Deiji knew of this. "It divides the world of Nigh right into two halves, the Known and the Unknown Worlds. Humans on one side, Mystics on the other. Prophesy claims that it will one day be one realm, but that has yet to unfold. Ancient lore speaks of the great division of Man. Perhaps I shall tell you more stories some night," he suggested brightly, and Deiji smiled.

"I had always wanted to visit the Unknown World," she mused.

Mangiat frowned. "I thought you were from the Unknown World. Mount Odel, right?"

She laughed. "No, that is the Known World. This is the Unknown World, here where we are now."

He smiled some. "Maybe to you. It is all a matter of perspective. We are unknown sides to each other."

They were sitting on the riverbed in the sun, sharpening sticks with rugged stones. "See, you want to turn the stick as you sharpen in, so all sides even out to a point," he said, leaning toward her, checking her work.

Every example he presented to her carried a lesson. Every lesson a moral. Deiji wasn't a particularly philosophical person, and sometimes found herself mentally overwhelmed by this creature, but somehow he managed to simplify even the most in-depth concepts.

"Thank you, Mangiat," she said, meaning it. She admired his grace, beauty and wisdom.

"It is my pleasure, Ju Ju," he said, blowing shavings off his sharpened stick. He glanced at her, his expression unreadable.

Deiji averted her gaze, feeling awkward. "Um, Mangiat? Why do you call me that?"

"What?"

"Ju Ju. You have called me Ju Ju on more than one occasion."

"Oh. Well, Deiji J Cu seemed like a long name -"

"It is three syllables!"

"- and Ju Ju just seemed to fit, is all. It's cute. Why do you ask? Is it wrong of me?" He looked suddenly uncomfortable.

"Oh, no," she assured. "It is what my father called me, that's all." She sat for a moment and thought of her parents. How she missed them! She worried for her mother's health. It struck her that J might be dead by now, and Deiji might not know it. She set her jaw rigid.

That is the sole purpose of these trials, right? She thought quietly. *Not only save the world, but to save my mother's life. This is my motivation*, she whispered in her heart.

In that moment Deiji grew up, in a sense. She opted for wisdom, courage and gratitude. After all, her intentions were pure. She accepted that she could stand to brush up on a few things, and learn something new as well.

She looked at her mentor and smiled.

Day Four – Earth

Deiji's days after this were long, and she felt her heart well fed. She especially liked the way Mangiat respected her, almost as if protecting her. At night he had escorted her to the mouth of her cave, and stood, watching the perimeter of the clearing for a time before retiring for the night, laying himself down against a tree.

On this day they were fishing off the riverbank with the spears they had made yesterday. They waded knee-deep into the river together. The river was thick with fish, and their movements probably wouldn't scare them off.

"Water distorts that which is around us," Mangiat explained. "Before you plunge your spear into the water, watch the current. Aim to the left of your target by several inches, perhaps at a pebble rather than the actual fish."

He thrust his spear and pulled it out, and sure enough, a fish flapped about on its end!

"Impressive," Deiji said, and she meant it, too.

Mangiat grinned. "Now you try."

Deiji stood, legs apart, feet steady just as he had told her. She remembered how she felt when she had failed on the island, and how embarrassed she would be if she couldn't do it this time.

She glimpsed a smooth pebble as her target just a little ways from the fish she had her eye on. She threw her spear! Nothing.

"Again!" Mangiat snapped.

She threw the spear.

"Again!"

After two more tries, she was delighted to see a fish squirming on the end of her stick.

"I did it!" Deiji cried, looking up, her eyes wide and shining. "I did it!" They were both smiling.

They walked to the shore together and, using a sharp stone, Mangiat showed her how to gut and clean their fish properly.

"Very good. Now," he said briskly, "we now will cover a very complex procedure, known as 'digging.' See," he knelt a little, "you scoop the dirt with your hands or an implement such as a stick -"

"Hey!" Deiji cried, indignant, "I DO know what digging is!" She stopped, catching the teasing look on Mangiat's face.

"Mangiat!" she cried, exasperated, but she couldn't help but laugh. She shoved her new friend, who caught her wrist, and they both tumbled onto the bank laughing.

That afternoon, after they had roasted and eaten their fish over Deiji's fire (which Mangiat had made her start herself, by hand), he led her deep into the forest.

"Bring nothing," he instructed. Easy enough, she figured. She didn't have much. She stashed her sword, spear and sling in her bedding and met him outside.

"We are embarking on a nature walk of sorts," Mangiat replied to her inquiries. "It is a spiritual, as well as physical experience. There is much to be learned of out here." Deiji said nothing, only fastened her cloak firmly at her throat. They walked for hours, mostly in silence.

"Shh!" Mangiat said suddenly, and he held up his hand as

they stepped through the underbrush. He gestured to a tree – a tree where two were joined into one trunk. They crept closer.

"Look.

Deiji saw nothing. No, she could see a little woven bird's nest, camouflaged in the crook of the tree. There were three little white eggs, and one of them quivered.

"Watch," Mangiat said, a glow of happiness on his face. As they observed the little eggs, the little birds inside began to struggle and kick until the eggs cracked. They sluggishly worked their ways out of the eggs until all three were free.

Their feathers were matted and sparse, but their little eyes were wide, and they looked with wonder at the girl and the Centaur.

"No," Mangiat laughed, "it is not us! But wait! Here she comes!" He stepped back and the mother bird flew into the nest with a bug in her beak. The three baby birds poked their necks out, beaks wide open, making quite a ruckus at the sight of her. Deiji and Mangiat left them to it.

"New life in the forest today," Mangiat said, smiling contentedly. They started walking. "Everyone takes their place in the forest," he continued. "No one takes or gives more than another. Everyone lives in a constant state of balance, bound by a common bond of utmost respect."

Deiji nodded, surprised at her own willingness to learn from this strong, proud figure.

"The people of the wood made their homes here well over two hundred years ago, bothered only by the yearly emergence of the Rockman. We live on this half of the continent, undisturbed, in mild fear that Humans may one day discover us. The time for them to learn of us is approaching, which will be a turning point, when the people of the forest actually meet Humans! You, for example, are merely the second Human I have ever met in my life. It is not very often that one of you comes into our midst."

They paused and Mangiat lovingly touched a flower.

"There is much speculation, but it is unknown what would really happen if the Mystical people were intruded upon, or what would become of our ways of life."

"Speculation?"

"Yes, especially as of late. I have heard the most disturbing rumor from a rabbit I met this morning, and though it is early, soon we will head southeast."

Deiji focused her sense of direction and thought about it. "What lies southeast?" She skipped a little to catch up to him.

"Toten Town."

They made their camp in the woods that night. Mangiat produced some dried fish from his leather satchel. Deiji built a fire.

Over dinner Deiji told him stories from her life on Mount Odel. Stories of Maia and of her parents. Tales of a life that seemed so long ago and so strange to what her life was now. And she told him of her adventures, of her time on the island, in the sea, and what it was to be in the Deep Forest now. And she spoke of Mowat.

When she said his name, Mangiat stopped and stared, his eyes wide. "You know Mowat?" he asked, surprised.

"Yes!" Deiji exclaimed, "I do! And you?"

"Yes! Yes! He is the Teacher of Life! Each element of Nigh has its own Keeper, and Mowat guides us all. He once took me under his wing and put me through many trials, leaving me in charge as the Keeper of the Deep Forest! He is Jayna's spouse, and often sends me messages through her."

"He *what?*" she sputtered, shocked. "Jayna is his *spouse?*"

"Indeed. Long ago he chose her as his link to the earth, as the Mother of all life and all elements. And so he chose, and she accepted, and this is what it is now. It is the highest honor that she would remain here in the element of earth for her roots. But she does have roots and branches that extend to other places."

"That is incredible." They sat silent for a while. "Why does Jayna always look so sad?"

"That," Mangiat said sternly, "you shall have to ask her for yourself."

Day Five – Earth

Deiji awoke very early under her cloak and waited until she heard Mangiat's movements before rising. They picked berries for a brief breakfast before heading on their way.

"We will fish when we get to the river," Mangiat promised as they hiked through the woods. "We are nearly there." They stepped into a clearing and Mangiat cocked his head, listening to something she could not hear. He grabbed her arm gruffly.

He turned toward her, looking very serious. "Believe me, Ju Ju, when I say this. It is of the utmost importance that you remain quiet and do not run. Motion will make you a sure target. Even if you do not like what you are about to see, you must be quiet. So be still and observe."

He knelt into the brush and Deiji followed suite, wondering idly of ticks. They watched the meadow quietly for a quarter of an hour. Deiji's legs were beginning to burn and cramp.

Then, she saw a mother doe and her fawn moving into view, to graze in the field. They grew silent and alert. Deiji wondered if the deer had smelled them, but then she saw it!

A cougar! It was crouched low, creeping forward in the grass.

"Does it see us?" Deiji whispered. Mangiat silenced her with his hand. She followed the cougar's gaze to the doe and her fawn, and the realization of what was happening struck her with horror.

She made to move from where she squatted, but Mangiat pushed her back down and kept his hand on her shoulder. She watched in quiet agony as the doe and her fawn leapt across the field toward the trees, fleeting, tails in the air. The cougar ran so fast its legs were a blur, and it leapt onto the back of the fawn, digging its claws in, twisting, and wrestling it to the ground. The mother never stopped running.

They watched as the cougar began to consume the fallen fawn. Deiji was at least thankful that the tall grass hid most of the details of the moment.

Mangiat finally spoke. "It is an old, redundant lesson that the young would die so the mature may live to give birth again. In these two days you have witnessed the ever old cycle of renewal and demise."

Deiji nodded. A hard fact to accept, but as she swallowed hard, more acceptance came to her than she would have thought possible.

"We need to continue," Mangiat declared. "We have a ways to go to find the river."

They heard the gurgle of the stream long before they reached it. She and Mangiat fished for an hour and had a small feast.

When they had eaten, and eaten well, Mangiat stood strongly. "It is only a moment's walk to the Town of Toten. Follow me, and keep low, as it is important that I not be seen."

Deiji nodded and the Centaur looked at her a moment. He took a leaf out of her hair but did not break his gaze.

"What is it, Mangiat?" She glanced around, and saw a bush of red flowers behind her. "They're nice, aren't they," she said, smiling.

He nodded and led her through the reeds of the riverbank and they could see a large village built on the opposite shore.

"What are we looking for?" she whispered as they peered across the way.

"It is rumored by the trees that the human King Jebhadsen has quartered an army on Toten Town. Or so the rabbits tell me."

"The king? Why would he do such a thing?"

"That is what we are here to find out."

Deiji glanced at him. "Well, you can hardly walk over there and ask them yourself. I think they might notice that you weren't quite the same. It would start a panic."

"I know," he said matter-of-factly, "that is why I brought you along." He grinned.

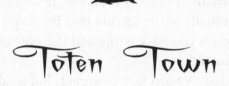

Toten Town

Deiji crossed the river at a small spot upstream around the first bend. The edges of the shore very nearly touched. A tree had fallen across the divide, and she had no problem walking precariously across it.

Once she entered the village she was surprised at the feelings of old familiarity, even though she had never visited this town before. How strange it was to see buildings and fences and huts and shops! Things she had not seen in near a month, although it felt like years. Villagers went about their daily routines, paying her little heed.

She walked through the village paths feeling very foreign. "How am I to find out the soldier's plans?" she muttered secretly to herself, noting the wild, hardened appearance of the soldiers who loitered about the huts, and the fearful, timid faces of the farmers.

Deiji stepped into the blacksmith's shop. "Please, sir," she asked of the soot-covered man who was beating heated steel with a heavy hammer. "Which way to the Elder's hut?"

The man grunted and nodded toward the hut at the top of the hill on the edge of the town. Deiji bowed in thanks and made her way along the path. She tentatively knocked on the splintered doorpost and waited.

"Declare yourself!" snapped a very disgruntled voice.

"I am Deiji J Cu of Mount Odel, your honored Elder, and I have need to speak to the village head."

"Enter!" the voice sounded. Deiji stepped inside, brushing aside the full-length curtain that hung across the threshold. It was dim and humid inside, and the whole place reeked of incense. A lone woman wrapped in a lavender tunic of sheep's wool sat in the middle of the hut like a goddess.

"What brings you so far from the mountain, Deiji J Cu?" the woman asked her steadily, taking a pull off a long, slender wooden pipe. She could see a cane propped against the wall beside her pillow.

"Honored Elder, I -"

"Sit," the woman commanded, breathing out a stream of smoke. "And I am called the Honored Lady Nia."

Deiji obediently sat cross-legged on the pillow dictated and faced the Elder. She accepted with a slight bow the pipe and flint the woman presented to her. After a few short puffs, for Deiji was not yet skilled in the ways of smoking, she passed it back to the woman.

"Honored Lady, I am here to inquire as to the nature of the soldiers who are quartered in this town. What purpose in duty do they serve?" She felt light-headed.

The Elder blew out stale smoke and pushed fresh leaf into the pipe with her thumb. "They have not said."

"Is that not unusual?"

"It is quite unusual, child. In all my years I have never heard of the king supplying no reason for his army's purpose. It is a strange thing indeed."

"Have you overheard anything unusual from the soldiers themselves?" Deiji pressed. "Even an idea of what their orders might be would be of some help."

"Who has sent you?" the woman asked suddenly, resting the pipe on her lip.

Deiji paused and chose to answer honestly. "Mowat, a great Teacher."

"I have not heard of this Mowat," she said serenely, and Deiji wondered if she had crossed a line.

"I do not know of anything," the Elder said with finality, and she stood. Deiji followed suit.

"If you will," the village head said, holding back the curtain over the door. Deiji bowed, then left, grateful to be in the fresh air and light once again.

She walked down the village path, searching for soldiers. The majority of them hung about the corral in the sun, lazily sharpening knives, kissing women or picking vermin out of their clothes. It did not look as if they were about to stand for battle, and Deiji wondered what they were waiting for.

Deiji saw a lone tree near the corner of the fence, and was struck with an idea. Casually she sauntered up to the tree and rested her hands upon it. "Jayna," she murmured. "Jayna, I need you to instruct this tree to eavesdrop on the soldiers stationed here, and let us know their plans. We need to know what their orders from the king are, and find out if we can stop it."

Deiji stepped away, feeling a pair of eyes on her. She turned and saw Nia staring at her with piercing gray eyes. She walked away into the village, resisting the urge to look again.

Deiji spent the next hour walking from shop to shop in the town, speaking to any and all that might listen. It was time to educate them all. She hoped she was doing the right thing. She headed back to the blacksmith's shed and the man acknowledged her arrival with another grunt.

"Please, sir, I ask only for a moment of your time." The blacksmith grunted again and carried a jagged piece of metal to a shelf.

Deiji took a deep breath.

"Mystical people live among us, sir, even as close as the opposite shore of this very river! Beautiful, sacred creatures of the like you could never imagine. Centaurs and Elves and –"

"Little girl, I have work to do," the blacksmith interrupted angrily. "Do you see the soldiers out there? They keep me working from dawn to midnight forging weapons for them! And for no wage but my very life. I have no time to listen to tales. Get out." He spat on the ground as she scampered away.

Determined, she tried the baker's hut.

"Please, ma'am," she propositioned the baker's wife, "the soldiers are set for some evil purpose, and –"

"What purpose of evil could be more than that which they have already done?" the brazen woman bellowed. "Get on with thee, we have no use for stranger's tales!"

Deiji saw a young boy with mousy brown hair carrying a bucket of water back from the river and she walked over to him.

"Hello there, little boy," she said kindly. "I am Deiji. What is your name?"

"Zechi," he answered quietly.

She leaned forward with her hands on her knees. "Zechi, do you believe me when I say that magical creatures live on the other side of the river? That we just do not know it yet? Centaurs and Fairies and even Dolphins live on our shores!"

Zechi shook his head slowly from side to side and looked down at his feet.

She saw a shallow pain in the boy's face and she sighed. She touched the boy under the chin and looked into his sorrowful eyes. "One day these shores will be joined again Zechi, and you will be of the first to see it happen. I pray such a day will come in your lifetime." She squeezed his shoulder and walked away.

She felt eyes on her again, and she turned to see the village head hobbling toward her, one arm clutching her purple shawl, the other pointing one, long accusatory finger. "Witch!" the woman shrieked.

"Oh no," Deiji groaned.

Deiji found herself encircled by villagers, all talking amongst themselves. Two strong-looking men were inching toward her with a length of rope. Zechi peeked from the edge of the circle, watching her intently.

"This girl speaks of evil!" the woman announced to the growing crowd. "She tries to sway you with clouded thoughts of magic and blasphemy!"

"She told me that magical animals live across the river!" the blacksmith called out.

Deiji glanced around nervously. It wouldn't be long until they got the soldier's attention.

"She asks questions that she should not," the Elder agreed, leaning upon her cane. "She makes inquiries that are not of her business. She wears men's trousers! She proposes evil, and such evil must be quelled!"

The villagers cheered.

"She shall be hanged!"

"She shall be burned!"

"She shall be drowned!"

"Oh, for heaven's sake," Deiji groaned. She pulled away from the advancing men. "*Cascata!*" she cried.

For one moment the crowd fell silent in fear. Then, a rumble, and the sound of rushing water. Deiji sprang from the crowd, snatched Zechi by the arm and scrambled up the tree next to the corral. Clinging to its lower branches and trying to climb higher, she snatched for the boy's hand and pulled him up after her.

People were screaming and running. Some were swept off their feet while others made it safely up the hill. They felt the tree buckle as a wave of water rocked against it.

Deiji watched the water recede and she jumped down from the tree. She ran toward the river and did not look back.

The Deep Forest

"So they thought you were a witch?" Mangiat asked, greatly amused.

"Oh, yes, it was quite funny. Next time you get to play ambassador." She stomped on ahead of him, slinking in and out of the brush.

Mangiat laughed good-naturedly. They were walking north through the grass, following the river away from the Town of Toten. "Did you learn anything of the soldier's plans?"

"No, I did not," Deiji admitted, "but I called upon Jayna through a tree stationed near the army, and I asked it to be a spy for us. Jayna may have the information when we return."

"And the villager's knowledge of us?"

"Completely unaware. I tried to tell them of all Mystical presence, but they did not listen to me."

"But they have been told."

"Yes." They walked further. "Will we go see Jayna now?" Deiji inquired.

"No, we have that which is yet to be done. We continue north."

They stopped in the early evening to fish and to rest. "Best sit and preserve your strength, Deiji," Mangiat instructed. "We have some long nights ahead of us." Deiji did not question further, but she was intrigued.

That night they made camp, but no fire. Deiji sat on a log and Mangiat lay next to her, folding his four legs beneath him.

"Tonight we look to the stars," he began. She followed his gaze skyward. The dome of the night sky was clear and the stars shone very brightly, and Deiji found a new appreciation in nature.

"Deiji, we are one planet of many. Each of those stars is the sun of a world as real as ours. We do not know if these others are host to life, or if they are anything like our planet here, but we do know their planetary trajectory routes and rotations in respect to ours. It is very mathematical, and bears incredible significance.

"There are twelve signs, classified by element. Those elements are fire, water, earth and air. They are the four quadrants representing ardor, emotion, power and intellect. A fire sign is inspirational, passionate, self-motivated and looks easily ahead to their own future."

She lowered her gaze to meet his eyes.

"You are a fire sign, Ju Ju."

"What does this mean?"

"It means you are stubborn, milady." He grinned. "But it also means you are joyful in your very existence. An adventurous spirit, pioneering courage, and a soul that cannot be restricted."

"Thank you."

"It is only who you are, my friend. You are graceful and dignified and determined."

Her eyes sparkled at this, reflecting the stars.

"You are also intolerant, patronizing, and dramatic," he finished quickly. Deiji was thankful that it was dark and he could not altogether see the flush that spread across her face. She laughed inwardly.

"Where did you learn of such things?"

"From Mowat," he answered quietly. "It is possible he chooses you as the Keeper of Fire."

Deiji nodded, absorbing this thought.

Continuing, Mangiat said, "the moon passes through lunar phases each month, resting for a night in each sign, affecting changes and the outcomes of all of us. In any case, the moon will soon pass through your sign, Ju Ju. There are changes coming, not only to this wood, but to the world."

"What am I to do?"

"Make your choices wisely. This is a very sensitive time. Within days the Rockman will rise and you will bear witness. I will require your assistance to protect Jayna. Can you do this?"

"I can."

Mangiat's hand found hers in the darkness. "Then let us gaze some more."

CHAPTER NINE

The Keeper of the Forest

Day Six – Earth

The sound of water gurgling over river stones... A gentle, warming sun and a soft breeze rusting the trees. Deiji was awakened by such peacefulness early that morning, frowning when it was interrupted by the sound of stamping hooves near her head.

She opened one eye warily. "Mangiat?"

He stamped on the ground again. "Sit up, Ju Ju."

She moved her cloak from her face and squinted into the blinding sun, but complied. Crossing her legs, she sat up straight.

"We will do stretches in the morning to greet the sun," Mangiat announced. He joined his hands high over his head and exhaled as he leaned forward.

Together they went through a series of stretches, stretching their upper bodies and arms, the waist, the spine, the legs... Deiji had never experienced such a transitional morning.

They rose to their feet and Mangiat suddenly shoved her shoulder, and she nearly fell. "Mangiat!" she said in irritation.

"Two legs! How on earth do you expect to stay balanced!" he teased. "But seriously, Ju Ju, you need to work on your stance. No one should be able to push you down."

Deiji focused her balance, spreading her feet apart and planting them firmly in the dirt as Mangiat guided her steps. "Wider. Okay, good. Now rest on your back leg, plant it like a tree. Bend your knees. More. Now transfer your weight evenly between your legs. Find your center of balance. Good, now give me your fist."

He took her hand and balled her fist accordingly.

"Now I want you to punch into my hand," he said, cupping his hand into a target. "As you punch, alternate fists, leaving the other palm up at your waist. Now, punch! Punch! Punch! Punch! Maintain your balance, now," he warned as she wobbled. "Punch! Punch! Punch! Punch!" He stepped back. "Very good, Ju Ju."

It looked as though they were finished. "What was that all about?" Deiji finally spoke.

"Part of my morning ritual. Some very basic things that I believe you can incorporate into your own life easily."

"Thank you," she said with a smile.

After their breakfast they continued on their way, Deiji growing more curious as to their destination with each step. Come afternoon, she was just about to ask for more details when Mangiat spoke up.

"We are far enough. If I am not mistaken, you can climb this tree here, and when you do, look to the east."

Curious, Deiji scrambled up the tree, high into the branches. She grinned at the ease that the forbidden trousers brought to her agility. As soon as the tree began to creak from her weight, she stopped and looked east. There, far away, above and beyond the Deep Forest, loomed the snow-capped Eastern Ranges, and Mount Odel.

"My home," she whispered. She could almost just make out the ridge halfway up the mountain where her mother still lived with Aunt Micid. She took a long, full look for her memory; a glimpse of what her mountain looked like from a distance. It put her world into sudden perspective. She could almost see a speck in the sky that she knew in her heart was Polk, and something in her chest grew very tight.

She climbed down slowly. "Why did you show me that?" she asked Mangiat as she hopped down the rest of the way.

"Because sometimes a person needs to be reminded of the reason they are fighting," he said readily. Deiji accepted this and they made their way back to Jayna.

They stopped in the early evening to make camp. Deiji was surprised; the sun could still be seen above the tree line. "Why so early?"

Mangiat smiled mysteriously. "You need to sleep now, for you will not tonight."

She asked no further questions, but took him at his word, lay down on the ground and tried to rest.

When Deiji awoke it was twilight. The sky was streaked with soft purples and oranges, but Deiji did not see this. All she could hear were the crickets, which were chirping loudly. There was something on her face cutting off her vision, and she yelped and touched the thing.

"Do not take off the blindfold," Mangiat said. "Drink. There will not be water until morning." He placed the wooden flask into her hands and she drank, dribbling a little down the front of her cloak. He slipped a piece of dried fish into her pocket.

"As you have taken on this task to be of my aid, I need to be sure that you will be calm under pressure, and be prepared to do what you must. I need to know that you know the forest well enough to use it as a tool."

He touched her arm. "I am going to leave you now, Ju Ju."

She drew her breath in sharply.

"What do you hear when you are silent in the forest?" he asked sharply.

"Not much, it's pretty quiet. Birds, sometimes."

"Unacceptable. The forest is alive with sounds and movement. If you know these noises, you can know what is going on all around you at all times. I want you to sit against this tree, and listen quietly. I want you to tune your ears to the forest. I am not going to tell you how long you will be sitting here, but when I toss a pebble at you, you may stand and remove your blindfold. Then I want you to track me in the dark. Use your ears, eyes and intuition. Do your best to walk without making a sound. I will see you at dawn."

Deiji reached out her hand but her fingertips touched air. Mangiat was gone. She sat down heavily and leaned against the tree trunk, her back straight.

After several long minutes she began to yearn for Mangiat's signal. She was growing fidgety. Finally she bit her tongue and chided herself. The Centaur had meant for this to be a learning experience, hands on work. Reality at its best.

Talking about things is not enough; the gaining of experience requires action and practice, she thought meditatively. *Too often one craves to obtain the knowledge, but is not patient enough to learn the lessons. Like myself,* she added as an afterthought.

And it cannot be rushed. While the end result is important, it is in the experience that we learn the way. It is in the experience where we find the most to gain.

Deiji began to think on these things until she had silenced her mind. Then, body and mind still, she found herself listening to the forest, picking out sounds and placing their source. For the next three hours she sat, eventually distinguishing the layers of animal and wind from one another.

The crickets were chirping.

And once she separated the noises, she was able to recognize the breezes that ruffled the trees and made them creak. She heard the soft padded feet of a bobcat slowly crossing the clearing. A fox's yelping echoing through the trees. The gurgle of the distant river. Fireflies. Amazed, Deiji was hearing movement in the woods that she had never noticed before.

She found herself wholly grateful that Mangiat would show her this. She smiled, and felt an unexpected weight land on the taunt fabric of her cloak, and her searching fingers discovered a pebble.

When she stood to remove the blindfold, she was very surprised to find the darkness as it was. It had to be nearly midnight; the only light was that of the moon, which seemed thankfully near its fullness.

Deiji scanned the tree line searching for Mangiat's form. Nothing. Focusing her eyes as they adjusted to the moonlight, she peered at the ground thoughtfully. When she saw a hoof print in the dirt she smiled and headed southwest. She had not told the Centaur of this gift she had retained, of always knowing directions.

Deiji made her way through the trees, trying not to make a sound or touch a single bush. She noticed easily with her newly trained ears the sounds of what was typical of the forest at night, and foreign noises, such as her own steps.

So she noticed immediately when there was a rustle in the

bushes that most definitely was not the wind. Deiji grinned. Mangiat.

As she stepped on in the darkness, she noticed a dark silhouette in the bushes. There was white, shaggy fur down its flank, quite distinguishable in the dark, and it was shorter than Mangiat.

Deiji froze.

It leaned its head back and opened its mouth and let out a long, steady howl that made her heart skip a beat. A wolf! It growled at her, opening its mouth, which was dripping thick white foam.

She backed away slowly, but knew it was no good. "*Someone! Help!*" she cried out in her heart, though she could not utter a sound for fear. The wolf inched forward, snarling.

Then, the sound of pounding hooves! Mangiat leapt into her path and grabbed her under both arms with surprisingly strong hands. "On my back!" he yelled as he swung her weight to the side and let go. Deiji snatched for a firm grip, and she found his shoulders. Pulling herself tightly to his back, she held fast.

The wolf growled again, hackles up; its hair standing on end. "We run!" Mangiat yelled, and they took off through the forest.

Deiji had never moved so fast, not even on Geo's winged back. The trees were a blur as they galloped, and the ride was quite bumpy. They leapt over fallen trees and through bushes. Deiji couldn't even look back to see if the wolf still pursued them, for fear of falling off.

She hugged close to the Centaur's body, praying he would keep his balance and maintain his speed, hoping she would stay on. Finally, Mangiat began to slow down. He settled into a trot, still not stopping. He was breathing heavily.

"Disease," he panted, wiping his forehead off with his arm.

"What?" She sat back, her hands still resting on his shoulders.

"There is a disease that has begun to touch the woodland creatures. In the wolves it causes them to act erratically. I am glad you were not bitten." He hopped over a small ditch.

Deiji leaned forward and hugged Mangiat around the shoulders. "Thank you," she whispered, burying her face into his neck.

Mangiat paused and lifted his hands to her arms, which were wrapped around his neck. They held each other this way, cheek to cheek, as the earliest stirrings of forest life awakened.

When they opened their eyes again the first light of dawn was beginning to show through the trees.

Day Seven – Earth

They stepped into Jayna's clearing mid-morning, weary but in good spirits. Deiji was not on Mangiat's back anymore; she had slid from her perch to walk beside him, almost embarrassed to have ridden so.

When Jayna noticed them, she did not wait for the usual obeisances; rather she called out his name at first sighting.

"Mangiat!" she cried out sharply. He left Deiji's side and hurried to his lady.

"Mangiat, my tree Sounet has informed me of the army's orders. At dawn tomorrow they are to ford the Longest River from Toten Town into the Deep Forest. They have been instructed to destroy any they come across; kill whoever or whatever they see."

The brave Centaur nodded, and Deiji knew his worst fears were confirmed.

"You know this is the eve of the sixth full moon of this year,"

Jayna insisted. "If the Rockman rises and we are defeated, the soldiers will destroy what is left, and it will be the end of us all."

"What must I do?" Mangiat stood straight, very serious. This was his moment.

"Go. Prepare for what is to come. I will speak to the trees to send the word for all to flee, and not to return tomorrow. We must clear out the forest and be ready for tonight. Go."

Mangiat turned, catching Deiji's eye for just a moment. She wanted to speak, but there was no time.

"We will be together soon, Ju Ju!" he cried as he leapt into the tree line. Silence fell over the clearing.

"Deiji!" Jayna was calling her. She turned.

"Yes, milady?" she asked politely, swallowing all emotion.

"You have done a very wise thing, asking me to have Sounet spy on those soldiers."

"Sounet?"

"That is the name of the tree you summoned my attention with." She curved her oak features into a smile.

"Ah."

"Furthermore, giving the village folk warning of our Mystical existence was extremely wise."

"Really?"

"Absolutely, my daughter. It will only validate the rumors when the truth is laid bare." Her smile faded, and she looked saddened again.

"Jayna? May I ask a question?"

"You may."

"I wanted to know... My new friend Mangiat told me of your unique relationship with Mowat. He is the Keeper of all Life, a bringer of hope, love and inspiration. Why then, my Mother, are you so mournful?"

There was a definitive pause in which Deiji felt sure she had said something wrong. But at last Jayna spoke.

"Sit, child."

Obediently, Deiji sat.

"My heart mourns because I feel my children's pain. It is hard to bear all the suffering of the children of this world without some sadness," she said with a small smile. "It begins a long, long time ago, when the first of the Humans, fresh from their journey from the sea, forgot all that they had left behind. Relant, the bringer of death, encouraged such willful separation, and within a few short generations, all knowledge of Man's history was lost.

"Mowat took me from the sea and placed me on the earth to do all I could to guide my lost children. But change does not come quickly. I chose to be placed in the Deep Forest where I could work through the Mystical people who had populated the entire continent before the birth of Man, rather than be placed in the midst of the Humans. At times it seems futile, but an ancient prophecy declares triumph!"

At this time Deiji opened her mouth to speak, and Jayna, seeing this, waited patiently.

"What is the prophecy, milady?" Deiji began. "I have heard of this thing before, and I need to know what it truly means." To her relief, Jayna had a ready answer.

"It is an ancient prophecy, prophesied by a wise Centaur from ages past. It is said that the Humans would continue to rise, unaware, and the broken continents would continue to shift on the sixth full moon of each year, when the Rockman rises and the earth quakes. The continents shift farther apart and the world remains divided.

"Relant, in his efforts to destroy the world, was to release a deadly fever that would target both Man and Mystical people. This sickness would clear the way for Relant's children. Relant has not yet revealed his children, so we do not know if the prophesy is complete. But it is clear that the fatal fever is on the rise. The air of the mountains is permeated. The oceans were affected but are now healing. The islands are also recovering, but we are still fighting for the forest.

"Mowat was to send One to relinquish the flames of the fever. They would come from a unique mother, a mix of Human and Mystical blood. They would be a joyous being, with many hidden strengths, and would crave knowledge above all else. With some instruction they would rise to be a great leader, a conqueror of each element. Hundreds of years have passed since this was foretold. The people of this world have slowly given over to despair, with no hope that we will all live in harmony one day. It has been a little over two hundred years since Man climbed onto the shore, and not one person has been born who fits the description of this prophecy. Until now."

Deiji waited, scarcely breathing.

"I have watched you before, Deiji."

She sat up sharply and frowned. "You have? When?"

"On the Dragon Islands. I believe you took refuge in my tree." Jayna smiled. "I guarded you against Adar."

"Oh, wow! It was *you* who spoke to me!"

Jayna nodded.

"Thank you."

"There is one you will encounter soon," Jayna continued. "His name is Taur, as you have heard. He lives underground in dark tunnels that extend for many miles. He emerges once a year, and when he finishes his work, the earth shakes and the continents shift farther apart. Absolute terror reigns in the forest.

"He will make six blood sacrifices to the moon and then he will come for me. The Keeper of the Forest will fend him off and keep him from completing his mission before the sun rises and Taur must retreat to his tunnels. The most sacrifices Taur has ever made were five; he has come close. Tonight he must be stopped for good. Relant is at his strongest and this chaos must be ended. The time is now."

"Does he have any weaknesses? Do you know of a way to stop him?"

"He is safe during hibernation. There is but one weakness he does posses. Being forty feet high and fully composed of rock, his only physical weaknesses lie in the strength he derives from the moon. To be cut off from the moonlight would utterly destroy him, and he would crumble back into the earth forever. In years passed the Keeper would allow himself to be chased until Taur receded at dawn. This year we end his reign of terror!" she finished with passion. "That is, if you are who Mowat thinks you are."

"What?"

"Do you not see? You are the Prophesied Jai. The One. You will save the world of Nigh."

Deiji was stunned. She could not think of anything to say to this. "I – I don't..." She was defeated. "Thank you for all you have given me, my Mother. Would you tell me of Mangiat's predecessor?" She asked this with urgency, as she was fearful for her friend's very life.

"Ah, yes," Jayna replied, once again mournful in such a memory. "One day, some years ago, there was a noble Centaur named Iden. He was the Keeper of the Forest; a title which none since have carried. He mentored a young Centaur, who got himself in a precarious position during one of Taur's deadly unearthings."

"That is what I heard, yes."

"The young Centaur was fixated on being the one to send the Rockman to his grave forever, but it was a mistake. He was wounded in the attempt and would have died if Iden hadn't arrived then. Instead of insuring Taur's defeat, Iden rescued the young Centaur. Once his student reached safety, Iden found himself cornered, and so became Taur's third sacrifice that night.

"The boy, shamed and saddened by these events, reluctantly committed himself to Mowat's tutelage, and after a series of intense trials, took upon the duties of Iden himself. He will be tied to these duties until the Keeper's death is avenged."

Deiji sat still for a while, contemplating. Animals began cutting through the clearing, fleeing north. The sun was growing late. "It was Mangiat, wasn't it," she said to the Dryad.

"That," Jayna said with a trace of a smile, "you shall have to ask him for yourself."

Deiji ran to her cave, snatching up her weapons and affixing them to her body then she sprinted down the slope. She found Mangiat on the riverbank, skillfully tying feathers to the ends of arrows in the fading sunlight. He was muttering under his breath, but looked relieved when he saw Deiji. Flocks of birds were flying north overhead, fleeing the wood and Deiji thought about the newborn babies in their nest who could not fly yet.

"Ju Ju!" Mangiat called out to her, and he pulled her into a tight embrace. "Oh, wait," he said, searching among his things behind them. He handed her a red flower.

"Thank you," Deiji said, giving him another hug. They stepped back, but did not let go. Her hand rested on his shoulder.

"Are you alright?" she asked him.

"I am full of anticipation. There is so much to be done." He pulled away and began gathering finished arrows into his holster.

"Will you teach me to make those?" Deiji asked suddenly.

Mangiat froze. He walked back to her and placed his palm

to her cheek. "I will teach you how to shoot, how to hunt and trap. I will teach you everything I know."

"Tomorrow," she said firmly.

His face looked rather grave, but he played along, as though following a script. "Yes," he offered her a weak smile. "Tomorrow."

He looked into her eyes and they both knew the truth. He frowned. "Deiji, your pendant! It is glowing!"

She looked down and saw that the vines on her medallion were emitting a bright green light around the Emerald. Turning to the river she saw the Dolphin surface, sending up quite a spray. "Arill!" she dropped the flower she still held clutched in her hand, and she plunged into the water, splashing wildly about as she sprouted her Mermaid's tail. She embraced her friend and he circled her in urgency. There was no time for happy conversation in the dusk.

"Deiji! It is time!" Arill cried. "It has come! The full moon rises! Taur will emerge from beneath, and whatever he does, the soldiers will be here at dawn to finish the job. You must stop both him and the soldiers."

"Both? But how?"

"I honestly do not know. Do what you can, my friend, you have my luck. I must go!" And with that he sank beneath the waters.

Deiji turned to the shore and saw Mangiat there, looking alert and startled. The full cover of nighttime had fallen in an instant. The ground began to shake.

She sluggishly pulled herself out of the water, gained her human legs and began to run, weaving up the bank, unable to maintain her balance as the earth wove and shook beneath her.

"Mangiat!" she cried voicelessly as she fell to her hands and knees, weighed down by the shifting earth beneath her feet.

CRAAACK! The earth began to split! A jagged tear in the dirt ran between her hands. A splash of red and she saw her flower fall through.

As the dirt crumbled away beneath her, Deiji found herself falling into complete blackness. After a moment or two she hit the ground and bounced hard. She heard a sickening snap and her left arm went numb.

More dirt and rocks crumbled and fell from above, and she covered her head with her good arm. Large boulders came loose from above and clattered down. The last thing she saw was a rock hurling from the air toward her head.

The full moon's light shone down into the crevice when Deiji opened her eyes. It was quiet. She quickly noted where she was, and examined her own damage. She rolled onto her aching side, tasting blood. Her head was throbbing and the pain in her arm was severe. She braved a look and saw bone. Broken.

Looking closer, she saw a vast series of tunnels spreading off in all directions. A large pile of boulders lay near. She could see the night sky above, and thought she might be able to climb out of the crevice. Suddenly, something moved.

Deiji frowned, looking for the source, then realized that the series of boulders that were stacked on one another were rocking a little. As she stared, mystified, the thing stood up, revealing itself to be a tall mound of gray rock, humanoid in body. It suddenly clicked in her head what she was seeing, and she scrambled to her feet and took off down a tunnel, the Rockman crashing on after her.

The boulders that might have been his feet rolled him along like the wheels of a wagon from Deiji's village. She sprinted through the tunnels as fast as she could, clutching her wounded arm to her body, but there was no way to outrun him.

She leapt to the left and hugged the wall, thinking to double back behind him. Taur tried to halt but skidded past her. His left boulder of a leg scraped her back raw as he passed and she screamed.

Falling back onto the ground, she lay gasping, when she heard a strange booming noise. She looked up at the Rockman and saw his whole body shaking in a fit of laughter, his cave of a mouth gaping wide.

Deiji jumped to her feet and limped back to where she had fallen into this place. She could hear him rolling up behind her, advancing quickly. She could see a way to climb up, but knew it was too late.

Then she heard the unmistakable sound of pounding hooves! An arrow flitted from the top of the crevice, and hit Taur's chest, knocking a chip of rock away. Infuriated, the Rockman roared.

Glancing upwards, Deiji saw a flash of a horse-like creature diving down into the crack with them.

"Mangiat!"

He leapt into the pit, his strong legs absorbing the impact. "Go!" he screamed at her as he led Taur down a tunnel. "GET ABOVE GROUND!"

Deiji dragged herself up toward level ground, looking to the open sky. She hesitated. Making a quick decision, she dropped back down into the tunnel and ran after them.

As she came around the bend, she saw Mangiat nimbly dodging the Rockman's deadly blows again and again. He was cornered against the rock.

Mangiat leapt once again out of the way, barely avoiding contact. Angered, Taur slammed a fist into the mass of earth and rock overhead. Pieces and pieces of rock fell, avalanching down the side of the tunnel.

The Centaur tried to jump, to leap from every falling rock, but a large one struck him in the side. Another hit his head, and another… He fell to the ground, bruised and bleeding.

And then the Rockman crushed him underfoot.

CHAPTER TEN

The Land of Man

She screamed and screamed. Terror and agony clutched at her heart. Taur looked up at her. For one moment they stared at one another, then he began to roll toward her.

Deiji ran. She climbed up the sloped rubble from the cave-in as fast as her legs would carry her, slipping and sliding while using her one usable arm to claw her way up. Up on land it was dark, but in the full moonlight Deiji could see the destruction his earthquake had already caused.

Trees were ripped up from their roots, and large fissures existed in the soil. The forest was eerily still and quiet and it took her a moment to place it: everyone had fled. Hardly a soul remained behind.

She ran as fast as she could, through the nearest, densest patch of gnarled trees. *"Keep him away from Jayna, just keep him away from Jayna,"* she told herself as she ran south. She wondered with a slight sob just how many more souls Taur would take before the night was over. With the Keeper of the Forest gone, hope for victory seemed very slim.

Glancing back, she was surprised to see that Taur had lost interest in her, hesitating to go into the thick trees.

"Oh, no you don't," Deiji growled, and she ran back to him and began to taunt him. "HERE!" she screamed with a new-found, vicious energy. "HERE!" She reached into her leather bag of rocks and fitted her sling. She fired them at him, one by one, and little flecks flew off his granite body.

Enraged, he followed her, and she led him into the forest. As she ran, the words of the Dryad echoed through her mind. *"To be cut off from the moonlight would utterly destroy him, and he would crumble back into the earth forever..."*

Deiji was huffing and puffing as she ran through a maze of trees. She ran south along the river, keeping within the tree line, finding her stamina in picturing Mangiat's murder, her veins flooding with adrenaline with every ghastly relived image.

She ran through the night, cold sweat enveloping her body.

Suddenly, the river! Deiji plunged into the icy water and Taur burst from the trees behind her. She, sprouted her fins, shot across the width and pulled herself up onto the opposite bank. Scrambling out of the mud, she regained her legs and ran into the village.

Toten Town was sleeping, even the soldiers lay soundly, ready to wake before dawn for the march. Accustomed to these annual earthquakes that carried no explanation, it was all just a matter of course to the villagers. Nothing ever happened when the earth shook.

Until this night.

Deiji scrambled through the village and Taur plowed on after her, crushing huts and knocking over shacks. Dogs began to bark and babies cried. People were roused from their beds, blearily asking what all the commotion was about.

She caught a glimpse of the village Elder Nia running up the hill screaming, her cane long since abandoned, and Deiji almost smiled. She had done something revolutionary: she brought one from the Mystical world into the land of Man.

She ran right through the corral. Soldiers jumped to their feet and began to shoot arrows at the Rockman. Losing interest in Deiji completely, Taur focused on the army of men scurrying about around his feet, and he began to kill them left and right.

Deiji ran to the edge of the village to catch her breath and watched the slaughter. She could see the little boy Zechi by the corral, his arms wrapped tightly around the tree Sounet, watching everything that unfolded.

She leaned against the nearest tree and shouted, "Jayna! Tell the trees to stretch their tops together and blot out the moonlight!"

Taur chased a handful of deserting soldiers into the forest canopy. He tried to stop, but it was too late. The trees creaked and groaned as they touched tops, and the Rockman stood in complete shadow. He stumbled backwards as he began to fall apart, rocks and pebbles clattering to the forest floor.

Deiji sneered and spat on the ground. "Well, there you are," she said angrily.

And he crumbled back into the ground from whence he came.

She had just about sighed with relief as she stumbled back toward the river, when suddenly the earth began to shake violently. The ground gave a great lurch. The scattered villagers cried out and many were knocked to the ground. The two sides of the riverbank moved and collided, the water pushed out to sea at both ends. Deiji felt as though someone ripped a carpet from beneath her feet.

She saw a glimpse of a Centaur across the way and she ran toward it, wondering offhandedly if it was Mangiat. When she got there she fell to her knees in agony because she knew the truth.

But the continents had joined.

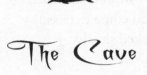

The Cave

Deiji sat back hard onto the ground, cradling her broken arm and hugging her knees to her body as she cried into her good arm.

"Oh, Mangiat," she sobbed.

"No," a gentle voice said. "Mowat."

She looked up, startled, for there indeed stood Mowat, a haze of rain and gray swimming about his person.

"Mowat," she moaned, "Mangiat is dead. He's dead! It is all my fault. I fell down the crack in the earth and he -"

"It is not your fault, Deiji. It was an honorable death, for he died trying to avenge his father, and he found great purpose in saving you. It was a double joy to him."

"And Jayna? And the people of the wood?"

"All damages to the forest have been repaired. There is great celebration."

"And the villagers?"

Mowat's eyes shone rainbows through the drizzle. "That is the best part," he said with some excitement in his voice. "Mankind is now becoming rapidly aware of the Mystical people. After your warnings to the villagers, confirmed by the sightings of Taur, people saw the truth. They have spread it through messengers to the rest of the world very quickly. Some have even crossed the creek where the continents now meet and have happened upon Centaurs and the like. It is one continent now. The world is aware, but the transition will be slow. Additionally, most of the king's armies have been destroyed or scattered. This is a major setback to Relant's plans."

Deiji sat back in awe and stretched her healed arm. All that should have been had come to pass.

"Mowat?" she asked slowly.

"Yes, my friend."

"When I took on these tasks you mentioned a reward of sorts… Anything I wanted in the whole world."

"And have you decided?" he asked patiently.

"Well, no, not quite."

"Go on."

"Mangiat told me that he had tutored under you as well."

Mowat's expression softened. "That is true."

"If I may ask," Deiji trembled, trying to hold back tears, "what was Mangiat's reward? What did he ask you for?"

"He was a lonely creature," he said with an edge to his voice, hesitating.

"What did he ask for?" she pressed.

"True love," Mowat answered simply.

Her heart caught in her throat and she barely managed to choke out, "okay," before she burst into full, sorrowful tears.

Mowat knelt down beside her. Putting a hand on her shoulder, he wept with her.

Deiji rested for four days. At times the grief was all consuming, and she found it difficult to lift her head from her pillow, but mostly she accepted her sorrow and swallowed it bitterly.

The day she met with Arill was a gray day indeed. When their foreheads touched Deiji's heart cried out to him and he was a great comfort to her.

On the fourth day Deiji took her customary bath. She felt

quite worn out. She put on her clean clothes and picked at her food as she waited for Mowat.

Out of the corner of her eye she saw a light flashing from the side of the cave. Turning to find its source, she saw Mowat, illuminated by a light that was flickering patterns of white and rainbow colors. The reflections danced across the cave walls.

"It is the day."

Deiji sighed and gathered up her weapons.

"I am sending you now to meet with the Four Monks of the high plane. Here you will sit with the Sages and discuss the current situation of the world as it now stands united. You must find out all you can as to their loyalties, for they have much influence in the world beyond ours.

"The Sties, as they call themselves, typically hold council to govern the four corners of the world only once a year. It is an emergency meeting that has been declared, and that is where you will want to be.

"Relant is rumored to have a hidden weapon that he will unleash as his last resort. A battle is to come, and it is with the Sties that you will prepare. I am sending you as an ambassador and representative of Nigh. Speak well for me. Do what you can."

"I will," she said stoutly.

"If you can save the world, then you can save your friend," he urged. "I am a Necromancer, after all."

Her eyes widened slightly, but she tried not to show this. "Then I will save him."

"Then you have my luck." He winked. "As well as a gift."

"More magic?" she asked eagerly.

"Indeed. Speak the words "*Terra Firma*" in a time of great need, and Jayna will heed your request. You may shout "*Ciechi*," and you will send a blaze of flint and rocks from your fists."

"Thank you."

"You have earned it. Good luck, Deiji J Cu." The white

lights separated from the colors in the rainbows. They flickered and danced around Deiji's head and she shut her eyes to their brightness. When she opened them again she fell back in shock.

Day One — Air

"There is a realm that is not earth, nor water, nor fire, nor air. It is not of this world, nor yours, neither from the sun nor the moon. It does not come easily, but it is not impossible. It is simply the end of suffering."

A chorus of voices sang out into the air in a monotone chant. Deiji could not make out the source as she stood and gaped at the world around her.

She was standing in two distinct planes of white and blue. Soft, fluffy and stunningly bright clouds stretched out below her feet for miles, as far as the eye could see. The sky was a brilliantly clear blue overhead. Deiji gazed at all that spread out before her and saw different terrains on all sides.

Some parts were flat where others were wispy; many parts were rugged and rough, and still others were smooth. Some clouds towered high, others dipped down low. Deiji was amazed. Amazed that the clouds - the very same clouds she had looked up at every day of her life - could hold her weight!

"This can't be real," she whispered in shock. After all she had seen, this was definitely unexpected. The unseen voices came again, with the same verse. "... *It is simply the end of suffering...*"

"Who said that?" Deiji demanded, pulling her knife from her waist. A soft sound of breezes rustling tree leaves blew by her ears.

"*Su Pita said it,*" a voice chanted, "*but he is not of this world, nay, he is of another earth.*"

"And who are you?"

"*I am Anaou, and we all sing his words.*"

"We?" She wished they would just *talk*.

Deiji tried to walk, to move around. The first thing she noticed was the feeling of weightlessness and airiness when she took her steps. Her feet seemed to want to lift from the clouds.

Delighted, she found herself caught up in this new thing, and all but forgot about the mysterious voices. Trying a small hop, Deiji was startled at how high she flew. When she landed she tried to launch herself as high as she could. Up and up she flew, over and across the clouds as though flying!

She laughed with glee as she floated down silently and softly, sending up a light mist. Deiji shouted with happiness as she launched herself again, and then saw she was headed right for a bare patch of clouds! She fell through, flailing her arms about desperately. She caught her hand onto the side of the hole, catching a glimpse of the earth, thousands of feet below.

She pulled herself back onto the clouds and fell backwards, gasping in fright. Peering over the edge she could almost make out the Trinity Islands, and north of them, the court and castle of Nigh.

"*They look better than on the blacksmith's maps,*" she thought offhandedly.

The extreme height made her nervous. Who knew how solid these clouds would prove to be? She sat back from the edge in pure wonder at this fluffy new world. Very near to enjoyment at this new discovery, she was suddenly struck with a pang of worry.

There were no resources here. No wood for fires, no caves for shelter, no food, no *water*... With each troubled thought, a greater panic filled her mind. "Well, what, then?" she called out to no one.

But there was someone.

"You must watch your step, creature, lest you fall into the world beyond," a voice rang out behind her.

Deiji whirled around and saw a woman there. But it was no ordinary woman. Her arms, her hair, her legs all melted into the air around her. They just faded away. She bobbed around restlessly, as if floating on a breeze. As awed and frightened as Deiji was, she was also relived.

"I am Anaou, Keeper of the Skies." Her voice was as if the wind moved suddenly through a grove of trees.

She hesitated. "I am Deiji." Although she could not explain it, she felt reluctant to give such a statement.

"And how did you come to our realm, little creature?"

"Mowat sent me on his behalf."

"Ah, Mowat did say he would send a diplomat," Anaou sang out, in a monotone chant. Diplomat? Deiji wondered if such wording was correct.

"Well, yes, that is true," she answered quickly.

"Then let us seek out my brothers."

There was a whirl of wind and a strong gust of salty air, as if just blown from across the ocean, and three more like Anaou came forth. They seemed to be male, and one of them looked distracted, while the other two looked reasonably intelligent.

"I am Eanle."

"I am Weyes."

"I am Fouthe."

They all sang in harmony, and Deiji bowed her head in greeting. "I am Deiji." They all stared at her, bobbing up and down. "May I ask what you are?" she said politely.

A hallow echo came from Anaou's mouth, which Deiji took to be a laugh.

"We are the Sties. People of the wind and Monks of the high plane. We live on the other side of the clouds here, and Mowat has broken the boundary between your world and ours so we could meet and discuss many things."

"How long have you been here?" she asked them in wonder.

"We have always been here, since before the creation of this earth." Weyes explained. "We come together now and then for our annual meeting, but this millennia we meet early to discuss a recent turn of events in the world below."

"Shall we get started, then?" Deiji asked eagerly. The quicker she was done with all this business the better.

"Not right away. It will be a time until our meeting commences."

"Alright," Deiji agreed evenly. "I need to ask you but one thing, then. What do I do for food, water and shelter here?"

Fouthe spoke first, his voice ringing out in a clear chant. "In this realm you do not hunger nor thirst."

"In this realm you may rest if you please, but nature will not scathe you for lack of sleep," finished Weyes.

Deiji felt some happiness at this. She wasn't even surprised to find that indeed, she was not hungry. In any case, it would be a nice break from scrambling about, trying to keep herself fed and cared for.

As if reading her mind, Eanle added cheerfully, "in this realm you may meditate peacefully without concern, and in strong contemplation."

"*This is going to be a long week,*" Deiji thought to herself.

The Sties left her in solitude that night.

As the light around her grew dimmer, she wandered around freely, frolicking happily, though avoiding such big leaps as before. Deiji shielded her eyes every few minutes against the blinding whiteness and surveyed her surroundings.

The whiteness of cloud spread out in all directions, to each horizon, and all was muffled; it was as if there was no noise at all. Just an eerie silence, a silence that seemed incredibly and suffocatingly loud.

Deiji found it difficult to focus on things, as if she were distracted easily and often. She spent a long, quiet night among the moonlit clouds, still bright, though blue. She stopped to rest in the early morning and actually fell into a light doze. She felt as though she was being watched.

Day Two – Air

Deiji woke instantly, blinded by the rising sun. She couldn't help but find the never-ending whiteness to be irritating. As so the silence and stillness. She walked around a little, confused and a bit lost in the lack of a morning routine. She wasn't to gather food, search for water, eat, wash her face or even meet a friend. It was quite unsettling.

After wandering around for the better part of an hour, she found her hands were empty and she did not know what to do with herself. This astounded her.

On the island, in the ocean, in the Deep Forest, even on Mount Odel there was always work to be done. Projects to finish. Keep oneself fed and maintained, play in the waves, feed the livestock, or pass a long afternoon working a monotonous chore in the cheerful company of a friend.

But here... This endless, unchanging white cloud that stretched out below her feet was all there was. Perhaps the most frustrating thing of all was that there was nothing to kick!

"Arrgh!" she finally vented in her frustration. "I will not be able to stand entire days of this! I wish to be done," she declared loudly. "What does Mowat want me to learn?"

"Patience, perhaps?" Anaou asked idly as she floated by. A light, howling wind followed her, blasting Deiji with such a refreshing breeze that she almost thanked her for it.

"Anaou!" she called out, relieved to have someone to talk to. But it seemed Anaou had no time for her words.

"The High Council will meet this day, three hours hence. We will summon you, and you shall have the honor of sitting in, o' revered ambassador of earth." Deiji couldn't tell if she was being sarcastic or not.

"Okay, then," she called after the retreating Stie, slightly disappointed.

"It is alright," a teeny voice offered from behind her. "I will be your friend."

Deiji whipped around, looking in all directions, her eyes finally coming to rest on a small creature sitting on the cloud behind her.

It was a small cat, fluffy and proportionate to the cloud she sat on, a kitten, really. She had a long, silky-soft grey coat and a fluffy tail, a perfect mix of fur and cloud. She looked up at Deiji with coy little eyes, as clear and blue as the sky above them, and she purred.

"Who... What are you?" Deiji asked the little cat, caught up in the loving gaze it gave her.

"I am Puff Puff," it squeaked. "I'm a little Princess."

"Oh, you are adorable," Deiji cooed, stretching out her hand, which the little kitten rubbed her face against eagerly, purring all the while.

"I am Deiji, little Puff," she said, and she nearly squealed with delight when the cat flopped onto her back, exposing her soft, furry belly.

"Love me," she demanded, purring and writhing around in ecstasy.

"Little kitty, where do you live?" Deiji asked her.

"I'm Puff Puff! In my Puff castle! You can sleep there tonight. I know you have other things to do until then, but I will be waiting for you." She hopped up off her fluffy little paws and leapt into the air, floating down a little ways away.

"Come play with me!" she called to Deiji, who laughed and bounded after her. They romped through the clouds, laughing and squealing, and Deiji felt elated, as if they were in a vivid dream together.

Finally they wound down, and came to rest upon a cloud. "I must go now, little Puff, but I will see you after," Deiji promised, scooping the little cat into her arms.

Puff Puff gave a squeak and purred as she gave Deiji little kitty kisses on the nose, sniffing and nuzzling her face. Deiji planted a kiss atop the kitten's head. Puff leapt out of her arms and bounced off. She frowned.

She heard the oddest noise – a sound of running water. She whipped around and there was Mowat! He wore his burgundy robes, a relief of color to her eyes, and he stood smiling.

"Mowat! What are you doing here?" she cried.

"I have come to show you a vision," he said simply.

She frowned, concerned. "A vision? Of what sort?"

"It is imperative to the mission that you retain this information I am about to divulge to you." He touched her cheek. "Just watch and listen."

He moved his hands through the clouds before them and a picture shimmered into view. "Some information is from a long time ago. The scene before us took place merely weeks before we met. These are things you need to know."

She leaned in and watched as they hovered over continent of Nigh and flew across the landscape. Mowat began.

On this earth it was the two hundred and thirtieth year, according to Man, its beginning having been marked by those who clambered onto land so long ago.

There was something new, a fever that moved along the people, both Humans and Mystics alike. A deadly, violent fever, it claimed the lives of thousands upon thousands and their bodies were burned on the hillsides.

The High Council of the Nigh Court held meeting on the Southern Peninsula of the Known World, aiming to uncover a cure. Doctors, Sages and knowledgeable people came from villages and cities to offer council to the king and his courtiers. Mowat came, also.

They gathered in the entrance hall of the Nigh castle where King Jebhadsen sat enthroned, looking out on the stone chairs that lined the stained glass windows. He stared into the gathered masses, seemingly without expression, so that one presenting a case to him could not quite tell if he were heard or not.

"Sire," a doctor of herbal remedy spoke with zeal, "this sickness is devastating the world. One in every four of my home in Hei Village have fallen ill or dead to this thing. Nothing I have in my stores has been able to quell this nightmare, or even delay it for a time."

Jebhadsen frowned.

"Go on," said a strong voice from the shadows. It was the voice of Telius, the king's royal vizier. He leaned against the wall behind the throne, and Mowat couldn't quite make out his face from where he sat.

The doctor's eyes flickered to the king, unsure, but he

continued. "I propose we lawfully quarantine any and all who show signs of the fever. Send them, damn them to the Unknown World before it is too late and we are all dead!"

"Hear hear!" The patrons in the hall stood, clapping their hands in support.

King Jebhadsen gripped his scepter until his knuckles turned white. His frown twitched and his eyebrows, already heavy with his age and his stress, furrowed in seeming anger.

"These invalids will be the end of us!" the doctor continued to the exuberant crowd. Raising his hands, he cried, "Send them off! It will buy us time! Away with them! Away!"

The king thumped his scepter onto the marble floor and the hollow thud echoed throughout the stone hall. Silence ensued. "Sit," he commanded calmly. Everyone sat, save for one. Mowat stood alone in robes of blue. Indeed, he had been sitting calmly while others were shouting.

"Identify yourself, Wizard," Telius spoke sharply from where he stood. There was no mistaking the condescending in his voice when he said "Wizard."

Wizards were a thing of the past, almost an insult, hardly given serious consideration in any but the most extreme of circumstances. This being one of those times, Mowat knew Telius would allow him a few words, though skeptical.

Mowat looked away from the king's face, and deliberately shadowing the unusual light that shone forth from his eyes.

"I am Mowat," he said softly. "I must say, it has since been proven that quarantine has made no difference in the people affected by this fever. It is not something that is contagious from one person to another, it affects only select people. We need to continue to care for these, not banish them where they will surely die."

"Then how does it spread?"

"That I cannot altogether explain," Mowat admitted. "Not

in a short phrase or two. There is much more at stake, and it can only be explained through words of truth."

"Truth," Telius said skeptically. "And what truth is this?"

Mowat sighed. "It is a painful thing that I must again be the one to inform you of the years of darkness you have wallowed in; the years you have spent in blind ignorance."

A murmur of anger spread through the crowd.

"It is not your own doing," Mowat said hastily, "but the forgetfulness of Man from over two hundred years ago. I told your grandparents once, and still they did not listen."

"Then enlighten us," Telius said mockingly.

"A little insight is key," Mowat agreed, not paying heed to the vizier's insult. "Let me start at the beginning, when Mankind washed up from the ocean..."

"It was the three hundred-thousandth year of the earth and of the sea. The closest thing to Man was the Merpeople who swam and built castles and fortresses in the bountiful ocean depths. They lived richly, and grew in number.

"But society came with a heavy price. The ocean holds many predators, but none so frightening as the Balla. It is a large, squid-like creature that hibernates yearly and stores food for itself in season. Attracted to the Mermaid's song, these people are helpless when the Balla comes for its prisoners. They are stuck in cages or caught in seaweed, awaiting certain death that comes when the great creature awakens. Very few escape.

"Individually, Merpeople are difficult to detect, but in large numbers, and it is a tragedy to acknowledge that they are a social people, their song echoes throughout the ocean, making them a mass target. The slaughter became so widespread that they feared for the very survival of their species.

"*They held an audience with their friends and allies the great Whales, and their logical, loyal companions, the Dolphins. The decision they reached was for half the remaining population to journey to the land's Western edge and dwell on its shores and mountains until the sea was safe again. The other half would remain in the ocean and strive with all their being to survive. They would have half a chance.*

"*Escorted by their large friends, the Merpeople climbed onto land, lost their tails, and became all-Man. These acts were meant to preserve the life and meaning of the Merpeople, but once ashore, they forgot. All memories of magic and mystery became unknown to them.*

"*They spread quickly throughout the land like a virus, and all of the earth's mystical inhabitants retreated farther and farther, and eventually fled to the other half of the broken continent, where they now live on the uncharted paths and territories on the opposite shore of the Longest River.*

"*Motivated by such a widespread division, and the degeneration of the Mystical communities, a great and evil being brought on the plague that now spreads among you. This creature wants nothing more than to ensure that Man will never remember, and thus your world will remain divided forever,*" *Mowat finished with flourish.*

The hall was absolutely silent. Then, a few bits of muffled laughter, which quickly turned into a roar, accompanied by the amused look of the king himself. The Jebhadsen's head to the Nigh army, General Morim, waited for the king's signal, though his face was doubtful.

"*I see,*" *King Jebhadsen said slowly.* "*And who, may I ask, is this evil force that releases this illness among us?*"

"*His name is Relant,*" *Mowat said steadily,* "*and he has cast a spell -* "

"*TRAITOR!*" *Telius threw himself from the shadows, stabbing one gnarled accusatory finger toward Mowat.* "*Guards!*"

Six men with war axes began to move toward him.

"You know of Relant?" Mowat asked, genuinely surprised. This was one thing he hadn't counted on. He glanced at the on-coming guards.

"How do you know this creature?" he called out as he stepped back into a corner, away from their advances. "He has not been seen in –"

"He came to my vizier in a divine vision," the king declared loudly, "with a promise to end this evil sickness. He has said it is a virus carried by people like you, people who cling to these ideas of magic and mutated people. You make us weak. We will spread the word to all ends of the land that the fever will be quelled, and we will venture into the Unknown World to destroy those undesirables who bring the fever upon us!"

"Relant has spoken the truth!" Telius shouted in agreement. "It begins today!"

"No!" Mowat held his staff close, pulling away from the lunging guards. "It is precisely the opposite! He has deceived you! The only way to destroy the fever is to reunite both Man and Mystics! It must be done. You cannot listen to him, he is evil!"

The king held up a hand and the guards paused, waiting.

"Sire?" Telius asked, nodding his head toward the Elderly Wizard.

Jebhadsen seemed to have frozen in thought.

"Sire," Telius cleared his throat, his face as ragged and hard-ened as an encamped soldier's. The king looked to him and nod-ded, giving him passage to speak.

"I propose we sentence this traitorous Wizard to death by hanging by the first light of dawn, on the grounds of heresy and blasphemy. Then we shall put out a warrant for all others who believe in such tales, and thus let the world know that this exter-mination of such liars has begun!"

"It shall be done," Jebhadsen proclaimed, looking thoughtful.

The crowd cheered and stomped their feet on the stone floor in approval.

"There is but one thing," Mowat said angrily, "you refuse to listen to reason, you idolize evil, you move to slay the innocent, and now you will intrude upon the Unknown World! So there is one thing you must know."

"And what is that?" Telius sneered.

"I am a Necromancer." There was a crack of thunder and a gale of rain swept across the hall and Mowat was gone.

"Search the grounds!" the king snapped. "Then clear the hall. I have a much more commonplace meeting to follow," he grumbled.

Telius ambled up to the throne respectfully and bowed. "It is not so common my lord."

"I went straight to the Odel village to find you after that," Mowat finished. "Now you know a little more to help you about your way."

"Thank you." Deiji paused. "Humans... We were Merpeople." She could scarcely believe it.

Mowat nodded. "Do not trust all four of the Sties. One of them is a traitor. I must go. It is your time, now." His body evaporated into a fine mist, and he ducked beneath the clouds and was gone.

Deiji watched, smiling, contemplating, when she heard another voice. "It is time, Deiji."

She turned and the four Sties sat like gods upon a raised platform of cloud that moved separately from the rest. She climbed onto this tower, thinking of the little cat with a smile, and took her place among them.

At the top they sat in their compass points, and Deiji seated herself cross-legged between East and the West, while the Sties hovered, always in motion.

"We are here," Anaou declared loudly in introduction, "for the seventy-thousandth four hundredth and fifty-second meeting of the Sties of the Four Winds. Sworn to the Code, we are here to discuss that of the world of Nigh and what is to be done in its recent changes. We speak so this year because the world is now one, and we have with us representatives from all four corners of the Wind. From the South, Eanle."

"Present!"

"From the East, Weyes!"

"Present!"

"From the West, Fouthe!"

"Present!"

"And lastly, from the North, it is I, Anaou, present."

Fouthe cleared his throat and looked from Anaou to Deiji pointedly.

"Ah, yes," Anaou sneered, as if it pained her to continue, "our visitor from earth itself. Deiji J Cu, of Mount Odel, representing Mowat, the Keeper of Life."

"Present," Deiji muttered quickly, reddening, taken aback by this sudden show of rudeness.

"Tea," Eanle waved his hands, and each found himself holding a simple, white porcelain cup of steaming green leaf tea.

"It is not for any necessity," Fouthe said, catching the look on Deiji's face, "it is more of a comfort."

"Now let us get down to business," Weyes said sternly. He seemed older than the rest.

"Right, right," Anaou agreed. Deiji sat up straight, wrapping her hands close around her cup, for a hot sip of the steamy stuff was indeed a comfort.

"For two hundred and thirty-nine years Man has remained separated in life from his Mystical brethren. Due to recent events," she shot a look at Deiji, "Man's awareness of such existence has reached a precarious point. Are the worlds truly ready to meet, face to face? Your thoughts, please." Anaou leaned back and rested on the wind.

"They are not ready," Fouthe said simply.

"This will lead to many wars, it is sure," Eanle stated. "Such a breakdown in the barrier between such extremities could not have been predicted or prepared for."

Anaou nodded in agreement. "Furthermore, Man will make their way across the Unknown World, and they will overcome and conquer all that lies in their path, as has happened before. The Mystical populace is doomed."

"I agree," said Fouthe. "The Mystical people will be run down, and Man will take the whole planet for himself!"

Words started pouring forth from them all, so many words that Deiji could not but follow a mere bit of it.

"– kill all in their path!"

"… avoid war at all costs, and -"

"- let them fight their wars! Those who come through in the end will have the rights to the world. Only the strongest survive."

"Stop." Weyes held up one blur of a hand. He, like Deiji, had not yet spoken.

"I think we can all agree that there will be war and conflict, regardless of any meddling we do. Fear of the unknown is an overwhelming thing, even if there turns out to be nothing to fear in the end. This sudden shift is a strong one, and people will not know where to turn, Man and Mystical alike. What are the people saying now? Let us look to the earth below us and watch the courts of Nigh."

The pillar of cloud they sat upon lifted into the sky, and Deiji watched with some surprise as they lowered themselves through the clouds down toward the continent below. They hovered, the view of the castle still far below them, and Weyes spread one hand over the middle of the cloud they sat upon, as if wiping it away, and a clear view of the grand entrance hall shimmered and focused into view.

King Jebhadsen sat enthroned, gripping his scepter, his eyebrows arched and angry.

"What do you MEAN they are DEAD?" he roared at the officer in front of him, General Morim. Telius stood nearby, looking quite pale.

"Sire, I was not even stationed in Toten Town," Morim explained. "A handful of soldiers escaped and reported this to me. The whole population of this continent is going on about the shores joining, and mythical animals – as knowledgeable as you or I – emerging from the other side, and mingling with our people! But aside from this, there is more."

"MORE?" The king's face was very red, and the veins on his forehead stood out fit to burst.

"There seems to be an awakening from the quiet volcano of the Eastern Ranges, Mount Odel," General Morim said nervously. "It is not lava," he said quickly, "but rather an army of dark creatures. Why they have emerged I do not know, but a Dolphin in the bay outside this very castle assures me that they are not of his Mystical people, but of a dark enemy of us all, named Relant. This army of black creatures are the carriers of this deadly fever that spreads among us, and they are marching for the Nigh Court as we speak!"

"Relant? He is... *evil*?" the king gasped and became very pale himself. He clutched his arm and seemed to be having difficulty breathing. "Telius?" He gasped, and looked to his assistant desperately, but Telius had gone.

"This audience with the king has not come to pass just yet, but in two days hence," Weyes said. "This gives us enough time to turn over the possibilities in such a matter. Deiji, your thoughts?"

Startled, Deiji opened her mouth, shocked to hear of this army of Relant's. Mowat hadn't said a word about it. She began speaking slowly.

"My thoughts on everything? I believe that the people do fear change, because they fear things wholly unknown to them. Even if things in the world are not well, people are more apt to take that suffering which is familiar to them, because it is a hardship that they know, over the unfamiliar that they fear.

"We must take the common people and thrust them into this new life with assuredness. There must be a better king to lead them than that which they already have; a leader familiar with the current state of the world, and all its new troubles. No one knows exactly where all of this will lead. All that can be said or done is to know that this war is coming, and we must make plans to stem the flow of battle as it begins."

"Here, here!" Weyes and Eanle clapped. Fouthe nodded. Anaou said nothing, but Deiji could feel the disproval radiating from her direction. Suddenly, her mind thought back to that cute little cat, and her thoughts became fuzzy and ill focused. She shook her head for clarity.

"With Relant's armies on the move," Weyes went on to say, "it will be a three-sided battle between the dark creatures, the common mix of Man and Mystical, and the addition of the king's army, led by General Morim. The latter will be the ulti-mate factor in the turn out."

"Here is a plan of action," Fouthe suggested smoothly, "Deiji will return to earth when Mowat sends for her. She will lead the army of the common people against this evil and keep them from reaching the courts of Nigh. She can hold them off until the king's armies arrive."

Deiji swallowed hard. "I am to go into battle? With common, untrained citizens?"

"Indeed." Weyes looked her in the eye with obvious pride. "You have the strength of Jai. You can bring the world to victory. Mowat chose you well."

"Then this I will do," she said boldly, sitting up straighter, feeling awful.

"This meeting is adjourned," Anaou spat forth nastily.

That night Deiji sought out the cat and her Puff Castle.

As she bounced along the dimming whiteness, she was sure she was seeing a tower of cloud in the distance. She saw the cat outside of it as she got closer.

"Hello! I am Puff Puff!" the kitty cried, running up to her in a flurry of fuzz and purring. "Welcome to my Puff castle!"

It was a large hollowed-out cloud castle, complete with turrets. Inside it was darker, with only a few rooms, but it had one long hall leading up to a fluffy throne.

"This way!" Puff Puff beckoned, scampering off. She led the way, her fluffy tail straight up in the air, into a side room.

They lay themselves down inside the room of cloud, and Deiji felt quite at peace dozing and waking beside an affectionate, purring kitten, who kneaded her sheathed claws upon Deiji's arm as if it were the most luxurious, pleasurable thing she had ever done in her whole kitty life.

Mowat

Relant growled at Mowat across the valley of their separate mountains. The electric energy in the air was taunt, as if it might burst into something terrible any moment.

"Do you see now, dear Teacher? My final weapon against your world will flood your continents with blood, and they cannot be stopped."

"An army," Mowat said, still stunned at what had unfolded. "Your children." It had been this, all along, after all these long years… He had failed. Long ago, he had failed.

He cleared his throat. "You have been brewing an army from within the depths of Mount Odel, all this time, under my very nose."

"Yes, an army," Relant sneered. "Of the like you have not prepared for! Ah, victory is sweet as the victim's blood!"

"Do not celebrate now, bringer of death. The souls have not been added to your stores just yet."

"But they will be. There will be a great slaughter, and it pains you that you cannot interfere," Relant laughed.

"Then it does not bother you that Telius has fled?" Mowat asked slyly. "Wasn't he your only sure link to the governments of Mankind?"

"He does not matter now. I thought I needed him to secure my victory, but it seems all has come about by its own means."

"And what of Mount Odel?" Mowat asked him angrily.

"Oh, that is my final move for victory, at the end of the slaughter," Relant taunted. "It *is* a volcano, you know. It will be a quick end to Man. I will make up for your years of injustice."

Day Three — Air

Deiji awoke to a purring Puff Puff curled in the crook of her arm, and she smiled. She could hear the sounds of song nearby.

"*This pilgrimage we make to thee,*
o'er forest, sand, sky and sea..."

She groaned and rolled to her feet, leaving the little kitty sleeping. Outside, the four Sties were floating in a line, bobbing as they chanted.

"*Four corners of the worlds of wind,*
someday we will meet again, O!"

They turned, back-to-back, facing their respective directions.

Deiji hopped over to them quickly. "What is going on?" she asked breathlessly.

"It is time for us to part ways and send our message to our corners of the world," Fouthe said curtly. "We will bring you allies in battle. I will send the Dragons from the West."

"I will send the armies of Man from the East," Weyes offered. "We will spread the message throughout Nigh. The battle will be won."

"The Pegasus from the North will be of good aid," Eanle stated. "As well as the creatures of the Deep Forest."

"I will summon the Wind," Anaou said with a smirk. The other Sties turned their faces away as though in shame, and Deiji frowned.

"Where is this battle to take place?" Deiji asked Weyes urgently, ignoring Anaou.

"Outside of the village, below Mount Odel. You are to cut them off as they come down the Mountain and attempt to leave the Valley. We must go."

"But what must I do? Where am I to go for now?"

"You will leave this place when Mowat summons you.

Meanwhile, train your mind, body and spirit with the tranquility of this place. Refine your strengths; meditate on all you have learned. After all, that is what the clouds are for. Not many of your kind are privileged to come to this realm." He winked, a very human gesture.

"Do not fret," Anaou threw in, "something tells me you won't be here much longer."

Deiji did not like the sound of that. "And what 'something' would that be?" she asked coldly.

The Stie did not answer.

"Farewell, my friend," Weyes said, trying for her attention, and a rush of wind carried the Sties in all four directions across the sunlit clouds.

The Keeper of Air

Anaou flew away hurriedly, straight to the little cat.

"Puff Puff," she said sharply. "What have you learned of the human?"

"Not much, my master. She is such a dull creature. Not even worth a good cuddle." She yawned, as if bored by such conversation, and she continued to bathe her face and whiskers.

"Well, whatever you do, do not let her focus on that which is to be done. Keep her distracted. We can't have her winning this war."

"Yes, yes, I understand. Honestly, Anaou, I don't believe she would win anyway. She's such a weak creature, as seen through her easy persuasion by my beauty and cuteness." She licked her coat vainly.

Anaou rolled her eyes. "Puff Puff is the curse of Relant," she muttered idly. If only she had been counted higher in his ranks! She was *exhausted* by this cat Relant had given her.

She grabbed Puff Puff by the scruff. "Can you keep her interest focused on you?"

Puff yelped but did not struggle. "Easy. She will be a simple defeat."

"That is a good assessment." She tossed the kitten back onto a cloud. "Keep her distracted until morning. Then we will deliver her to Relant."

"Yes, my master," Puff Puff said loyally, smoothing her ruffled fur.

Air

After the Sties had gone, Deiji made to calm her mind and body through a series of gentle stretches, much like the ones Mangiat had begun to teach her. Unable to do much beyond the beginnings of what he had shown her, she improvised as she went along.

The girl sat in the clouds cross-legged and focused her mind on clarity. When her normal thoughts and anxieties filled her mind, she did not violently shove them away, but rather dismissed them passively. She let thoughts turn over in her head until they were exhausted in themselves, and the distractions ceased.

Of anything, she wanted to be clear of the apprehension toward the events that lay ahead. The idea of battle and the end of this fight was both exhilarating and unnerving. She hoped the Sties would come through for her, and for the world, but she remained quite skeptical as to Anaou's loyalties. She remembered Mowat's statement in regards to the Stie's allegiances with a frown.

Deiji planned to rest her body well that night. She knew these events were spiraling quickly to something she could not quite foresee, but she knew it was something incredible.

There was much to be appreciated in this current realm. The fact that she did not have to focus on the basic needs for food and shelter was quite a blessing. "Survival is exhausting," she decided. Because of this lack of natural need, Deiji found herself with ample time on her hands, and was able to focus on many other things.

Her aim was to think on her inner-self, more thoroughly than she had ever done. She knew that all of these experiences within the elements had shaped her severely as a person, in a flow of constant changes.

But Deiji heartily embraced such change. Through change she found the beginnings of wisdom.

That evening grew into further meditation and contemplation. Just as she was growing quite accustomed to the quietness of her mind, she felt the tickle of fur brush across her arm. She tried to ignore it, but Puff wouldn't have it.

The cat dug her claws into Deiji's arm, and she opened her eyes and brushed the kitten away. "Go, on, I'm busy!" she snapped.

"But it is time for us to sleep for the night," Puff Puff squeaked.

"Fine, okay," she sighed, knowing she had lost the moment already.

Deiji went back to the cloud castle, thinking of Mangiat and missing him terribly. The little kitty gave a squeak at her, and rubbed about her knees, as if asking for a treat.

"Oh, little thing," Deiji cooed, leaning over a bit to pet her a bit, then walked on. The cat tagged along at her heels as she walked, and she nearly tripped over her.

"Cat!" she cried in slight agitation.

"I'm Puff Puff!" the cat threw itself down on the clouds, squinting up at Deiji with a contented expression. "Love me!"

Deiji felt somewhat tranquil when she looked into Puff Puff's eyes. "You're a sweet little thing, aren't you?" All of her irritation had vanished. "Are you a magical kitty?"

"I'm Puff Puff!"

It became clear to her that she would get no logical conversation from the cat. She sat in the clouds through the evening, with the purring kitten in her arms, stroking it as she watched the sky grow dim.

CHAPTER ELEVEN

The Darkness

Day Four – Air

When Deiji woke Puff Puff was gone. She crawled out of the cloud castle blearily, and had hardly begun her stretches when she heard a noise. In the stifling silence above the clouds she was instantly aware of it. It was the sound of wind rushing, moving fast, tearing through the sky above.

The sky darkened to an eerie bluish-gray, and the sun ceased to shine so brightly.

Suddenly, a beam of white light pierced the dimness around her, and she glanced down. The medallion! The clear stone shot a narrow beam into the whiteness.

She turned about searching the clouds, and saw Arill arise a ways to her left. A light mist of cloud rose into the air as he breached slightly and hovered beside her.

"Well, this is odd," Deiji said as they touched foreheads, trying to make light the dread that engulfed her stomach.

"There is no time! This is urgent. I am here to warn you, and I pray you do well. You must be strong, my friend, for this will be a difficult day to endure. Do not forget what you have learned."

"I won't," Deiji said bravely, and she kissed the top of his head.

"Keep your sword close to you. There is a special stone symbol on its hilt – the Rune of Life – and it will keep you from sure death."

"Alright."

"You are a true warrior, Deiji," Arill said proudly. "I will see what I can do to help you."

"Wait! Where are you going?"

"Toten Town!" He dove into the clouds and out of sight.

Rain and hail broke from the sky and Deiji was swept off her feet by a gale of wind and water. Lighting flashed, and the sky rumbled angrily.

She went back into the castle, searching for the cat. She didn't have far to go, for as when entered into the long hall she saw a familiar form sitting on the throne, stroking Puff Puff, who was curled in her arms.

"Anaou!"

"Greetings, human!" the Stie called out above the roar of the storm. The top of the cloud castle was wisped away by the wind, leaving them exposed.

"Puff Puff?"

"Oh, this is my shape-shifting pet," Anaou said with a laugh. "You have already met the immortal Djin, Princess Puff Puff. She is under my complete command." The sky darkened as ashes, and more lightning etched itself across it in brilliant yellow and white patterns.

The kitten jumped down from Anaou's lap and gave Deiji a cute little wide-eyed look. "Hello, Deiji," she said sweetly. "What a day we seem to be having."

Deiji stared, confused, as the cat puffed itself up. Her fur stood on end, and she continued to expand.

"What on earth…" Deiji backed away.

"She can become anything I wish," Anaou bragged. "Such a useful little pet, do you not agree?"

Puff Puff grew into a tall, towering whirlwind, sucking the surrounding air and cloud into her funnel-shaped windstorm. Deiji turned and fled from the castle.

Outside the wind raged still. Deiji looked back at the advancing tornado. Shockwaves of wind began to blow across the clouds; she fought to remain standing as each one rocked powerfully against her.

She stood and something promptly plowed into her, knocking her over again. Her sword slipped off her shoulder and dropped with a wisp into the cloud floor. She looked up at her offender.

"Anaou! Stop!" she cried.

She stood, openmouthed as Puff Puff's new form slowly grew on the horizon, moving her way.

The funnel-cloud spun faster and faster, sending the clouds beneath it into a whirlpool of darkness. A harsh gust of wetted wind knocked Deiji over again.

Anaou screamed with laughter, and flew high above her. "Go on, get up, Deiji!" she taunted. "Be careful of that hole there, you might go somewhere dangerous!"

"Just tell me why, Anaou."

"Because you are meddling in the affairs of the world. You a thorn in the heel of my master, and you are hindering progress!"

"Would your master happen to be Relant?" Deiji spat angrily.

"Yes, and you shall meet him soon."

"Then tell him I look forward to it," she snapped, lifting her arm as if to punch the traitorous Stie. She shouted, "*Ciechi!*" and bits of rock and flint flew from her fists, striking Anaou out of the air. She didn't watch to see what became of her enemy. She did not care.

Gritting her teeth, Deiji stood. She marched boldly, seemingly unfazed, into the gist of the storm. She approached the whirling tornado with her arms open.

Deiji was surprised at her own lack of fear. Her body was cold, but calm. There was nowhere to run, and her fate was readily acceptable. So she took it. If she were to meet death today, she would face it head on.

The tornado rolled and whirled toward her.

Something knocked into her, and she was nearly sucked into the twister! She clung to the clouds, her legs gravitating to the tornado.

"Anaou!" she said, surprised. The Stie laughed, though injured.

"You have not killed me yet, Deiji!"

"'Yet' is correct phrasing, Anaou!" she cried, and she loosened her precious hold. She snatched her knife from her waistband and threw it at the Stie.

"Oh!" It stuck Anaou in the heart, and she stumbled backwards. "You…" the Stie sputtered, but she never finished.

The tornado circled around toward Deiji.

She looked up, her hair whipping around in the wind, water and hail ripping against her face, her jaw set in cold defiance. The funnel-cloud lunged at her, and the whirlpool at its base flew straight under Deiji's handhold. She fell through!

A quick glimpse of rock below, and the world turned upside-down. Deiji gripped the edge of the clouds with her fingertips, and pulled herself up until one foot touched the edge. She kicked off and flung herself up through the hole and high into the air.

She rose into the sky and fell in a perfect arc to safety, when the twister suddenly sucked her right out of the air! It attacked, pulling her near its very center, twirling her in circles.

Deiji found herself tossed around, completely disoriented. She reached out, but there was nothing to grab onto but air. The force of the wind tore at her skin like a million little animal claws.

She was lifted, higher and higher to the top of the twister. Her hair flapped around into her face, cutting off her vision, and she was choking on a huge wad of it. Her body was thrashed about mercilessly, and little cuts began to form all over, where the skin was breaking from the pressure. Drops of blood were pulled forth, and traveled slowly across her arms and face and into the air.

Already exhausted, Deiji threw both her hands into the raging wind around her and focused on one last, wild thought.

"*Terra Firma!*" she screamed to Jayna, the words lost to the wind.

She felt a strong energy surge from within, and she called out with passion and strength for what she really wanted at that moment: "Life. LIFE!"

The silver sword dropped into her hands, the rune sparkling in the harsh light.

"YES!" Deiji screamed in exhilaration, and swung the sword in a smooth arc all around her, in one quick motion. There was a roar of wind and the tornado spit into pieces. Deiji swirled down into the bottom of the twister, faster and faster...

And then it dropped her on a hard, rocky ground.

FIRE, WATER, EARTH, AIR

eiji stood up carefully, gripping her sword. The air around gave off a static blue haze, and almost seemed like it wasn't real. She was high on a mountain she did not recognize, on a long stretch of a ridge of steep ground.

A little cat dropped at her feet.

"I'm Puff Puff!"

"Oh, no," Deiji said in warning, "you are NOT coming with me."

"I'm Puff Puff?" The cat looked confused, and cocked its head to the side.

"What do you want, cat?"

"I am yours to command now. You killed Anaou." The kitten nuzzled against her shins, purring.

Deiji rolled her eyes. "Then evaporate into air until I call for you, okay?"

"Okay!" And the little kitty rolled up into a ball and disappeared with a puff.

Deiji took a long look across the valley below. She recognized Mount Odel, and was startled because it was giving off smoke, but she seemed to be standing on a mountain she had never seen. In fact, she was quite convinced this mountain had never been there before.

She frowned…

Suddenly, Deiji felt eyes on her. Turning around slowly, she sensed a dark presence.

Splash!

She jumped. Looking down, she saw a pool of thick red blood had gathered at her feet, rippling from the drops that had just fallen. Her heart leapt with fear, her concern growing stronger with every second. Where was it coming from?

Lightning flashed overhead against the eerie blue-gray sky, and she looked up and nearly screamed in terror.

Perched upon a peak, not too high above her, was a dark, evil creature. Its silhouette struck sharply against the sky. The creature had enormous talons that gripped into the mountain rock, and they bled a deep, dark red that was almost black. It dripped down the rock face in thick, hazy traces.

The creature's leathery wings were pointed proudly and ominously toward the gray sky, shifting about in the heavy mist.

It looked down at Deiji, right into her eyes. His empty eye sockets were a soulless, bloody black, but such a dark light flowed from them that Deiji knew that it possessed a soul of an evil she had never encountered. He stared right through her, almost into her mind, and Deiji felt vulnerable, as if he could see her deepest fears.

"Deiji J Cu," he growled, his raspy voice sending shivers up her spine. He gave off a few clicks, assessing her form.

"Relant," she confirmed boldly, in an unexpectedly steady voice.

"That's Keeper of Fire to you, child," he said quietly. He eyed her sword with a lingering gaze, and Deiji gripped it harder and lifted it up, prepared to use it.

"Look around you, Deiji!" Relant cried loudly. "Look to your mountain! Do you see your family? Go ahead, look."

Deiji did not even glance away. She held her ground, bending her knees and pointing her sword at him.

"Look to Mount Odel," he insisted, "Does your father live, after all your efforts? Has your mother recovered from the fever that ravages her mind and body? Perhaps she is already dead. Did you get to say goodbye? I think not."

She tried with much effort to keep her face unchanging as he goaded her.

"Do you see the blood that flows from my claws?" He shifted further into the shadows. "It is a sweet blood, sweeter than the finest honey. It is a never-ending flow of the blood of my enemies that I have slaughtered. Your mother's blood runs in it, and yours will soon join it."

The corners of her mouth twitched.

"Yes, yes," he continued loftily, "I killed your mother myself. There is no sense in false hopes. Now, you have managed to push aside my legions of the elements that I put in your path – pathetic, weak creatures, I must say – but it is all at an end. Do you not see that the message of those damned Dolphins will never be spread throughout the world? Did you actually think that your sacrifices would merit the end to all evil? No one can pass me, Deiji. No one defeats me, not even Mowat, with all of his moralizing." He spat a black clod of blood onto the rocks.

"You have done all of this, and it is still a waste! The prophecy brings nothing. And now you must face the consequences of your foolish actions. Now you must face *me!*" He lunged forward in a mock-threat.

Deiji did not flinch, nor blink.

"Or perhaps," he drawled, "you should face *them*." He nodded his head toward the ridge of Mount Odel.

The sound of hundreds of footsteps marching down the mountainside echoed across the valley below. Deiji tore her eyes away from Relant and ran to the edge of the cliff. She put her hand to her mouth. Hundreds of Dark Dragon soldiers marched down the mountain toward her village, each a deadly mixture of tooth and claw. They seemed to look exactly like Relant himself, though much smaller. Their bladed tails were held high behind them as they headed to the village.

She was instantly flooded with fear for her friends and neighbors. What were these things? She had never heard of them before, not once.

"The armies of death approach your people," Relant said calmly. "A thousand of them, in fact. Nothing can be saved. The world is theirs now."

"I will save them," Deiji declared boldly, and she held her sword tightly and leapt over the side of the mountain.

Relant grinned, his bloody mandibles bared against the cool mountain air. "Good," he growled with satisfaction.

Deiji slipped and stumbled down the slope. She did not like what Relant had just said. A thousand! Were there even so many Humans in the world?

It was so steep she could scarcely keep her footing. She nearly lost her balance, her feet not moving fast enough to keep up with her speed. She stopped herself by throwing her body into a skid, breathing heavily in the dirt.

She looked around. There had to be a path… It seemed that all she could focus on was the dreadful blackness that was pouring out of Mount Odel.

Glancing to the sky, smiling distantly in her mind when she saw the clouds from underneath them, Deiji noticed a familiar outline gliding overhead. Enforced by her need, and by the incredible urging of her own mind, she let out a screech that echoed across the valley. Again and again she called out these pleas for help, calling to an old friend.

A faint screech of reply floated across the divide, and she was filled with hope.

"Polk!" she screamed. Polk cried out again, circling closer across the sky. Deiji lifted her hands up, calling to him, trying to communicate her fear and distress. He circled away, still screeching.

"Polk, *please!*"

For one muted moment despair seemed to flood her soul. Her heart sank as she realized she wouldn't make it to the village in time.

Then she saw him follow a smooth arc in the wind, gliding back down to her.

"Polk!" she cried in joy.

He screeched again in reply. Then, the noises she heard next brought to her heart the utmost hope: birds. Dozens of birds.

They came down all around her – large ones, small ones, all beautiful in her eyes.

Falcons and owls snagged her arms, legs and hair with their talons, and they lifted her from the ridge where she stood. Polk flew ahead, leading the way. They glided off the mountain, and fell swiftly but lightly toward the valley below.

Deiji laughed and shouted loudly with exhilaration as they fell to the village. Their claws pinched, but it was okay. She would make it!

The birds released her a little ways above the ground and she stumbled to her feet. As soon as she touched the valley, she came out of the blue-gray haze and into the greenness of the Odel Valley, where the sky was scarcely overcast.

She looked back to the mountain she had just fallen from but saw nothing, though she could still sense Relant's watchful eye. The sky was full of birds.

Deiji turned her gaze to the Odel Village and broke into a run. "Everyone!" she bellowed at the top of her lungs as she burst onto the paths between the huts. "The dark army approaches! They're here! Everyone, listen!"

People stepped out of their huts and barns, startled by the noise. The sight that met their eyes rendered each and every one speechless, and Deiji had to grin, despite the situation at hand.

She knew she was changed. While she had never been a gentle or proper maiden, she had always been pretty. Yes, very pretty. And here she was before them, somewhat weatherworn and tanned, looking quite strong in body, and wearing trousers. She was changed, and this was written on their faces.

Out of the village huts two people came forth: Pav and Micid. They emerged from the baker's hut with looks of utter surprise struck upon their faces.

"Deiji J Cu!" her Aunt cried out, astonished and infuriated. "Where in all the world have you *been?*"

Deiji gave a small laugh. "Exactly where you just said. But there is no time for that," she added hastily, catching the look of outrage building on Micid's face; for she had not used the proper greeting or apologies that one would be expected to offer.

"Deiji -" Pav said warningly, but the young warrior cut her off boldly.

"There is no time," she urged, rushing to their sides. The entire village had gathered now, to watch the spectacle.

Micid raised her hand as though to strike the girl in the face. Deiji caught her Aunt's hand by the wrist in mid-motion. She gripped it firmly and hissed into her face, "*don't.*"

The crowd around them gasped.

"How dare you!" Micid breathed in indignation. Deiji pushed her arm away forcefully and turned to the villagers.

"The army of darkness approaches!" she announced, stepping onto a wagon cart so she could be seen. The crowd began to murmur anxiously.

"Be silent and listen!" A hush fell over the puzzled crowd,

which quickly turned into alarm, as the distant rumble of a thousand footsteps grew ever louder.

Pav pointed up the mountainside and gasped. Whipping around, she screamed, "they come! They come!" And she positively *fled*.

Everyone followed her frantically shaking finger and saw the mass of black Dragon Bats pouring into the valley. There were shouts and screams from the villagers as chaos and confusion reigned.

People milled around, grasping for loved ones, snatching up possessions, some simply breaking into an aimless run from where they stood. A handful of people could be seen following Pav onto the twenty-mile trail to Hei Village.

"Stop!" Deiji yelled. One hundred villagers or so stared at Deiji for a few moments. She could see the realization dawning on them that the girl before them had a firm knowledge of what was going on.

Finally, an Elder stepped feebly forward. "And what do we do, Deiji J Cu?"

"We fight," she proclaimed from the cart, and she lifted her sword to the sky. The Dragon Stone of the Rune caught the sun's light and sent a dazzle of rainbows across the villager's faces.

They all gasped and pointed to the sky. Deiji followed their gaze and saw a glorious sight.

"Geo!"

The crowd screamed as Deiji laughed. "It is okay!" she assured them all with a grin. "He is my friend, and he is here to help us!"

Geo landed next to her, looking noble, proud and modest. She threw her arms around his great scaly neck.

"Oh, Geo, you've grown so much!" He was a full-grown Dragon now, no longer dog-like. His wings were proudly held back, and his head was held high. His curved green eyes seemed to smile radiantly.

"You are here to help?" she asked her best friend, her hand to his face. He gave a curt nod, and they turned to the waiting crowd who still stood, their mouths agape.

"Those who are young, elderly or sick, flee north to the village of Hei. Stay on the trails and support each other to your destination. Send for reinforcements, for we are in great need of some help. Geo," she turned to her loyal friend. "I have a special task for you." The Dragon nodded eagerly, ready to take the job.

"Take this Elder," she gestured to the older man who stood in the front of the crowd, "to the town of Sartica. Honored sir, please proposition any and all who may come to our aid. Swiftness will win us this battle. Go!"

Geo leapt to the Elder's side, who clambered on carefully and they were gone. Deiji watched them disappear over the horizon.

A few dozen of the more delicate of the villagers turned to the woodland trails and began the slow walk to Hei Village on foot, suddenly refugees. Micid trailed behind them, glancing back at Deiji in shock every few steps.

Deiji looked away, and back to the minute army she had acquired, some seventy men, women and children, and she stared at them blankly for one endless moment. The footsteps of the marching armies grew deafening. What was she to do? She suddenly broke from her reverie.

"Blacksmith!" she shouted. The man stepped forward. "Any weapons you may have crafted – bring them to us now!" The man nodded and ran to his shed.

"My friends and neighbors, arm yourselves with whatever you can! Hurry, now!"

They scattered, regrouping quickly, exchanging a wide array

of cooking knives, pitchforks, a few amateurish swords and other such simple weaponry.

"Follow me!" she cried out with bravado, and she raised her sword and pointed it toward the mountain.

The Nigh Court

Zechi was shaking as he stepped into the grand entrance hall of the Nigh Court. The events of the last few weeks had led the little mouse-haired boy to believe that something drastic had occurred in his world, and he might have a chance to help it along. Or so someone had once told him…

On the day after the Rockman had destroyed his village, Zechi had awoken after being struck by a soldier. There was a Dolphin in what remained of the river, and it had squeaked at him urgently.

When he approached the Dolphin it leapt up at him, as if wanting to speak. He cautiously leaned forward over the riverbank and it lifted its head to his. When they touched, Zechi nearly fell in. The Dolphin had spoken to him.

"Hello, young master, I am Arill," it said pleasantly.

"I am Zechi," he hesitated. "Why were you trying to get my attention?"

"Because you are of a position to help us," Arill had explained kindly, and he stated his purpose.

And now, at the Dolphin's urging, Zechi decided he had nothing left, and nothing to lose, so he made his way from Toten Town to the Nigh court to seek out King Jebhadsen and the remainder of his army.

He shivered a little as he approached the empty throne, his

canvas pack thrown over his shoulder, causing him to hunch over more than usual.

"You there!" a general called out to him, and the timid boy nearly fainted.

"Please, Sir, do not kill me!"

General Morim rolled his eyes. "What do you want, boy?"

"I must speak to King Jebhadsen. I have an urgent message from the, uh, the Mystical people of the Unknown World." He felt a little silly, and was surprised when the general did not laugh.

The general looked out a stained-glass window solemnly. "His Royal Highness is dead. The shock of the world's current state took his life just today. His vizier, Telius, was something of a traitor and it did not end well. He has deserted us."

Zechi gulped, feeling faint again. "Who, then, is standing in his stead, sir?" he asked, breathing hard.

"There is no one. What message is it that you have to give? Perhaps I can be of assistance? After all, I am the head of the Royal Army, for the time."

Zechi stared at the man's honest, compassionate face and decided he was well enough. "Alright then," he said finally, "this is what I know."

Mount Odel

Deiji was trying not to shake in terror when she saw the Dragon Bat army at eye-level. Seeing them from atop the ridge was one thing, but this… It would be a massacre. She looked over her shoulder at her small army, who looked back at her.

"Do not show your fear," she told herself, clamping her teeth

to keep them from chattering. A harsh wind blew, and Deiji shouted out to them with as much force as she could muster.

"Do not be afraid!" she scanned the crowd of those who stood beside her. "For this is the end of evil!" She wanted nothing more than to fill these humble farmers with the courage and confidence it would take to march into such certain death. The odds of this battle were quite obvious to all.

"This is it," Deiji whispered, steadying her shaking hands. It wouldn't be long now. She drew in a sharp, steady breath, remembering how sweet the cool mountain air of home was.

Suddenly, a blinding white light pierced the sky in a line above them. A silver hole in its center began to spin slowly, growing wider every moment. Both armies turned their faces skyward, frightened and in awe of this new phenomenon.

A single white horse emerged from the spinning hole and spread its beautifully feathered wings. A Pegasus!

"Eanle. He did it." Deiji smiled. The Sties had not let her down. Two more were close behind. The people gasped as more and more horses floated out of the sky and took ranks among the villagers. Hundreds had joined them in a matter of minutes.

Deiji swung her leg over the nearest horse and thus encouraged her people to do the same. Raising her sword she pointed it toward the Black Army.

"We live!" she cried, and so led them into battle.

The first collision was absolutely beautiful, Relant thought. The stark contrast of black on white, and the way the black Bats tore through the whiteness absolutely fed his heart.

"Do you see, Mowat?" he asked from his separate mountain. "Do you?"

Mowat stood atop his own, looking at the smaller mountain

between them where the battle was just beginning to turn ugly. Relant smiled at the look on his face.

"She has inspired bravery," Mowat said slowly.

The villagers below fought and quickly died, torn to pieces by the Dragon Army. The Pegasus flew above with riders on their backs, sending streams of white fire upon the Bats. Many of them were falling from the sky. Would it be enough?

"She has led them to their deaths," Relant rejoiced with confidence. "This will be a simple feat for me."

"We shall see," Mowat said slowly. "She is Jai."

Below them the battle raged!

Deiji's Pegasus carried her high enough above the battle to keep from harm, but low enough to keep all in reach of her sword.

The horses were stunning with their white fire and incredible enthusiasm, but they were still outnumbered and many fell.

The villagers fought bravely, these people Deiji had known and grown up with. People with families and kin who lay dying around them fought with zeal at her side without question. She saw the miller's wife slashed by a dark Dragon, and she toppled over, disappearing into the crowd.

Deiji steered her horse and they descended upon the woman's attacker. "Hold on!" she cried as she swung her gilded sword. With her balance slightly off-kilter, a black soldier slammed into her Pegasus and Deiji was thrown from her horse.

She found herself flung into the heart of battle, lying amidst a flurry of stomping claws and hooves. She rolled and swung her blade in a smooth arc around her and cut the Dragon soldiers' legs.

Once she could see a spot of sky, Deiji jumped to her feet and fought the blackened creatures hand-to-hand with everything she could muster, blindly attacking in all directions with her sword.

She found herself face to face with a Dragon Bat. His body was black, as if he had been dunked into a vat of tar, and his wings were stumps. His face was ugly, like a squashed Dragon's, and his teeth were sharp, black stained and bloodied.

"*We need help...*" she thought disjointedly, as the desperate swing of her sword removed his head.

"Screech!"

She glanced up for one brief moment. Polk! Her falcon was soaring overhead, bringing with him the flock of falcons and birds, and they joined into the chaos, diving onto the Dragons again and again, ripping and tearing and clawing... Deiji would never forget the blood.

A Pegasus blew a gust of white flame that nearly singed her where she fought, and she fell back from the heat.

"*Ferula Imperio!*" she cried, remembering the magic Mowat gave her. The flames would not harm her now.

Suddenly...

Dragons began to drop from the sky! Not black ones, but good ones! Green and purple, gold and crimson they came, taking the Bat's attention to the sky, gnashing their teeth. Fouthe had done as he said.

The fire was everywhere now. Deiji leapt onto the nearest Pegasus.

"Retreat!" she called to her people. "Villagers of Odel, retreat!" There was no need for them to die in this. "Pegasus, carry the humans to safety!" she screamed.

She saw the white winged horses begin to lift from the crowd with people clinging to their backs, and was satisfied. Deiji followed them to the village and onto the edge of the battle. There were maybe a dozen left, sitting atop the white horses, mute and in shock.

"Go, all of you," she commanded. "Go to your loved ones. Carry them the rest of the way to the village of Hei. Take with you the message of the dead. Comfort those left behind. Go now." They stood silent a moment, lonely islands in a sea of the dead. "Go!" she shouted at them, and they slowly took flight.

Deiji turned back to the battle, which had raged beyond anything she could ever have imagined. She took a deep breath, finding it difficult to step back into the frightening mix of tooth and claw. She lifted her sword and prepared to return to the fray. Then, a horn blew!

Deiji turned to the north and relief filled every corner of her heart. An army of man, on horseback, down from Sartica. They had arrived.

She steered her horse to their leader, a man in a black silken suit leading an army of one hundred men. He knew her by name.

"Deiji!"

Startled, she peered at the man, who straddled a brown saddle horse.

"Men," the dignified man called out, "CHARGE!" The men obeyed and plunged into battle, fully armored, wielding their superior weapons.

Deiji bowed to the man who led them, who seemed to be a little too well bred for such a position.

He bowed back. "Deiji, I have heard much about you. I am pleased to see you are in good health, for the rumors stated otherwise."

"Yes," she was a little confused. "Who are you, sir?"

"I am Maia's husband, Par Jacque, and Head of Sartica."

"Oh my goodness," Deiji cried in shock, hopping down from her horse.

"Yes, yes, it is so good to finally meet you. Maia has always spoken very highly of you, and with great admiration. Many fine tales of your youth together, as well." His eyes twinkled and he slid off the side of his mount.

All at once Deiji's heart was flooded with forgiveness at this. Her eyes almost started to tear up, but she felt very full inside, as if she had finally crossed a very long bridge.

Par Jacque put his hand to her shoulder. "Maia is well, and she sends her hope for this battle. She swears a Mermaid told her to prepare for battle. There have been rumors of such a war in the courts of Nigh, and Maia spoke non-stop of this fight. She convinced me to partition in the town square for Sartica's finest. And halfway here during our march, the Odel Elder flew down to us – upon the back of a Dragon, nonetheless! It has been very exciting."

Deiji closed her eyes in silent thankfulness to her friend. She looked at Par Jacque. "Thank you," she said simply.

"Let us get to this, shall we?" he asked kindly. They returned to their horses and turned to the battlefield.

As if this wasn't enough to strengthen hope, another horn blew from the east.

Relant's smile faded, and he gripped his bloodied talons deep into the mountain rock.

"It seems that the Sties have successfully brought word to the four corners of the world," Mowat said with a smile. "The armies of Nigh have such a glorious reputation."

"This will not end easily, Mowat," Relant growled. "And I will have *her*, in any case!" And he raised his wings and flew toward the battlefield.

Three hundred soldiers, of Man and Centaur, and the promise of more to come. The armies of Nigh had joined that of the Deep Forest, and came together to fight against such evil. The war was almost won.

Deiji raced over to the general of the Nigh army, and after hastily introducing herself, exchanged information.

"I was awoken by an odd spirit, by the name of Weyes," General Morim explained. "He gave warning to such a war, and told me the battalions of Centaurs were approaching to assist us. I was quite conflicted by such a prospect, and it was only confirmed when this young boy here approached me from Toten Town and told me his story. It all seemed to add up."

Deiji looked behind the man and saw a young, brown-haired boy crouching meekly behind him.

"Zechi!" she cried in happy surprise. She leaned down a little. "Just promise me, Zechi, no matter what happens here, stay away from the fighting. I do not want you to be hurt." She fumbled about her waistband and pressed the seaweed bag of Sapphires into his chest. "Keep these safe for me," she whispered.

He nodded silently, pleased when she gave him a big grin. "Thank you for bringing the army here, Zechi." She tousled his hair with a smile, then turned back to General Morim.

His soldiers had joined the fight with enthusiasm and it seemed the battle was very near its end. Deiji was very glad for this; she did not like to witness the slaughter of her kin, and would not rest well with it.

She sat out of the battle for this time; she was confident that it was nearly over, and those more knowledgeable than she in the ways of fighting had taken over for a swift finish. Only a handful of black Dragon Bats remained.

Then...

Men began to scream, not out of pain, but in terror. The birds and Pegasus lifted from the battle and flew away.

Deiji snapped to attention as a giant Dragon Bat swept down from the sky into the heat of battle. It was Relant. He let out a shrill cry and the men seemed unable to move!

"He has frozen them!" Morim cried.

Relant bore down upon the stationary soldiers and tore into them, human and Bat soldiers alike. The Mystical Dragons from the Dragon Islands dove at him, nipping, tearing and slashing, but they were a mere third his size.

Relant let out a sharp cry that seemed to freeze Deiji's blood and she saw the Dragons become still in mid-air – stunned – and they dropped to the ground below. Once mobile again, they flew away in great haste. The ground gave a great lurch.

"All men, forward!" Morim commanded to his soldiers.

"No! Hold back!" Deiji screamed.

"What?"

"Get them out!" she said quickly. "Get them all out, now!" She galloped away and rose high into the air out of sight.

"Retreat!" General Morim shouted. "All men back to the trail!" The horn blew. "Retreat!" He ushered Zechi ahead of him.

Deiji circled overhead, looking down on Relant as he attacked those attempting to flee. She watched those who were able break ranks to run into the village and beyond, glad they were able to get away. The ground continued to rumble, and black smoke and ash began to erupt from Mount Odel.

"Oh no," she whispered. Deiji felt helpless as the earth shook below her and orange and red lava began to gush forth from her mountain. *"If that gets to our soldiers they are all finished,"* she thought, her heart pounding.

She changed course and dove into the valley on her winged horse. As they glided across the battlefield, Deiji called out a spell with all her voice. *"Cascata!"*

There was a rumble from the west and a rush of water as

a monstrous blue wave crested through the valley. The few Dragon Bat soldiers that remained tried to flee but could not.

Dolphins leapt in and out the wave as it made its way across the battlefield, with Mermaids just behind them. Deiji darted ahead of the wave, but found herself overtaken, and she fell flimsily into the water from her horse, who flew on.

She was frightened that she would be swept away by the wave, but once inside it, she transformed.

"*Yes!*" she cried, kicking her Mermaid tail, and she heard the gentle moaning of a great Whale behind her. She rode the surface of the wave easily and whistled for the Pegasus.

The wave struck the lava, instantly cooling it, hardening it, stopping it in its path. It bore down upon the last of the Bats and the dead that remained, washing the filth of the battle from the earth and out to sea.

The Pegasus landed beside Deiji, who stood on the marshy ground with legs once more. She pulled herself onto the back of the winged horse and they rose into the air.

She sat on her mount in silence, staring down at the muddied, washed-out valley below. They had protected the people of this world, she knew. The sacrifice her friends and neighbors had made on this day would always stay within her heart, and that of the entire world.

Suddenly, something struck her harshly, and she was knocked from her horse and fell a dozen feet to the ground. "Umpf!" She hit the ground and rolled upon impact. She saw an ominous shadow cross the muddy earth in front of her, and she scrambled to her feet and ran. Deiji felt fear as she heard the rush of air under Relant's wings as he came after her, but it was fear as if in a dream. Strangely aware, she felt she had a plan.

But wait! Her sword! She must have dropped it in the fall. She circled back, feeling terror and adrenaline course through her veins as the shadow descended upon her. Relant's talons closed tightly around her shoulders and he lifted her from the ground.

"No!" she screamed, her legs motoring in the open air. He drove one claw into her side, penetrating her ribs. She felt her skin and flesh tear and she screamed in agony, blood running to her ankles.

He flapped them higher into the sky and dropped her. She saw the ground rushing up, and then, incredibly, something swooped under her feet and caught her on its back!

"Geo!"

Surprised, Relant froze for one moment, giving Geo time to gain a head start.

"No, Geo!" Deiji panted firmly, holding her wounded side, "go to my sword, on the ground back there. It is time to finish this." She closed her eyes and rested her head against her friend's neck. She listened to the wind rush by, and felt him change course.

Geo flexed his well-tuned tail muscles and steered them down against the valley floor. They barely skimmed the dirt, and he closed his talons around Deiji's sword and flew into the sky. Deiji knew the evil Dragon Bat Relant was right behind them, and she could sense her Dragon's fear.

He tossed the sword into the air with his talons and dived forwards toward the ground. As he turned back to the sky, making a complete circle, Deiji reached out and snatched the handle as it fell.

Geo turned, and they flew at the dark Keeper, sword and claws extended. Deiji lunged as they flew past him, her sword nearly grazing his body. She heard the steel cut through air, not flesh, and they turned once more, cutting their speed, facing him again.

Relant flew at them, his wicked talons exposed, screaming in exhilaration. Geo shot straight at him, turning sharply at the last second. They flew at each other again, and this time Deiji felt her sword nick his shoulder.

He screamed in pain and rage and twisted around. Geo and Relant locked talons, and went for each other's necks with their teeth as they rolled about in the air. Deiji held on tightly as the world and sky swirled together.

Geo dug his poisonous claws into Relant's talons, and the green rot spread quickly.

Then, Relant shouted, *"Debeo!"* shooting his black fire at the green Dragon, stunning him. Geo blinked, seemingly frozen, then Relant dug his teeth into his throat. Geo gave a gurgling cry and his wings fluttered, then gave. Relant released his hold on Geo's talons as he fell away. He dove after the falling Dragon and snatched Deiji right off his back.

She felt his weakened claws dig sharply into her shoulders and the two of them rose into the sky again. Geo was gone. Relant laughed with triumph as he dove toward the ground with speed and threw her against it.

CRACK!

The bones in her legs snapped at the thigh, she felt her teeth break and she barely had time to register the pain when Relant yanked her back into the air once more.

But she didn't drop the sword this time.

She could only tell distantly that she was screaming, and she was quite dizzy.

"Oh!" she cried in surprise. Something glided into Relant's face and was clawing and pulling back and diving into his head again and again.

"Arrrgh!"

"Polk!"

The falcon seemed to know it wouldn't be but a slight bother, but its gesture seemed to aggravate Relant enormously.

Deiji watched, exhausted and as if in a dream, as her friend clawed at the Dragon-bat persistently. Relant swiped at the falcon with his claws, and Deiji distantly thought of the happy little dream-like kitty, and realized...

"Puff Puff!" she shouted in her haze of pain, "I want you to take Relant's form and fight him! And save me!" she added.

Out of the sky there came a wisp of cloud, which twisted and grew and turned a deep black. Relant turned his attention to this thing in complete awe, after hearing Deiji's plea and seeing what came after. Polk continued to attack his face, but the dark Keeper was too stunned to fight back.

"No!" he gasped. "She is not yours. She couldn't be!"

Puff Puff turned into an exact depiction of the Dragon Bat, claws and teeth and all. She sneered, and made as if to attack him.

SCREECH!

Relant struck the pesky falcon with his spiked tail in irritation, separating Polk's head from his body.

Deiji's mind was struck violently with clarity as Polk fell to the earth and she watched the Puff Puff attack Relant, tooth for claw. They struggled and fought, but the Puff was equal in power and body. Relant even had a disadvantage – his talons were occupied, as he was still carrying Deiji. He flew away from Puff, rather than fight her.

They rose higher into the sky, Puff Puff close behind them, and Deiji could see the village far below. How small it looked against the whole region! She knew he was going to drop her.

"It is time to meet your end, Deiji J Cu!" Relant shouted down to her in a sinister voice. She closed her fingers tightly around her sword.

"That was my *falcon*," she hissed menacingly. She pointed the sword up at his underside, thrusting it upward with the last of her strength. It punched deep into his innards and he screamed!

Dark blood, blood that was almost black gushed forth from the wound, drenching her from head to broken toe. It clouded into her eyes and she could taste it in her mouth.

She vomited.

The loss of her own blood began to wane on her strength. Relant was flapping aimlessly in his agony, swooping loosely from side to side. Deiji slipped from his talons and free-fell, dropping the sword, closing her eyes to the rush of the wind and the pull of the world.

She thought she saw the Puff Puff in Relant's form diving to catch her, and her eyes rolled into the back of her head as she reached for the darkness before meeting the ground.

CHAPTER TWELVE

The Island

The Cave

CHAPTER TWELVE

A few black moments passed and Deiji opened her eyes to the looming face of Mowat, who smiled kindly. A flock of birds lifted off in flight behind him, and Deiji closed her eyes. There was no more pain.

"Mowat."

"Yes, Deiji."

"Did I make things right? Is the world okay?"

"Yes, you did. All is well," he answered gently.

She breathed the deepest sigh of relief she had ever breathed in her life. It was over. After all that had passed she was finally relived of this burden.

"You died," Mowat continued conversationally.

"I *what?*" Deiji sat up straight.

Mowat chuckled and rays of sunlight shot through the cave ceiling and spotted the floor.

"After you took Relant's life you fell to your death, though your little cat," he paused while she rolled her eyes, "tried to save you. I did not lie, Deiji. I told you there was much risk to be taken. But as you took Relant's life before he took yours, all damage inflicted by Relant's influence has been undone. Including your death. Including all deaths caused by these recent events."

"My mother and father?" she asked quickly. "Polk? And Mangiat?"

"Waiting for you in the next room," he answered readily, nodding to the door leading out of the cave. She looked at it apprehensively.

"But there are many others who wish to see you, Deiji. You have paid the world a great favor. I do not wish to overwhelm you," he said with warning, "but they have been waiting for quite some time, and the world waits to thank you."

"Okay."

"Bathe and dress quickly, then. The ceremony begins soon."

Deiji fell back into her hot, foamy bath and breathed in the steam, her heart happy. It was over! Finally over!

Stepping out of the bath she found a beautiful purple and white, full-skirted dress waiting for her. Fit for a princess, its pinching corset bodice and sleeves that flared over the hands were breathtaking to behold. It was truly the most exquisite dress she had ever seen.

Deiji pulled it on and cinched up the corset, marveling at the discomfort. She felt quite pinched and entirely restrained. She definitely did not like having her hands covered by the sleeves, nor her legs entangled by the skirts.

Her lustrously thick brown hair was down past her shoulders, loose and brushed smooth. She set a circlet of white and green flowers atop her head and stepped out from behind the curtain. Mowat was waiting, smiling. She grinned back shyly.

He offered his arm and they left the room. Very curious as to what lay beyond Mowat's cave, Deiji nearly rolled her eyes when she found herself walking across the court of Nigh.

They formally breezed up the steps and into an ornate hallway. There was the grand entrance door at the end of the hall, and Deiji could hear muffled music from within.

"This is it," Mowat said proudly, and the double-doors swung open to admit them.

The hall was brightly lit, and set up for a grand banquet. Lovely music floated out into the hallway, played by a small ensemble of Elves, and the sudden collective noise of the chatter of Man and Mystical voices and the toasting of wine goblets was a little startling.

A large gathering of all sorts waiting, mingling; Centaurs and Humans, Dragons and Elves and Unicorns. Colorful Mermaids and Mermen hung beautifully about the sparkling fountain in the center of the room. She caught sight of Elail and they both waved, grinning.

The little glowing lights of fairies could be seen flitting from corner to corner on the high ceilings.

Mowat leaned over to whisper in her ear after she had a moment to take it all in. "Before the feast and festivities I am going to present you publicly to your people, and then you shall claim your reward."

She nodded, struck by the thought of this. In all the weeks she had to ponder this she had not yet made a decision.

"Consider carefully," Mowat added, as though reading her thoughts. "It is your life."

She remembered what Mowat had said in the beginning. "... *I will grant you your personal freedom, free of all social obligation. Once you have seen the world, and understand your place in it, you may choose any life you please, and I will send you there. And no one, nay, not a single soul will judge you harshly for your decisions..."*

"This is a heavy decision, and I never thought it would come," Deiji muttered to herself as Elvin attendants scurried around her feet, straightening her skirt as she and Mowat prepared for her debut.

"There she is!"

"She's here!"

"It's her!" Members of the crowd gasped as they began to notice her presence. Deiji blushed hard and looked away. Mowat winked at her. He knew she found this tiresome.

The crowd applauded at their entry, lining up along the sides of the red carpet that led the way to the king's now vacant throne. All of the stranger's faces were mostly as blur as each fell into a bow, though a few in particular stood out strongly. Deiji nearly yelled.

"Deiji!" Her parents called out to her. They were waving their arms wildly and breaking the line, rushing onto the carpet. She slipped away from Mowat's side and the three of them fell into a strong embrace.

Seeing them smiling, alive and well again was enough proof to Deiji that it had all been worth it. She reluctantly tore herself away, and had scarcely taken a step when Mangiat stepped out of the crowd. They threw their arms around each other tightly.

"Ju Ju," he whispered.

But even this could not keep her from her fate. It was time to stand before the crowd.

Mowat supported her hand on his and escorted her to the throne. She felt a moment of elation as she looked out into the sea of faces before sitting, somewhat awkwardly, on the throne, her face flushed and burning.

"Ahem!" Mowat began. The murmuring of the crowd

subsided. "I have a few announcements. Weyes the Stie has taken Anaou's place as the Keeper of the Skies. I find this to be an appropriate placement. The other two Keepers, Mangiat and Arill, will maintain their stations. But we need a new Keeper of Fire." He turned to Deiji. "This is Deiji J Cu, citizen of Mount Odel and its neighboring village." Thunderous applause cut him off. "This girl," he continued over the roar, "sixteen years in her age, has saved our world. From the day I met Deiji I knew of her infinite potential. I could see from her example as a kind spirited individual that she alone might be brave enough to face what must be faced. Well, I was correct in my thinking.

"Deiji has faced solitude in foreign environments, self-reliance in terms of survival, and even tutelage under those more enlightened than she." Deiji caught Mangiat's eye and they grinned.

"She has taken on the most horrifically dangerous creatures of this world, and even Relant himself. She has been victorious against the most ultimate evil of this world. And she has made friends," he added softly. "Friends of such a strong degree that you or I would pray to have such friendship in our lifetimes."

The crowd was hushed, absorbing the legend. Mowat went on.

"She has fought, learned much, and has overcome all trials. She has made shown her strengths!" There was more applause. Mowat turned to her.

"Deiji, the 'J' in your name isn't just a letter. It stands for 'Jai,' which is the essence of a secret strength, a boldness that will remain light, even in the midst of the darkest evil. The prophecy named you. This is your new name – we give you a new name!"

"Jai," she whispered, sounding it out.

"For all these things that Jai has fought for we honor her today," Mowat said with finality. "But there is more to be said. As everyone now knows, the continents of Nigh are now one.

Man and Mystical, having dwelt separately for hundreds of years are now living amongst each other.

"The people of this world are in a time of peace with this new awareness. People of all races and cultures are meeting together, learning from one another. But even in the midst of something so fortunate, we cannot afford to be foolish."

The hall fell silent.

"We need a ruler, someone who understands both sides, one who is wizened and experienced. And I do not think King Jebhadsen is, shall we say, up for the job," Mowat added with a chuckle. The crowd laughed appreciatively. Deiji's heart sank. She knew what he was going to ask of her.

He reached for her hand and she stood to meet him.

"I present to you this medallion," Mowat announced, stepping to the side of the dais and receiving a small box of gold plated antler from an attendant. He opened the box and lifted the pendant for all to see.

She had worn it through all the elements, and it had become tarnished and dull. Mowat had it polished and shined up wonderfully, and the entire circle of jewels was alive with glowing colors.

"Jai, I once promised you the ultimate reward of placement in this world. I ask you to make that choice now. Will you find the strength to lead the world into its new age?"

The people fell silent, listening intently with bated breath. Deiji couldn't find her words. She stood for a moment that felt like an eternity. How to make such a decision?

When she thought on politics and leadership, she suddenly became very tired. Did she really have what it took to lead a whole world into a new era?

Her eyes spotted her parents in the crowd. She knew she was too world-weary to return to Mount Odel with them, back to the ignorant, constricted life of daily routines. Her gaze lingered on Mangiat. What better life was there than love? They could walk the world together. But would she be satisfied? Mangiat...

She opened her mouth to speak, but promptly shut it again. Wait! Mangiat! Something brilliant surfaced in her mind and something she had longed for deep inside her soul was within it. These thoughts welled up so quickly she could scarcely contain them.

She leaned over and whispered urgently into Mowat's ear for a few minutes. The man's face looked startled, then he smiled warmly, obviously proud of her.

She bowed her head and Mowat held the amulet up to the crowd.

"The Keeper of Fire has chosen!" he announced, placing it around her neck, then lifting his hands in joy, and a rainbow shot up from behind him, and it arced to the other end of the hall as the crowd cheered.

Jai stood on the raised bluff of the southernmost of the Dragon Islands with Mowat, scanning the skies for Geo.

She was wearing a much more comfortable sari, which was perfect for the island's temperature. Her sash was tied tightly around her waist, her knife girded to it, and she toyed with the medallion.

Deiji remembered her first days here, and wanted to relive that special satisfaction for a time. If they wished to leave, Geo would simply fly them anywhere in the world they wanted. She knew this was her true path.

"There he is!" she cried, pointing as the green Dragon glided down to perch on the edge of the bluff, looking over his shoulder at her. She laughed as he beckoned her to climb upon his back. She made to move, then stopped.

Her eyes met Mowat's and she saw the wholeness of the entire world, the land and the water. Her brow furrowed in concern, for he had passed to her a majority of his magic, and seemed somewhat emptied.

"Do not worry," he said strongly. "Mangiat will rule well in your stead. It was a great decision you made, for he is wise and will lead the world easily."

"He will be a fine king. Your sword," she said respectfully, holding it out to him with a bow.

"No, for it is yours. I am to retire in a few short years. The Rune of Life on its hilt will make its possessor The Keeper of Life, and it is time I passed on such immortality and responsibility to someone else." He winked and held out the sheath.

Deiji laughed for sheer joy and gave him a great hug, her eyes sparkling as the ocean under the sun. She sheathed the sword and turned to Geo. She climbed upon his back, her sword slung across her shoulders.

"Let's go, Geo!" she cried, and he took off, his powerful leathery wings beating beneath them.

Jai and her Dragon flew high into the light blue sky and the man grew smaller beneath them. Mowat looked at them as they faded into the world above. The sun reflected in his eyes and he smiled.

"You did it, Jai."

The End

ABOUT THE AUTHOR

©2016 Photo by Lisa Chadwick www.bootsnbloomers.com

Davina Marie Liberty (yes, that's her real name!) works as a traveling Equine Sports Massage Therapist and Holistic Hoof Care Practitioner across northern California. She takes her own horses in Endurance rides and horse shows for fun and in her spare time (it does happen!) she writes and travels internationally.

Davina lives in the northern California redwoods with her husband Lu Liberty, and their dogs and horses. This is her first novel.

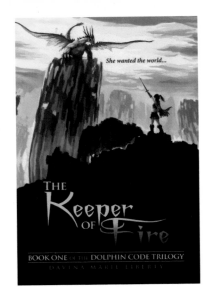

Thank you for your purchase!

I would be honored if you would take a moment to post a review on the following sites, listed on the back of this card.

The Keeper of Fire
By Davina Marie Liberty

Review At:

■ www.amazon.com

■ www.goodreads.com

■ www.powells.com

■ www.barnesandnoble.com

■ On Facebook: The Dolphin Code Trilogy

COMING SOON!

*Take a Sneak Peak into the next
adventure of the Dolphin Code!*

The King of Nigh

BOOK TWO OF THE DOLPHIN CODE TRILOGY

Zechi burst into the grand entrance hall breathing heavily, his clothes sopping wet, and Nia's lip curled at the pools of water collecting on the marble floor beneath him. His student stood before him now, looking, for the first time in Mangiat's recollection, eager to speak.

"What have been doing, my friend?" he asked the boy, looking him up and down. He was quite a mess.

"Training," Zechi answered quickly, "but there is that which I wish to say!"

The king nodded, giving him the floor. Zechi paused, as if unsure of what to say first.

"Say on," Mangiat urged.

"It is Mowat. He is missing."

Mangiat stood up straightly and lunged forward. "What is this you say?"

"I met Arill in the bay. He says that Mowat disappeared four days ago, with no explanation. He suspects he has been kidnapped!"

Mangiat frowned. "Perhaps you are both mistaken," he said gently. "Mowat has powers far beyond that which you and I understand."

"That is what I said," Zechi insisted, hardly able to contain himself, "but we are both wrong. Mowat relinquished most all of his powers five years ago. He is as any man now."

Both Mangiat and Morim stared, openmouthed. Even Nia and Gance stopped writing for a moment. Mangiat quickly came to his senses. He said, very seriously, "does Arill have any idea of where to look?"

Zechi hesitated again and Mangiat's eyes narrowed. "What is it, boy?"

"There was something he wanted to tell Deiji," he answered softly. "He took a small boat and rowed himself across the sea. Arill traveled alongside him until they were caught in a storm... They were separated and Arill found the boat later. But Mowat wasn't in it."

Mangiat put his hand to his aching head. This could not be.

"Master, Mowat knows nothing of Jayna's death. Arill has requested your assistance."

Mangiat nodded. Mowat was his friend, his Teacher and mentor. He had to find him.

"Sire?" Zechi sought his gaze. How unusual. Zechi was one who avoided eye contact at all costs.

"Yes, say on." He looked awkwardly flustered and he knew it.

"I think we need to start where Arill left off."

"Meaning?" His Centaur's heart sank and rose quickly, a sickening motion.

"We need to speak to Deiji," Zechi said firmly. There was a hollow silence and Mangiat looked away.

"I shall, er, write her a letter then," he said briskly. He rose, nodding his excusal and made his way to a side door and into his private quarters.

Printed in the United States
By Bookmasters